THE ULTRAS

EOIN McNAMEE

The Ultras

faber and faber

First published in 2004
by Faber and Faber Limited
3 Queen Square London WC1N 3AU

Typeset by Faber and Faber Limited
Printed in England by Mackays of Chatham plc, Chatham, Kent

A CIP record for this book
is available from the British Library
ISBN 0–571–20775–8

2 4 6 8 10 9 7 5 3 1

THE ULTRAS

The door of the Three Steps Inn stood open, casting light across the dirt surface of the car park, yellow light gleaming off the roofs of the parked cars. It was a time when car manufacturers still used chrome, and bumpers and trim gleamed in the dark, lending this night an opulence it did not deserve. The Triumph Dolomite was parked at the back of the car park, in the shadows. Robert's gun was locked in the glove compartment.

The following morning fragments of teeth and bloodstains were found on the parapet of a bridge two miles to the south. The tooth fragments and blood have always been presumed to belong to Robert, although there is no actual proof. The documentation of the find suggests rudimentary dental forensics, blood tests not performed, botched crime scene analysis. However the find does match the Townson account of what took place. The mishandled interrogation, the pistol-whipping.

All accounts place Robert in the bar. He sang Danny Boy. It was a favourite. He was attracted to the bogus émigré charm of it, the attempt at swamping melancholia. He had been there for several hours. He told the other drinkers that he was a PIRA operative called Danny McErlean from Belfast. They knew that he was lying. Robert went in without backup. That was the way he did it. He drove the red Dolomite from Bessbrook Mill to the Three Steps Inn. He said that he had to meet an unnamed informant. Robert said that he specialized in low-grade intelligence. He implied that he was on the verge of a major breakthrough. That he was monitoring things on the ground. He felt that people instinctively liked him. That they saw him as goodhearted and open to the unconstrained evocation of masculine virtue. That they were drawn to his public school languor.

His last contact with Bessbrook Mill came at 9.58 p.m., twenty minutes after he had left. He said that he was going into the Three Steps and that he was breaking off contact.

It is thought that Robert made it to the car. The driver's side panel and wing were badly dented and there were blood-stains on the ground. It is thought that he was trying to reach the weapon which he had left in the glove compartment. The weapon was a 9mm Browning pistol with its handgrip filed and a larger than standard safety catch.

Robert's body was never found. There are tales of night and dreadful murder. Some accounts speak of his body being buried in Ravensdale Forest. However, the most compelling evidence points to the disposal of the body in the nearby Anglo-Irish Meats plant.

Robert would sit in his room and stare at the map until it became an abstract thing. He tried to get beyond the actual terrain of the border. He tried to see it as cartography. He related the names of informants to contour lines, looking for patterns, edgy formulae of the peripheral. He thought in terms of substrata, edging his way into a zonal framework. He thought that Major Kitson's work on low-level intelligence gathering was seminal.

Local witnesses said that Robert went to the toilet three times in rapid succession before he left the Three Steps. Intelligence sources suggest that he knew he was in trouble and was attempting to destroy vital documentation. Or that he was making contact with an asset in the toilets. Or that he thought he might be able to climb from the toilet window.

Robert had been singing with the band. The bandleader knew that Robert was in trouble. As they started to pack their gear, the bandleader told Robert to come with them. He said that he would get Robert out of there. Robert refused. He would have had to leave the Q-car, the Dolomite, in the car park with the Browning in it. He would have had to explain what had happened to the car at Bessbrook Mill.

The serial number of the Browning was IT774. It was one of a number of weapons that Robert was seen with. He also carried a Remington Wingmaster folded butt shotgun. In addition he was said to have been seen with a Star pistol. The Star pistols were part of a consignment brought in through Galicia in 1972 and distributed to members of the IRA. If Robert had a Star pistol either it came from a PIRA arms dump or possibly from the assassinated John Francis Green, also known as Benny Green. In addition, the Star pistol provides a link between Robert and the murder of three members of the Miami Showband in July 1975.

By the time of Robert's death the undercover paramilitary units were starting to acquire a literature, passed around among themselves or carried in specialist publications like the SAS magazine, Minerva and Mars. They displayed photographs of themselves with their faces crudely blacked out, lounging around on an assortment of civilian vehicles and carrying a variety of non-standard weapons. This was important. That the firearm was different. They used phrases like custom-made. Lounging around in grainy black and white. A mazy idiom of interdictions, free-fire zones. There was a sense of textual density.

The lengthy interrogation. The pistol-whipping. The Browning pointed at his head misfiring four times.

They kept him at the bridge for a long time. Enough time for one of them to drive to the Lisdoo Arms and come back with the shooter, Townson, who had been drinking there, to explain to him that they had the British captain and to drive him back to the bridge. Robert made one attempt to get away from them but they dragged him back. You have a sense of shallow breathing, lacerations to the head and face, convulsive seizure. Mystery already starting to adhere to the moment.

The men wait for the shooter, glancing at each other, beset with uncertainty. They realize afterwards that they should have interrogated him.

One of the men had to be treated in hospital afterwards for a gunshot wound to the leg, sustained accidentally when Robert tried to break away from them.

At one stage, they said, Robert had asked for a priest and so one of them had pretended to be a priest to see if he would open up to them, tell them what he was doing in the bar, what he was doing in the country, what it was all about? Why, for instance, did he go into a bar and pretend to be a man from Belfast when they had all seen him walking through the countryside with military patrols?

They made him kneel to shoot him in the head. The men were cursing now. A low sound, almost a collective moan, almost a devotional quality to it. It seemed important that Robert should be kneeling, his head resting on his chest, an undercurrent of assent in his posture.

The men cursing. The gun misfiring four times. The blood matted in Robert's black curly hair.

We know that Robert had a brother who died when he was fourteen. We know that he had two sisters. We know that his family has made many attempts to have his body returned to them.

When Robert was eleven his father showed him how to dissect an eye. His father practised ophthalmic surgery. Ophthalmic meaning of the eye. They went to a butcher's shop. The butcher took them into a corrugated shed at the back of the shop. There were organs in zinc buckets on the floor. There were three cows' heads sitting on a stainless steel bench. The hide had been stripped from the heads but otherwise they were intact. You noticed the teeth first, large and yellowed and exposed in a dire, lipless grin as though death had exposed them to a ghastly cosmic drollery.

His father removed the eye through the back of the skull.

He set it on the stainless steel table. A fist-sized pulpy object turned a deep blue colour. Robert thought it was a thing without mercy. His father showed Robert the blade. A fenestrated scalpel. Fenestrated meaning drilled. The soundless incision. He showed Robert how to maintain hygiene in a theatre environment. In later years Robert dissected frogs and rats but he never again dissected an actual eye.

As his father named the parts of the eye, the processes, the anatomical principles, Robert looked up at the remaining heads and it seemed to him this time that they were engaged in a process of glassy-eyed arbitration, of implacable judging.

His father explained each part of the procedure, the reason for it. At home he would get Robert to look up words in the dictionary and repeat back what was written there. He discussed diseases of the eye. He defined each term that he used and made Robert repeat the definition, what it meant. The conjunctiva. The macula. Retinal meaning of the retina. His father intended to show him the lens, washing it first and holding it out, a mica disc with a machined look, a look of fine grinding and polishing about it. The structures of the eye. The ducts. Sclera meaning stiffness. The vitreous humour. The iris. Lacrimae meaning tears.

He spoke to him about disorders of the eye. There were visual phenomena, bright lights, flashes, floating black specks. The processes of seeing were fraught. It was important that you paid attention. It was important that you attended to the details. It was important that you were watchful. People came to him who had been careless about variations in their vision and he had watched them descend into blindness, the world fading away from them. Robert had seen them in the ophthalmic wards, sectioned off, the newly blind. He had seen them sitting on the edges of beds in pyjamas, walking with halting steps and arms outstretched, sometimes bumping into each other softly, momentarily grasping a sleeve or a hand, perplexed, lost in the darkness.

* * *

The darkness had begun to fall for Robert. He could not see beyond the men who stood around him. He had said many times that he would die in this place. People had said that they didn't know if he meant it or not. They thought he might like the drama of the statement, its element of bogus predetermination. He remembered that his call sign was 48 Oscar. He remembered dissecting an eye with his father. He was tired and confused. There is evidence that he had experienced difficulty in comprehending the world for some time. Other agendas kept seeping in. Covert meaning secret. He could barely see the men standing around him. He remembered his father told him about images that imprint themselves on the back of the eye and do not fade, phantom images, shadowy and equivocal. He was kneeling and kept falling over. Every time he fell someone put him back on to his knees. He could hear a river nearby. Riparian meaning rivers. He heard a metallic click in the distance. In the event of misfire, remove live ammunition from the chamber then rework the slide until the internal action of the firearm is functioning smoothly then reload. To avoid muzzle burn at impact point, hold the weapon at a distance of eight inches or more from the target area. He had known that it would end here but he had not known until now that it could end like this. He had not anticipated these dense, introspective moments. He tried to reach out to the men around him, feeling that he was failing them, that they were due some largesse from the moment. He thought he heard an owl or some other nocturnal bird. Nocturnal meaning of the night. He heard the metallic click again, then again and again, four misfires in total. He closed his eyes. Lacrimae meaning tears. Nocturnal meaning of the night.

2

Blair Agnew kept an archive photograph of the Miami Showband on his desk. Five people had died when the operation to
plant a bomb in their van had gone wrong. The incident had
taken place on 31 July 1975. Those involved included Robin
Jackson, Wesley Somerville and Harris Boyle. He also possessed a photograph of the aftermath. Emergency personnel
wearing oilskins worked under lights. Armed police in silhouette. The wreckage of the van. A white ambulance stood
in the foreground. It did not seem to belong there. There was
a dated look to it, high-backed, with heavy chrome bumpers.
It seemed to refer to civic virtues which had no place in the
aftermath of massacre.

Agnew kept returning to the faces of the Miami Showband
members. They had long hair and sideburns. At first they
seemed quaint, open and guileless, dressed in satin shirts and
flares. Figures that invited you to sentimentalize, tottering on
platform boots, barely upright, all their vulnerabilities on
show. After a while you started to wonder whether they had
brought the whole thing upon themselves. The way they
inhabited the photographs. The way they looked at you with
their heads tilted to one side, oddly knowing, exuding a
tainted juvenile sexuality. Damaged princelings.

Agnew considered that he had sufficient evidence, in addition to his own eyewitness statement, to place Robert Nairac
at the scene of the Miami Showband massacre.

Periodically Agnew had meetings with journalists on the
subject of Robert Nairac. He was aware that they regarded
him as damaged goods. He talked to them in bars. He was

aware that his fingers were stained with nicotine. He pulled pieces of paper out of his pocket and dropped them. His world of whispered conspiracies, webs of deceit. He tried to explain to them that everything was connected. He told them that he had spent time in a closed psychiatric institution but that was for reasons of addiction to alcohol and did not imply any mental instability on his part. That was the point at which he began to feel it slipping away from him. He tried to make them see the connections, putting Robert at the scene of a number of different atrocities, trying to make them understand how the logic of these killings differed from the logic of other killings. How the thinking evolved from Robert's early career, the calamitous abstractions involved in the contact with Robin Jackson, the Miami Showband killings. He wanted them to understand what became of Robert, the governance of his last days. He sometimes caught a glimpse of himself in a mirror. A man in his early sixties wearing an open-necked shirt, gesticulating with a cigarette.

He seemed to carry an aura with him. Of grievances nurtured. Of long-held prejudices.

'I can give you details,' he heard himself saying, 'names. I can put people in specific locations. I can identify the gun type, the prominent businessmen who conspire.'

Agnew had a sense that no matter how much trouble you were in, it was possible to find some more. His marriage had disintegrated. He had started to avoid the town-centre bars, had started to work his way towards the periphery, the housing estates built on the sites of the stockyards, the railway marshalling yards, the filled-in canal basin. Sometimes you could see the metal of a railway track underneath the tarmacadam. You had the sense of a ghostly infrastructure. The estates where you could smell fires when night fell, a yearning for smoky dusk. The air was damp, full of coalfumes. Everyone smoked. There was a tendency towards the chronic respiratory condition, the uncontrollable coughing fit. Ailing men in their early sixties took their daughters' arms to reach the bar.

The bars were shoddily constructed, with thin industrial carpet laid over bare cement. There were fake gilt mirrors, chipped wood veneers, damp stains on the thin walls. There was an air of people taking their pleasure where they found it. Women wore white court shoes with jeans and tights. On Friday and Saturday nights there was an expectation of violence, crimes against the person.

He felt that it was safe to drink in town-centre bars in the morning. He went to the Clipper most mornings.

'There used to be hooks under the bar for hanging your jacket,' he said. 'What happened to them?'

'You always say that. The only hooks you get around here is the ones sat at the bar,' Daphne said.

She poured him a brandy and port. He lit a cigarette and ignored the drink for a while. It was something he did. Not looking at the first drink. Demonstrate a disregard for it. Show that you could take it or leave it. Besides he wasn't ready for the minor dose of uplift that it would supply, the necessary subterfuge of wellbeing. He felt that there was still some mileage in the sense of bleak accountability that accompanied him most mornings now.

'You going to drink it or look at it?'

Daphne turned away as she spoke. Letting him know that her heart wasn't in it, that it was a rainy morning with the desultory to the fore.

The door behind him opened and he turned to see Mallon standing in the doorway. Mallon wore a hacking jacket with leather patches on the elbows. He didn't like to look like a policeman. He liked to look as if he had just come from a gymkhana, that there was a horsebox parked outside, a dissatisfied pre-teen daughter in jodhpurs and riding boots.

'Jesus, you're a sad bastard, Agnew.'

'Tell me something I don't know.'

Mallon took the stool beside him and ordered a drink.

11

'I hear you're talking to journalists again.'

'I am.'

'Nobody gives a fuck, Agnew. Give it up.'

'I wish I could.'

'Look at this town. Look at the whole place. Things are all changed now. You don't get proper riot footage any more. Look at the police. They're all black flameproof suits, Kevlar and flameproof balaclavas. Somebody's sat down and worked out how to make them look sinister.'

'That's the point. They're not sinister any more.'

'What could be more sinister than a rural policeman with a baton in his hand? Longheld generational hatred and mis-understanding mixed with fear in his eyes. The smell of teargas. The sense of events taking a turn that no one could have predicted, events spiralling out of control.'

'That's what we're missing in this situation.'

Mallon made an impatient sound.

'So what, you want to get all wrapped up in Nairac , all wrapped up in the past? You think it's going to help you, some of the things you done? Is that it?'

'Maybe. Maybe not. I don't know.'

'You done your crime. You done your time. Same as half this fucking town. Let it go.'

'You're the man to be talking. You're as caught up in it as I am.'

'I'm a different case, so I am. I'm getting paid to do it. It's my job.'

Agnew shut his eyes. He saw Jackson. He saw Clyde Knox. He saw David Erskine. He saw Robert half turned towards the camera, a group of children around him, the children picking up something from him, recognizing the storybook charisma. They swarmed around him, small hands plucking at his battledress, trying to catch his eye. Robert knowing there was more to the moment than met the eye, feeling the forcefulness of the children's attention, a grave attention at work under the noise of their voices.

'Robert Nairac is dead this twenty-four years,' Mallon said.

'They never found his body.'

'What odds they never found his body? He was took out of the Three Steps and shot dead and that's the end of it.'

'Then where is the body?'

'We know what happened to the body. The meat factory.'

'That's just a story, Mallon. People like to tell it. The shining young captain coming to a terrible end.'

'He's dead, Agnew.'

Agnew didn't reply. There were those who did not believe that Robert was dead. There were those who believed that he had been spirited away. There were reports of four men with English accents being seen in the area immediately after he was abducted from the Three Steps. There were unconfirmed reports of a man being lifted into a car in the car park of the Border Inn several hours after the abduction had taken place. Unnamed eyewitnesses said that the man had been moaning but was still alive. The car was a green Ford Cortina. This detail was repeated with each telling of the story. It was the detail of the car that gave authority to the account. The car was said to have driven off north at high speed. This was another satisfying detail. The car was behaving as it was expected to, driving off at high speed. You had a sense of a shadowy apparatus being brought into play, opening the whole episode to levels of meaning, giving structure to the dread that people felt, the shifting unease. The night along the border full of tec whisper, microwaves in the air around the hilltop listening posts, the antennae, the unexplained structures. Their domestic animals were dying of unex- plained causes. There were leukaemia clusters. They needed Robert to help them dream their way through this.

'Who do you think Nairac was?' Agnew said.

'Fucked if I know. I think he reckoned he was one of them boys you would see in films and that. You know, the Com- mando boys. Face blacked up. Cutting a sentry's throat and blowing up something important, a vital installation.'

'Piano wire.'

'What?'

'Piano wire. They didn't cut throats. They used piano wire.'

'Is that a fact? Let me tell you another fact. You did what you did when you were a peeler and you got to live with that and I don't give a fuck if you lie awake at night playing a fucking invisible violin for yourself and your immortal soul. But you got a daughter to look after and you're not helping her by trying to find forgiveness for yourself by chasing after a dead man.'

Agnew wondered if that was what he was doing. Or if in compiling a case against Robert Nairac, he was assembling a dossier that he could use against himself.

At dusk he drove out to Angela's to pick up Lorna, turning into the avenue as the light began to fade. He felt that he was developing a habit of being summoned at dusk. He felt that people were aware of his weakness for sentimentality. The gravelled driveway curved and was lined by mature shrubs so that you couldn't see the house from the road. It was a 1920s two-storey house with leaded lights. The paintwork was new. The windows gleamed. The house had high chimneys, a glass conservatory to one side. You were meant to experience nostalgia for lost values, the undervalued unhappinesses of the newly wealthy. He realized that Angela had told him to call at dusk in order to maximize the feeling of disappointment, of things not being worth the effort.

Several times lately, when he came to leave Lorna back on a Sunday night, he found Angela drunk. It seemed that her new husband was never there. She would invite him in and sit on the arm of his chair, eyes bright, questioning him. There were accidental touches, her breast brushed his shoulder, she placed her hand on his thigh in order to make a point. They were light whispery touches. She stood in doorways with the light behind her, holding a glass.

14

She seemed conscious of a certain ruined glamour. The mother of a teenage girl. She told him that she had found a card with the number of a call girl agency in her husband's pocket after a business trip. She was smiling when she told him, as if it was important to confirm what was going on in his despicable heart. She said that when she confronted him about it he said that he had taken a walk through the red light district and somebody had pressed it into his hands. Agnew only half heard what she said. He was lost in the way she had spoken the words call girl. There was something dated about the term. He imagined girls with pan make-up. He thought about old-time erotica, badly drawn.

Later he was troubled by the image of her husband walking through a red light district. The downtown of some great mercantile city, Rotterdam or Frankfurt. Rain-slicked streets. A feeling of trade about it, of transactions arrived at.

Angela opened the door for him. When she wasn't drinking she treated him with indifference and she turned her back and walked away from him without waiting to see if he came in. She was wearing a pleated tennis skirt and tennis shoes. Her legs above her white tennis socks were tanned. He could see the small gold hairs on them as she walked in front of him towards the kitchen. Her hair was tied at the back.

'How are you anyway?' he said. 'Anything strange or startling?'

'Post-marriage small talk,' she said. 'You don't have to, Blair.' She spoke in a tone of low-key and formalized bitterness, part of the codified acrimony of their marriage.

'I can't be bothered,' he said.

'That was it, wasn't it? You never could be bothered. Couldn't be bothered going to bed, couldn't be bothered to get up, couldn't be bothered taking your head out of a bottle and just looking at your family for just one single minute.'

'We're not married any more,' he said. 'I don't have to.'

'You're Lorna's father.'

15

'Don't make that an accusation as well.'

'Don't take her to that caravan this weekend.'

'Why not?'

'Why not? Why not? It's not hygienic. And those boys that hang about . . .'

'The unhygienic boys.'

'Don't be funny about it.'

'Where's the new husband?'

'Working.'

'Meaning I'm not. Is that a smirk? I thought I saw a smirk.'

Angela picked up a tennis racquet from the worktop. She ran her fingers over the strings. She held it up and turned it in the air as if something in it could come to their aid, as if there was something instructive in its tensile laminate, disciplines of the unyielding.

'How is Lorna anyway?'

'Not good. She can't concentrate at school. She gets blackouts.'

'I don't get blackouts. I get hypoglycaemic episodes.'

Agnew turned. Lorna was standing in the doorway. She had on a shapeless black dress. Her hair was parted in the middle and she wasn't wearing any make-up. For a moment she resembled a medieval saint, a pale-faced postpubescent with her martyrdom depicted in an ancient stained-glass window. Angela opened her mouth to say something then closed it and looked away. Agnew understood. It was the way that Lorna had spoken, the tone of detached, forensic observation that she brought to the comment on her own condition.

They drove most of the way to Cranfield in silence. As he turned into the entrance to the campsite she turned to look at him.

'It's a cliché,' she said.

'What's that?'

'An eating disorder. Your parents both drink too much.

Their marriage breaks up. You're an adolescent girl, so you get an eating disorder.'

'If you were a boy it would be minor public order offences.'

'Don't make fun.'

'You're not the cliché. You can't be a cliché at sixteen. I'm the cliché. Sixty-year-old ex-con gone to the dogs. A corrupt cop kicked off the force. An unhealthy obsession with the past. I'm not even a cliché. A cliché is more interesting.'

It was the way they spoke to each other. He parked outside the caravan. It was Friday evening and there were cars towing caravans coming through the gates. There was something comforting about sitting in the car outside the caravan with the sand hissing in its aluminium chassis. Women in nightdresses walking through the darkness towards the toilet block. Nylon pinks and blues. They seemed unfixed, wandering. Cars labouring in from the city. Retired couples touring. There was an atmosphere of the makeshift, the impermanent.

He had bought the caravan in the summer of 1989, five years after he had got out of prison. He was looking for a backdrop to a failing marriage. Angela went along with these holidays because it aroused a sense of compassion for him. It seemed that she coveted the sense of crushed morale that he brought to the marriage. For a while it seemed that she craved desultory sex in the foldout double bed. She uttered small, dispirited moans and sighs. The caravan smelt of cooked food and drains. The chassis creaked when they moved. There was a sense of communality among the married couples on the site, of knowingness, a sense that this was what they were there for, of marriages in transitory states. As the holidays went on she thought she saw the other women take on a voluptuous nature. They walked about the site with an air of being physically coveted. She went to a small local hairdresser and returned with blonde highlights. She read Titbits and began to smoke Player's No. Six. She began to identify with the wives in the magazines. There were recurrent motifs of jealousy, premature ejaculation, of unresolved longing. She began to insist that they read their horoscopes to each other every day. She felt it was her duty to be alert to calamity in every possible way. The night was full of raised voices, the voices of children abroad at midnight, of girls in platform boots and other signifiers of marginal lives. Three months later she left him.

He carried Lorna's bag into the caravan. When they were inside she went to the fridge and got a drink for him. They liked these small courtly gestures. Their weekends were hedged about with formality. Angela had told him to make sure that she ate, that she didn't hide the food beneath her tongue and spit it out, that she didn't mash the food on her plate so that it looked as if she had eaten some of it. Something in him admired her. There was an ascetic quality to the illness she had chosen for herself. She was given to casual insights which he found devastating. She had discovered whole layers in herself, strata of denial, self-loathing. She brought a steely determination to her task. He thought about the whole range of insightful disorders that teenage girls had brought into being. Variations on themes of self-harm. At night he lay awake, listening to her making herself vomit on the grass outside the caravan. A harsh, pietistic sound, the incoherent names of the deity. Sometimes he met her in the kitchenette at night, barefoot, wearing a towelling dressing gown. She seemed to be trying to illustrate degrees of wanness. Once or twice he tried to get her to sit with him, before he realized that her night was tautly structured. There were observances to be performed, episodes of malign introspection. He respected this. He knew that drinking generated its own surly observances.

When she was young he would come home drunk and fall asleep somewhere. On the corridor. In the bathroom. Often he would make his way towards the hot press and fall asleep there, slumped, slouched, his body finding improbable geometries in the house. If Lorna woke during the night she would step over him as if he wasn't there. He would wake in the morning, his body aching but feeling strangely refreshed.

She never mentioned the bales of newspapers that were stacked everywhere in the caravan, the autobiographies of minor military figures, the works of reference, the volumes of parliamentary debates, the badly annotated files, the library books, the yellowing photographs, the curled-up microfiche. He knew that she had her own means of compiling documentation. Angela had told him that Lorna kept a diary. She told him that she had searched the house for it but could not find it. She said it was in a plain red notebook with lined paper. It occurred to him to wonder how she knew that the paper was lined. She suspected that it was hidden in the caravan. She wanted Agnew to find it. She thought that it might reveal something which would help her fight the anorexia. Agnew believed Angela, her eyes bright with anxiety, knowing that the diary was something forbidden to her. He sensed the tension that the diary represented, the sense of forbidden text. It wasn't a thing that he wanted to go near. There were aspects of dangerous lore he felt he should avoid.

There were elements of the relationship between his wife and his daughter which made him think of post-Inquisition sects, schismatic, swirling with heresy, prone to cruel and intimate punishments.

Sometimes he saw her writing in the diary, sitting on the sand dunes in winter with her coat wrapped around her, a huddled archivist.

Agnew didn't think that the boys who came from the city were threatening. They dressed in black, were possessed of a feral watchfulness. They sat on the low fence of the small wooden-walled shop. Or they leaned against the sea wall. Agnew noticed that she never looked at them. He saw how she felt that they understood her inattention, took it as a gift. He knew she appreciated the seriousness they brought to watching her, the laconic bounty of their gaze bestowed upon her. They seemed to know why her face was pinched and unsmiling. They seemed to know what it involved, the wearing of loose clothing, baggy and shapeless. If Agnew was worried about anyone he was worried about the boys. They were too still. He wished rites of passage upon them. There seemed to be an adolescent suicide pact hovering at the edge of their collective consciousness.

There was an undercurrent of secret record in the caravan. They were both in pursuit of something coded, allusive.

He left Lorna in the caravan and drove into town. He found Mallon in the Sugarhouse. Mallon was wearing a sheepskin coat. He was standing at the bar with a bright-eyed woman in her early forties.

'Have you met Margaret?'

'Hello, Margaret.'

'This is my old friend Blair Agnew. A man with a past.'

'Take it easy now, Mallon, take her handy. There's no call to be going into the past.' He realized that Mallon had not stopped drinking since the morning.

The woman was looking at him now. She had dark hair and wore gold jewellery. Agnew looked at her hands. You could see the white band on her finger where the wedding ring had been. Agnew thought of teenage children, family therapy, an uncontested divorce, a progression through states of mild unhappiness.

'Tell us,' she said, 'what did you do?'

She was smiling now, saying that there are indulgences to be gained no matter what, that it was a matter of exposing yourself to all the grace available, even if it did fall short of forgiveness.

'He was an accessory, that right, Agnew?' Mallon said.

'Accessory to what?' the woman said.

'An accessory to mayhem, same as the rest of us, isn't that correct?' Mallon said.

'Were you in prison?' the woman asked.

'He done five years, max security,' Mallon said. 'He's a right terror, our ex-Sergeant Agnew.'

'People are looking at us,' the woman said.

Agnew noticed that there was a small ladder on her tights, that there was lipstick on her teeth. She swayed slightly as she spoke. Agnew knew that she wanted to tell him about her life. That if he stayed he would end up sitting in a banquette while she told him about the failure of her marriage, the charted lows, the stoic nights.

Agnew decided that he wasn't going to stay.

'You're wrong, you know.'

'Wrong about what?'

'I'm not trying to save my soul with Nairac.'

'What is it, then?'

'I can't explain it.'

He went home and read an interview with Robin Jackson carried by the Sunday World in 1998. The interviewer said that Jackson had terminal cancer. He said that Jackson showed no remorse.

Sometimes he thought he knew why he was drawn to Nairac's story. It was the rumour that Robert had been taken to the meat factory. It was the rumoured use of the factory mincer. It meant that there was a newness to the crime, a modernity to it. The amorality and existential vacancy of it. It prefigured the subculture drifters, the loners, the basement dismemberers. There was a sense of cognitive dysfunction which was missing from other border killings. The culvert bomb, the multiple victims, the historical carnage.

3

There is a theme of popular band music running through Robert's narrative. The presence of the band in the Three Steps Inn. Robert on stage singing. The band leader trying to rescue him. Come on. Come on to fuck. Get in the van. There is the persistent speculation that Robert was present at the murder of four members of the Miami Showband outside Banbridge on 31 July 1975. Robert seemed to be drawn to the places where you heard country music. Where men and women know the jivesteps. The sound of steel guitar. Women with their hair high and lacquered. Women sitting over drinks with a hardpressed look. An air of lethal sentimentality in the place. Young men on the edge of violence, working towards the moment in the car park afterwards, the torn shirt, blood and saliva dripping, the breathing coming hard and tight, a feeling of lonely night like a catch in the throat.

You wonder if that was one of the things that Robert was looking for, the car park after the dance, the dense intimate moments, the fights, girls in print dresses being fondled by boys they had known all their lives. Not one witness had come forward to tell what had happened in the car park. Many people must have seen Robert being abducted. There would be a closing of ranks, but there seemed to be something more to it. A sense of not interfering in a decision freely made. A sense that, for whatever reason, Robert had chosen this place.

In the early days Robert would spend days at a time in the field. He would be dropped by helicopter at night. In a few hours he would scrape a shallow foxhole, finishing it before dawn. He liked the basic fieldcraft. It was one of the things that he understood. It was one of the places where he stayed with the manual. The construction of a bivouac from branches. The use of plastic sheeting to collect rainwater or dew. The bagging of your shit when you moved on. Days in the open were no problem. He saw himself as a naturalist. He spent New Year's Eve in the field in 1972. He observed wildlife from covert positions. He divided his immediate landscape into fields of fire, defiles, firing points.

Robert liked to go out on patrol with the police. He liked the interior of the Saracen. The sense of old munitions, armoured interiors. The chipped green paint and the two-inch plate.

In February 1972 Robert was at Gough Barracks when they brought in a group of internees. The men were in the back of a truck. It was seven o'clock in the morning. Most of them wore shirts and trousers. Some were barefoot. Some had been beaten. There was a timelessness to the scene. Soldiers waited with dogs. Soldiers waited with rifle butts. The men looked sullen, defiant, frightened. They embarked on stumbling, fearful runs through a gauntlet of soldiers and snarling dogs. They had blows showered on them. They would stumble. They could have been Slavs or Poles or Ukrainians. There was an atmosphere of nationhood in retreat. The soldiers made rough jokes among themselves. The men hung their heads and did not make eye contact. There was a careful iconography of civilians in mass transit to be observed.

Robert went into the barracks. There was dried blood on the walls. He walked along a corridor looking into rooms. In one room they were playing white noise through a raffia-fronted loudspeaker. The police interrogators were florid men in shirt-sleeves. When they walked, they let their arms hang slightly away from their bodies, as if their hands had been exposed to a contaminant. In another room two plain-clothes men were standing over a crank-up generator with electrodes leading off it. There was an air of bad science about the place.

23

Robert had boxed at Ampleforth. At Oxford he was responsible for reviving the boxing club and became a boxing blue. He liked the smells of chalk and sweat. The sound of leather against skin. Robert like the idea of men in competition, men stripped to the waist. He boxed in front of a full-length mirror, watching himself and his muscles moving beneath the skin until it seemed as if he was looking at an anatomy illustration from one of his father's books, the skin stripped away to an actual webbing, a machinery in there. He liked moving round the ring, the canvas talced, the ring gritty underfoot. He liked the moments that you arrived at halfway through a fight when everything slowed down almost to a halt and you could see your opponent like a photograph, gloves high, eyes watchful. You could see the blood smeared on the gloves, blood and sweat. He did road miles early in the morning and went to the Avoca cinema to see the American fights. Joe Louis. Sonny Liston. Sitting there in the dark, watching Sonny Liston shuffling forward. He believed that he knew how the Negro felt. He had a trick that he used. He imagined that he was punching a spot two inches behind the back of his opponent's head. That way you got the maximum impact out of the punch. You felt the jolt travelling up your shoulder.

4

David drove from Theipval barracks to the city in a blue Viva that he signed out from stores. He carried spares for the reel-to-reel at Gemini and Kodak for the still camera. He kept the shortwave Storno handset on the seat beside him, tuned in to 14th Int. Once every ten minutes or so an operative would come on and give a position or ask for a suspect to be run through P-card. There was a phlegmatic feel to the conversations. 14th Int liked to be seen as cool under pressure. It was important to be thought languid. There was a sense of short-wave transmission, crackling static, strained frequencies. David liked the wartime feel of things. He routinely proposed curfews at staff meetings. He had spent time in Berlin and was attracted to the historic aspect of operations there. It seemed to him that the East Germans had a more advanced sense of continuity. He liked the studied grimness of their checkpoints. There was a poetry of harshly lit installations, conscripts in ill-fitting uniforms. There were complex listening devices, overtones of peasant brutality. It was important to cultivate levels of intrigue. He thought about bringing in surly conscripts with blunt Slavic features, sending them out on the streets in lorries with canvas tops. He thought that the city would benefit from a Middle European dimension to things.

He had concerns about morale at Gemini. There were also issues of hygiene to be addressed. He felt that it was important to be able to detach, to stand back. It was a requirement of PsyOps that you were able to switch off. He knew how people's minds worked. He knew that the sexual impulse was a weakness. He had identified it as a weakness in himself. He thought that someone in the corridor at Theipval might have a cure, something like bromide that you put in tea.

All the intelligence agencies shared the corridor. The corridor had distempered walls and wooden floors and metal-framed windows. There was MRU, PsyOps, 14th Int, MI5. There was a smell of wet overcoat. Each room had a filing cabinet, a kerosene heater and a wooden desk. Men wandered from room to room with pipes in their mouths. They liked to project an image of enthused amateurism, cheerfulness in the face of adversity. They wore worn tweed jackets with leather elbow patches. A large tea urn was replaced twice a day by cheery Wrens with open homely faces. Men were given to bouts of staring into space, then scribbling feverishly on scraps of paper. Juvenile nicknames were employed. The boffin. The prankster.

Clyde Knox was MI6. He was tall and rangy. His hair fell forward over his eyes and his corduroy trousers were too short. You were meant to think boyish and eager. You were meant to think absent-minded. Knox collected insects at the weekends. He kept some in his desk drawer in the corridor. He showed them to Erskine once. They were in a wooden tray lined with cotton wool.

'You suck the yolk out with a little straw,' Knox said.

There was a smell of formaldehyde in the case. The insects were tiny and ornate, pinned to the box. There was a sense of work in miniature, minute and tooled. Knox showed Erskine how you put the living insect into a jar and then placed cotton wool soaked with formaldehyde into the jar until the insect was overcome. Other men came in to watch.

Knox had spent time in Moscow. He seemed to bring a cold-war edginess with him, an aura of dead drops and miniature cameras. He was a fluent Russian speaker and had been assigned to the Berlin station for a year. He said that he would sit alone in a room with headphones on, listening to transmissions on military frequencies, soldiers' voices coming in on bursts from command posts on the Baltic. Anything military was coded, he said, but it was his function to assess morale among the Soviet troops from their personal conversations with each other, their talk about their wives, the quality of their loneliness, sudden detectable changes in their voices. David wondered if you could invent a machine to measure their solitude. He imagined a fine needle, an infinitesimal wavering.

Knox was an authority in the use of disorientation techniques in interrogation. He implied that he had spent time at Langley. He used the phrase 'sensory deprivation'.

'Chinks came up with it in Korea,' he said. 'The clever little buggers. Bring some poor bastard in, three days later he doesn't know which end of him is up. Best way to get the truth out of them.'

He showed Erskine a brown glass jar filled with a white substance. 'Amphetamine sulphate,' he said. 'Put it in their tea, ten minutes later they're singing like the proverbial.'

'Bit too technological for me, chum,' Erskine said.

'Works better than the old electrodes, less messy.'

'I prefer the psychological, work on the mind, dig up a bit of dirt. Everyone's got a bit of dirt hidden there.'

'And if you can't find it, provide it. That right, chum?'

It was like that in the corridor. You had the impression of new fields being opened up, promising angles being explored. Erskine liked to think that his techniques complemented those of Knox. His were about exploring new angles in psychology, Knox's were about new scientific applications. The boffin. They saw themselves in terms of being pioneers. Knox used the phrase low-intensity warfare. He mentioned the six techniques.

Knox had access to miniature technology. He promised Erskine that he could get a Minox camera for him.

'Two inches long,' Knox said. 'The quality is excellent, though, spot on.'

Knox liked to help in the darkroom when Erskine was

developing the photographs from Gemini. Erskine didn't like anyone else being there. Especially Knox, who seemed to take up all the room, distracting Erskine with awkwardness and apologizing. Knox was only interested in seeing who was in the photographs. He lacked an awareness of melancholy fate as the clients' bodies began to emerge from the tray of developing fluid, nude and compromised. David thought that Knox did not show a proper appreciation of the men's vulnerability. A middle-aged man's body deserved respect, Erskine thought. The roll of fat at the waist, the curly dark hair on the shoulderblades, the unexamined paleness of their flesh. Their partially glimpsed faces, jowled and subject to disquiet. Their bodies know what lies around the corner. The coronary infarction, the unexplained lump, the sudden dizziness that leaves you pale and sweating and grasping the corner of your desk. The willpower it takes to avert the certain knowledge of ageing. He understood why they were drawn to the Polish girl, her limbs without tone, her half-hearted moaning, the way she endured the men and their compromised lusts.

When the photographs had dried they took them to the corridor. Erskine kept them in a locked filing cabinet. He did not want them sniggered over. There was that schoolboy thing in the corridor as well. On the back of the toilet door someone had drawn an erect penis in blue biro.

In the corridor there seemed to be an accumulation of terse, abbreviated forms of communication. 1st Int. IntCom. There was a sense that what they were doing acquired a textual density. SigInt. SatInt. David had the sense of elevated communications, amassed forms, almost classic in their brevity and use of obscure grammatical protocols. There was a feeling in the corridor of insight coming in salvoes, that a sudden and complete grasp of what was going on might some day come in a dense acronymic burst.

It was raining when David got to Gemini. He rang the door-
bell, looking round as he did so, trying to adopt the persona
of a small businessman converging on sexual adventure. He
liked the name Gemini. It had a modern feel to it. The sign
over the door, Gemini Health Club, expressed aspirations
that he knew many of the population shared.

The club was in the basement, behind rusted wrought-iron
railings. The Gemini logo was repeated on the bell. The stairs
were streaked with dirt. The logo was good, but he didn't
want things to be overly clean. There were necessary incre-
ments of the furtive as you went further into the club. He
wanted clients to perceive themselves as shabby and open to
misgivings on a spiritual level. Inside the carpet was threadbare and there was a smell of damp. He wanted to promote
themes of solitary self-abuse. It was important that a client
started to feel himself detached from his former life. He
wanted them to be subject to devastating images of matrimo-
nial fidelity, of radiant children, of a wife tear-stained and
chaste. That was what made somebody vulnerable. That was
when they could be turned. Joyce opened the door. She was
wearing a flower-pattern dress belted in the middle. She wore
American brown tights and slippers with a fleece lining. She
made David think about News of the World stories of wife-
swapping. She possessed an aura of down-at-heel sexuality.
David imagined her in lingerie, against a background of G-
plan furniture, her face crudely blacked out, working within
the persona of debased suburbanite. The heels of the slippers
dragged on the carpet as she walked down the hallway in
front of him.

There was a new girl at the club. She was Polish, blonde and
sullen. She refused to smile and her room was a disgrace, Joyce
said. There were cigarette butts on the floor, soiled underwear.
She had been back to England for several abortions. Her hair
was often greasy and hung about her face, but the clients loved

her, Joyce said. Her air of Middle European decadence. Her heavily intonated English. They didn't seem to mind that she was sexually unresponsive. They thought that this was what they deserved, unsatisfying sexual encounters.

'She's a cow, but the punters can't get enough of her,' Joyce said. 'You can't believe the stuff they ask her to do. Unbelievable.'

Erskine brought girls from the Black Cat Club in Blackpool to work in Gemini. He made sure that they attended the Theipval MO on a weekly basis: 'The last thing we want is one of these sports catching a dose,' he said. He went for foreigners, but Joyce preferred experienced girls with colloquial accents and liked to promote a spirit of cheery self-reliance among them.

'How come a working house is always in a basement?' Joyce said. 'I never seen one that wasn't right at the bottom of the house. The smell of damp in this place would skin you. Pleurisy is what you'd get working in a place like this.'

David thought that the smell of damp was a good thing. It contributed to the unwholesome atmosphere in the place. Joyce had taken a small back room as her office. There was a table with a chipped Formica top in the centre with a tin cashbox on it. One corner of the room was filled with recording equipment, reel-to-reels in battered black metal cases. A cased camera, the casing lined with kapok for silent exposures.

'One of them techs is upstairs, trying out the cinecamera,' Joyce said.

David was experimenting with Super Eight cine film. The lighting was the problem. Faces were lost, sexual acts were indistinct, as though they were engaged in some hypothetical act.

'Any players in today?' David asked.

'Not a one, far as I can tell. Just the punters, a few regulars.'

David turned up the volume on one of the mikes. It was linked to a room occupied by a girl called Jackie, who had asked Joyce to send policemen to her.

'It's the uniform,' Joyce said. 'The little tart likes the feel of the uniform.'

The conversation between the punter and the girl sounded strange, archived. As though it had taken place a long time ago. The man was talking about his wife, about all the things that she would not do for him, the girl making little noises of assent from time to time. David found himself listening intently. There seemed to be something that he was required to deduce from their conversation, that the man was engaged in giving some kind of testimony to the nature of his life and the completeness of his solitude.

'Give us a penny for every man ever talked about his wife,' Joyce said.

David stood behind her and rubbed the knuckles of his right hand along her spine. It was something he liked to do. He appreciated the way that Joyce kept on talking as though nothing was happening. He often thought that working girls had a grasp on the true nature of espionage, the ambience of need that had to be maintained, the sense of unspoken appetites. Joyce would leave milk at the back door of Gemini for the stray cats that infested the back gardens.

He liked to hold her ankle in his hand, run his hands along her bare arms. There was a pastiness to her that he liked, a running to fat, a sense of poor post-war diet. Her underwear was ill-fitting. He liked the fact that she was unresponsive when he slept with her. She liked him to touch. She liked him to call her mother. He liked to tug at her slack flesh.

One of the techs came into the room. Without speaking to either of them, he drew the curtains. He erected a screen on a stand and switched on the camera. There was a smell of hot film in the room, an atmosphere of mild toxins. David sat down to watch the footage. Joyce started to wash cups in the sink. The film had been shot in the upstairs bedroom because the light was best there. The tech had been concealed in the next room, with a hole cut into the wall for the camera. David had discussed it with Joyce and they thought it was unlikely that a client would notice the lens or the faint sound of the camera running. They were usually dry-mouthed, respectful, fearful of transgressing. They chose first-timers as less likely to notice anything wrong. From the moment they entered the house, they were aware that they were subject to a code of behaviour that was unfamiliar to them, a dread etiquette that had to be maintained. The footage was grainy and indistinct. The figures onscreen had a feeling of odyssey about them, of labouring into the night; the sounds were hisses, wordless exclamations, strained falsettos. You had a sense of the husbanding of resources. You wanted to weep for them. The women had an Eastern European look to them, a dark radiance. They turned their faces wordlessly upward, bathed in historical sorrow.

5

Knox sat in the Rover in the car park of the Royal Victoria Hospital. He found places like this soothing, large areas with a municipal dimension to them. Spatial vectors, urban renewal. From where he was parked he could see the entrance to casualty. He tried to read the injuries of patients being unloaded from ambulances by the demeanour of the accompanying relative. He guessed gunshot wound. He guessed blunt force trauma. There was a brief burst of activity with people suffering from multiple shrapnel wounds being helped from taxis. As the last taxi pulled away, the passenger door of the Rover opened sharply and Agnew got in. He wore a brown raincoat which he pulled up as he sat down, moving his service Webley round on his belt so that he could sit comfortably.

'Cunt of a thing, a Webley, so it is,' the policeman said. 'You'd never get it out of the holster if you needed it. No use to man nor beast.'

Knox waited for him to complete the operation. Agnew was always restless. Some part of him was always moving. His mind as well. Looking for opportunities, for a deal, for leverage.

'You better mind yourself with that knocking shop on the Antrim Road. If PIRA get wind of it, you boys is fucked.'

'Not really my concern. Gemini is Erskine's op.'

'What's the story with Erskine anyhow? Who is he?'

'David Erskine is attached to the corridor. He's PsyOps.'

'PsyOps, my hole. He's running a brothel. Do them boys tell him anything or what? Do they spill the beans when they're on the job? I got an Armalite in the attic, my love.'

'Not the point. They become assets as soon as they set foot in the place.'

33

'Blackmail.'

'Crudely put.'

'Do what I tell you or I'll tell the wife.'

'Perhaps. Although it doesn't often have to go that far. They are, after all, filled with remorse. They are grateful to you for knowing their secret.'

'Too complicated for me. You got anything else for us?'

'Not at the minute. Just keep things low profile for the time being.'

'Jackson's not going to like that. That boy likes to be in the thick. He could take off, settle a few things on his own account.'

'I don't want Jackson freelancing.'

'I don't think the likes of you or me is fit to tell the likes of Jackson what he should be doing or not doing.'

Agnew was reluctant to talk about Jackson. It seemed that it was better not to speak too much about him. The words you sussed about Jackson tended to hang in the air long after they were uttered. There was a sense of arcana about his name, of dread usage.

'He said this army boy got in touch with him.'

'What army person got in touch with him?'

'Some boy by the name of Nairac. You know him?'

'I've seen him in the corridor. I didn't pay him much notice. Struck me as a bit of a lightweight. Naïve. Bit of a Boys' Own type.'

'If he's a lightweight, then he's punching well above his weight with Jackson. He'd want to watch his step there, so he would.'

'I think I'll have to take a look at this Nairac. Army Int are in general not the most subtle of people.'

'What is he, a major or something?'

'A captain, I think. A Guards captain if my memory serves me. Attached to SAS.'

'Wonder what Jackson thinks of that? A Guards captain sniffing around him.'

Knox made no comment on what Jackson might have thought about Nairac. He was aware that Jackson's thoughts were unknowable, but he suspected the presence of deep-seated psychic carnage.

He could smell whiskey from Agnew. He knew that the policeman was gambling heavily on horses and dogs. Both activities were common among policemen in the city. You saw them standing at checkpoints with Heckler & Koch rifles. Burly men with compact families and a tendency to nihilism. He had seen the same traits among native policemen when he had been posted to Yemen. Agnew told him that he had taken to sitting in the dark with his revolver on the table in front of him, an open bottle of whiskey in his hand. The sitting in the dark went with the gambling and the drinking, Agnew explained. He seemed to be saying that a certain level of unexplained suicide among middle-aged men was not necessarily the worst psychic outcome in the situation they were in. It implied a level of self-knowledge not attainable in peacetime.

'Where is this Nairac based?'

'Bessbrook Mill, near the border. He goes on patrol with the regular army. Carries a shotgun under the arm.'

'Why?'

'Don't know. Walks along like a squire. Calls the locals by name. They all think he's not wise. He goes into the local bars and sings for them. They call him the British captain.'

'This is a joke.'

'No joke, honest to God.'

'What kind of songs?'

'Carrickfergus. Danny Boy.'

'The man is a menace.'

'The same thought come into my own head. A menace to the world.'

'We have to find out who his direct superior is.'

'We ask around?'

Knox thought about it. You didn't ask around. You never went for the direct route. Information that came to you obliquely was more valuable. It picked up nuances on the way. You found yourself acquiring peripheral wisdoms. There were complaints from GCHQ that there were too many organizations on the ground and that they were interfering with each other's work. Knox didn't agree. He encouraged the entry of other branches into the field. It was important to have inter-agency rivalry, people working in layers, laying false trails for each other. Groups of highly trained men stumbling across each other at night. Knox knew that confusion was important. A sense of unstable government was vital to good intelligence work. You wanted there to be shifting patterns, shadowy allegiances, overtones of corruption and sexual scandal. There were unexplained incidents of violence, widely witnessed, which were later denied on all main media. As a consequence people could no longer rely on their own perceptions and were driven to depend upon less obvious means of interpreting what was going on around them. They were forced to acknowledge tonal variations in the matter of their lives, attend to psychic currents, place meaning on certain patterns of weather. They became grateful for violent death. It was the one fixed thing which gave perspective to everything else.

'Let's just observe him, keep an eye,' Knox said.

'I don't know about leaving him be,' Agnew said. 'There's plenty of mischief for him to be at.'

'Maybe we could involve him in a little mischief of our own.'

'Might be we could,' Agnew said thoughtfully. 'It might be we could. But how would you get him into our way of thinking?'

'I got you into my way of thinking.'

'I'm different.'

'Different how?'

'I don't give a fuck about none of you.'

Agnew liked to think of himself as a rogue cop. He liked the transatlantic sound of the phrase. There was an edgy, modish feel to it. He liked the sound of rogue cop and he liked the sound of out of control. He imagined the words being whispered about him in the barracks. Agnew's fucking out of control. He was given to bursts of sudden uncontrollable rage during interrogations and the whispering of death threats to suspects being led into court. Frequently now he had the sense of being a disinterested observer of his own actions and knew that it was only a matter of time before he killed someone, and felt that this elevated him above his colleagues.

He had a girlfriend at the time. She was a tall, pale girl with a history of spousal abuse. Agnew thought that he provided her with what she needed, that his drunken rages and infrequent bouts of clumsy, inconsequential sex, heavily laced with blame, were the things that held her together. She needed to be told that she was not beautiful, that she was stupid. She needed her friends imploring her to leave him, the pitying looks of neighbours when she left the flat. She saw herself as clinging to the rudimentary dynamic of self-blame that ran through their relationship. She would sit on the edge of a red vinyl armchair in the small living room of her flat in Whiteabbey with mascara running down her face, woebegone, defeated.

'What is this boy at anyhow, this Nairac cunt?' Agnew asked. 'Does he not know he's going to get himself stiffed?'

'It seems that he is operating to a different agenda.'

'What fucking agenda? The dead captain agenda? The stiffed and single gunshot to head and dumped on the border agenda?'

Knox said nothing. He was beginning to sense a structure in the things that Agnew was telling him. There was a thematic progression which was stark, modernist, but with a feeling of something more feral about it, Nairac out there, wanting the natives to like him, identifying with them.

'He's a fucking head job waiting to happen,' Agnew said. 'He's an innocent abroad in a nasty world.'

Afterwards he noticed that Knox had not made any comment on the subject of Nairac's innocence.

'Let's leave Nairac alone. Meanwhile, there's the subject of Jackson to deal with. You have to talk to him.'

'I don't have to do nothing, Knox, just you mind that.'

Agnew knew that Knox owned him, but felt an obligation to mark the moment with some hard bluster, feeling that it was expected of him at this part of the conversation. The point of hard talk usually preceded the point of weary ironies.

'Inform Jackson that he is an asset. At the minute. Inform him that assets can turn to liabilities very quickly.'

Agnew could tell that Knox was pleased with the phrasing of that. Assets and liabilities. There was a menacing equilibrium to the sentence. However, he doubted that it would mean a fiddler's fuck to the likes of Jackson, whose life was posited on different orders of equilibrium, on the fundamentals of carnage.

'A man would wonder how much of it makes any bit of difference anyhow,' Agnew said.

He had his instructions now and was willing to sit back and watch nurses leaving the hospital, the white of their uniforms stark in the gathering dusk. You had the sensation of signals coming through, systemic in the darkness, of semaphore.

'I like nurses,' he told Knox. 'I want to marry a nurse.'

He liked to look at them when they were unaware of him, bent over a patient or writing notes on a chart at night, the geometry of the uniforms, the way they used your first name no matter what. He could see himself standing in a registry office with a nurse, an RN in her mid-thirties with a good heart. He saw himself waking up beside a sad-eyed altruist, smelling faintly of disinfectant.

Six months earlier he had checked into an alcohol clinic in the Downshire Hospital. It turned out to be an enclosed unit. An old part of the hospital with long distempered hallways. The alcohol unit was in the same wing as the psychiatric patients. There were padded doors with no handles, meshed grilles on the windows. The psychiatric patients queued up for their drugs. Clozapine. Haloperidol. There were classes in basket-weaving, rug-making, remedial activities with a folksy edge to them.

He liked it for a while. He developed a shuffling walk. He talked to doctors without meeting their eyes. When he spoke to them he tried to develop the persona of a man on the edge of unravelling, letting his speech tail off mid-sentence. He slumped. He twitched. He gave in to bursts of uncontrollable rage, followed by long periods of unnecessarily severe remorse. He began to spend time with the paranoids. He found that there were areas of agreement between them, matters of common concern.

He would not have believed what they told him about full moon. At full moon they locked up the cutlery and confiscated shoelaces. The mildly depressed sat in corners, talking to imaginary foes. There were multiple attempted suicides and retreats into catatonia. Patients talked of owls fluttering against windows, of actual bats in the corridors. Harbingers of madness arriving unannounced.

Every second afternoon he had therapy with Dr Greene. Dr Greene had a psychiatrist's wispy hair. Agnew told him outrageous lies. He seemed to believe that this was required of him. That he should enter fully into the baroque structures of madness, that there should be a wild-eyed element to his narrative.

At full moon he lay awake, listening to bare feet running up and down the corridors.

One day he was told to put on his street clothes. He was shown into the room where Professor Greene had talked to him about the addictive personality and about the twelve-step programme. Agnew knew he would laugh out loud if he had to stand up at a meeting and say hello my name is Blair, in a damp basement room with fold-out chairs and posters sellotaped to the wall. He saw himself saying things like hello you bunch of sad alco bastards. He saw himself saying anyone for a drink, by fuck I'd skull a double vodka.

39

When he saw Clyde Knox sitting in Professor Greene's chair he thought a psychiatrist, a mumbling cunt with a fringe hanging over his face and a hole in the elbow of his woollen pullover. Knox told him to sit down. Agnew expected therapeutic talk, roaming in the broad confessional spaces. Instead Knox took a photograph from a folder and placed it in front of him. The photograph showed a cratered country road. An armoured Cortina lay on its side several yards away. There was a sense of aftermath, of dazed survivors. Knox said two names out loud. They were the names of men who had attended basic training with Agnew. He could see them at their passing-out parade, marching past the dais, eyes right, in white gloves and spit-polished boots, with the band playing a jaunty air, everything aimed at creating a finely tuned semi-militaristic pathos, melancholy images of ambush and sudden death encompassed.

'Dead?' Agnew said.

'Killed by a culvert bomb. Four hundred pounds in a beer keg. Detonation cord leading to a nearby hillside.'

Agnew knew that it was a recognized technique. You worked on people's grief. You worked on their bewilderment and pain. You pointed out aspects of brotherhood. You offered them a structure to work within. Six weeks later you found yourself conducting an unsanctioned checkpoint, wearing civilian clothing, the body of a man lying at your feet.

Knox pulled Agnew's service Webley from the bag at his feet and pushed it across the desk. Agnew looked at it.

'I'm in the madhouse,' he said. 'I could shoot you. They'd never convict.'

'Shoot away,' Knox said. 'I'm offering you an opportunity.' He tapped the photograph. 'These are men with girlfriends, with mothers beside themselves with grief. Where is Blair Agnew? In a hospital while two former colleagues are lying cold and dead.'

'I'm being recruited.'

'We're asking for assistance from like-minded men. The place is falling apart. There are civilians gunned down in the street for no apparent reason. Commercial life is at a standstill. The courts are weak. Blair Agnew sits in a hospital.'

Knox stopped talking. Agnew looked at the Webley sitting on the table. It looked weighty, chipped, exuding a dullish authority. The black barrel, the brown handgrip, a thing of surprising heft with a feeling of covenant about it, of avowal and consequence.

6

David had seen Robert on the corridor for the first time in January 1974. Sleet was sweeping in across Lisburn. You could hear it against the wooden walls and tar roof of the building. It was four o'clock, approaching dusk, and the corridor gave the impression of being the base camp of some character-testing expedition, with men coming in from week-long treks with a grizzled look, haunted by peril and hair's-breadth escape. Robert was standing at the end of the corridor, talking to an NCO. He was wearing a donkey jacket and old trousers and had his back to David. As he turned away from the NCO, David glimpsed Robert's face. He realized after Robert's death that it seemed this was the only way he had ever seen Robert, turning away from you with a half-smile on his face, glancing at you with an air of amusement. He had dark hair, almost black. The kind of hair that is described as unruly, overtones of boyishness, of mischief. David moved closer. He had never seen Robert before but he knew it was him. The donkey jacket was often mentioned when people spoke about Robert. It was what he wore when he went out into the field. David could see why. It gave you the authority of burly men, big-knuckled, raw-boned. David noticed that Robert had a Guardsman's stance, which the donkey jacket went some way towards concealing, although you could see that he had a Guardsman's jawline, and the way he moved his hands as he spoke hinted at something clipped and regimental.

Robert spent several hours in the corridor. He would walk into an office and start to question its inhabitants about the projects they were working on. He made them feel the urgency of their task. He was based in the city at the time and he brought the city to them. He told them about mystery gunmen, about nail bombs, about pogroms, about mutilated corpses in the street, about arson, riot, the night-time city with dark miscreants abroad. He brought a drama and urgency to their workaday existence. David could see into the offices through the glass windows that formed one wall of the corridor. He was taking IntSum files from the boot of his car and bringing them to his office. Robert seemed to be working his way up the corridor from office to office. David couldn't hear what he was saying but he could see men exchanging shy, grateful glances among themselves as Robert spoke to them. At one stage he seemed to be orating. There were four other men in the room and they seemed to be rapt. Though David couldn't hear anything he knew what was going on, the words seeming to travel through the fabric of the building. There was disturbance in the air, a sense of a tent evangelist's metaphysic clamour.

David made a last trip to his car. It was now seven o'clock in the evening and the barracks were quiet. It was Friday and civilian employees had left the base for the weekend. Half-melted sleet lay on the ground. Antennae glistened on rooftops. The buildings were flat-roofed 1960s functional structures, dreary in daylight but coming into their own on a night like this, taking on the attributes of a baleful northern-latitudes listening station, low-slung monochromatic buildings of sinister intent.

David carried the last box along the corridor. When he looked through the first pane of glass, he saw that Nairac was in his office. He seemed to have the authority to be there. He looked as if the office formed part of his jurisdiction. He was turning over papers on David's desk in a casual way, his face lit from underneath by the desk lamp. David remembered it afterwards. Nairac's affinity for striking poses of unconscious heroism. He carried the box into the room and put it down on the desk. He held out his hand.

'David Erskine.'

43

'Bob Nairac.'

David realized that there was technique in the way Nairac took his hand. The way he squeezed it firmly and then held on to it for a moment too long, holding David's eye as he did so. There was a self-taught feel to it.

'Sorry about just walking into your office, David. Couldn't resist a look at your map.'

David had a PhotInt image of the city from the KH-9A satellite pinned to his wall. It had been copied from a high-resolution image and blown up on to paper. It had a blurry feel to it. The streets were indistinct in places, shadowy and ill-defined. The purpose of the image was to provide a clear strategic overview, but in fact it suggested shadowy activity, something barely discerned flooding in from the suburbs, the far-flung industrial estates. Knox had commented on the image with approval and asked for a similar image to be posted in his own office. It appealed to his sense of social decay, economic structures imploding, covert activity filling the areas no longer under the control of civil authority.

Nairac went over to the map. He put his finger up to it and appeared to be tracing imaginary lines on it, lines that went to the margins and beyond.

'You hear what they're saying at HQ? They say, and I quote, they are confident of disrupting enemy supply lines. Supply lines, mark you. They still think this is France 1944. They think they're at El Alamein. You and I know different, David.'

'Hearts and Minds?' The Hearts and Minds policy had been in force for several months. Soldiers were encouraged to be friendly to the local populace, to gain their confidence. It was accompanied by photographs of cheery soldiers in battledress chatting to young boys.

'Hearts and Minds is fine, but it's not for me. Hearts and Minds is about getting people to like you. I want to get inside their heads, fuck it. I want to know what they're thinking.'

'How do you do that?'

'For an instance, the accent is important. You must appreciate that not all accents are the same. I can do Lurgan. I can do Belfast. Go into the fucking bars. Smoke a fag with them. Gain their confidence. I do a Belfast accent. For fuck's sakes, give us a fag. That's the Belfast way of talking.'

David wanted to hear the accent. He wanted to hear the Guardsman do a Belfast accent, work his way into the consonantal squawks, the post-industrial falsetto, the semi-hysteric tailing off. But Nairac didn't do it. He leaned towards David confidentially.

'You know, David, I have a feeling that they're going to get me here. I have a feeling that I won't be going home from this place.'

David stared at him. Robert looked back with the air of having exchanged a confidence, something forceful and intuitive and fundamental. David was surprised that a man like Robert could utter something so banal. But afterwards he realized that it was part of the persona. That charismatic men were drawn to cheap sentiment and facile self-dramatizing. It was part of their trajectory, the appeal to the popular consciousness, the way you looked at yourself in a maudlin way. It was part of your entitlement, to address yourself in grandiose terms, to enter people's lives and transform them by means of softly spoken confidences delivered without irony.

Robert picked up a shotgun from David's desk. David couldn't believe that he hadn't noticed it there before, among the papers. It was a hunting gun with delicate chasing on the trigger guard. You knew, to look at it, that it was hand-made. There was a bespoke allure to it. Holding the gun by the barrel, Robert slung it casually over his shoulder. He shook David's hand again.

'I'm going out with the Greenjackets tonight. Mustn't keep them waiting,' he said. David watched him walk off down the corridor, smiling at people as he went. He saw the rolling inexorable walk, the predator's gait, and he watched through the window as Robert crossed the car park, his lips pursed, the faint strains of a whistled tune reaching him and, although he could not make out the melody, the sight of the whistling man conjured up an image of something jaunty and ill-starred.

7

Agnew drove towards Lurgan. He had to deliver Knox's message to Jackson. He was stopped by several checkpoints as he approached Lurgan. He showed his warrant card. The men seemed to know where he was going. They handed back the warrant card with a knowing look. He tried to remember what he knew about Jackson. He knew that Jackson had been taken away for training. Cyprus had been talked about. The local branch officers laughed about that. Jackson the only man that winter in Lurgan with a tan. Knox had sent Agnew on a similar course in Ashford. Tactical firearms training. Close-quarters assassination. The hollowing out of bullet points. He attended lectures on the subject of infiltration techniques, agent extraction. Secrets of dark espionage. Agnew drank whiskey with the physical combat instructor, a burly, light-footed man in his mid-forties. The man had served in Oman in the late 1950s. He described in detail an affair he had conducted with a fourteen-year-old native girl. He kept describing her as willing. He showed Agnew photographs of his estranged wife and children. He apologized for not having a photograph of the girl. Agnew seemed to find himself drunk late at night in the company of men with complex longings.

Agnew had a feeling that Jackson would not have spent his time in Cyprus drinking. The instructor had served in Cyprus and he told Agnew that it was a place of tunnelled mountains, isolated gorges, secret military installations. In the winter you could freeze in the mountains, contract skin cancers on the plains. A detective inspector from Lurgan told Agnew that he had seen Jackson in Larnaca when the policeman was on holiday. He said that Jackson was in a beach-front hotel, drinking with four or five other men. They were wearing work shirts and camping boots. The detective inspector said that he knew they were Special Forces by the way they moved, a kind of self-absorption to them. Jackson was the still centre of the group. He said that they sat around Jackson in a manner which suggested that he was cherished.

Jackson's house was on a small estate in Lurgan. The houses were well kept, with trimmed lawns and garden furniture with a hand-made look. It was the kind of place where you expected full employment, men working in small engineering firms – fitters, mechanics, small resourceful men with a mechanical bent. Compact family cars sat in driveways. You expected episodes of minor suburban dismay. Jackson's house was in the middle of a row of identical houses. It had a post and rail fence painted white. Agnew pulled up outside and turned off the engine. There was no one else on the street. It was cold and overcast and some leaves blew down the street. He looked up and saw Jackson standing in the doorway. He was in his stocking feet and had a china cup in his hand. He remained in the doorway as Agnew got out of the car. Jackson held the glass door for him.

Agnew sat in Jackson's living room. He wondered who had been responsible for the way the room was decorated. There was a deep nylon carpet, a salmon three-piece suite with tassels on. There were net curtains edged in lace on the windows and shepherdesses on the mantelpiece. It struck Agnew as being a retired man's room, a place of accumulated comforts, the ornateness of the furnishings. Agnew knew that most of the other houses on this estate had a similar room. The velveteen cushions, the framed embroidery print of birds, the sense of no expense spared within limits. Normally Agnew liked these rooms, but he didn't like being in Jackson's living room. Jackson was a small man, balding, unemphatic, pitiless. He was the kind of man who made you brag to your friends how scared he made you feel, strain to find words to describe the creeping terror. Fear as

48

a language, difficult to enunciate, visceral, harshly intonated.

'Knox thinks you should take it easy for a bit.'

'Thon cunt.'

'Could be right so he could.'

'Knox has no notion what's happening here.'

'I'd watch him still and all.'

'You watch him, then. I've better things to be doing.'

The eyes never changed, Agnew thought.

'Knox says to sit still.'

'Sit still like fuck I'll sit still.'

'Says it, so he does.'

'There's more boys than Knox that's not for sitting still.'

'What boys would that be?'

'Boys that would be in my line and boys that would be in Knox's line.'

'Come on, boy. Don't talk shite. There's few enough boys in the same line as you, never mind the likes of Knox.'

'I never asked you here, Agnew, nor give you the speak to believe or misbelieve me.'

'I hear tell a few people seen the British captain in these parts.'

'What people?'

'Just a few people that says they seen an Englishman in a donkey jacket.'

There was a sense of things having gone too far. Agnew found that he couldn't stop talking. He had a sense of future retribution, of being flagged down at a fake checkpoint, of a hail of bullets, glass shattering.

'If you got any plans with the British captain, maybe you'd better put them on hold.'

He was in the grasp of a massive hopelessness now. He could see himself sitting in the small room, gesturing apologetically.

'Nobody knows what the British captain is at, who is running him or anything. Fuck knows. You find yourself in trouble and nobody's fit to get you out of it.'

Agnew had the feeling that Jackson had been working with Nairac all along. That some dreadful plot had already been hatched, something tortuous, Elizabethan, with overtones of small-hours treachery. Jackson was smiling now, nodding gently as Agnew talked. He could feel sweat running down the inside of his shirt. He felt that Jackson was working on a way to take him out, an elegant, nuanced operation. He saw a baleful tableau of murder; something dark and arterial flowing from his head.

Afterwards Agnew went for a drink in the Blues Bar in Portadown. The town was empty except for youths who sat at the wheel of customized cars. Escorts, Capris. Sometimes they started the engines and drove in convoy around the town, moving according to no discernible signal. There was the impression of careful ritual taking place. The empty places had to be patrolled. Agnew kept finding himself in towns like this. Places strange, windswept, bare.

There was horse-racing on the television above the bar. Some part of him knew that he would find Hoppy there. Hoppy was a shapeless man with an air of failed business ventures about him. He wore a sports jacket and carried a large bunch of keys on his belt. He was the only person who seemed to spend any time with Jackson. He seemed to have the ability to tolerate the sense of amoral void that Jackson projected, of mercy abrogate.

'Well, Agnew, having a steadier? You look brave and shook. I seen your motor up at Jacko's.'

'Me and him had something to talk about.'

'You're not the first boy I seen come out of that house looking a bit white around the gills.'

'How's things in the disco business, Hoppy?'

Hoppy had a mobile disco which he ran from a trailer he pulled behind his car.

'Away and fuck yourself, Agnew.'

'Only asking a civil question.'

'I'll tell you something,' Hoppy said, sitting down beside Agnew, 'you mind people were saying that discos was going to finish off the live band? Well, them people is talking pure shite. Far as I can see, the live bands is ripping the arse out of the disco business. Can't get work for love nor money.'

Agnew wondered if Hoppy's association with Jackson had anything to do with the fact that he wasn't getting any bookings. He thought that you didn't want the likes of Jackson turning up on a Saturday night.

'Mind you, the British captain wasn't too worried. He just walks clean up to the door, not a bother on him.'

'What British captain?'

Agnew was aware that the question had come out too sharply.

'Always the peeler, that right, Agnew?'

'Only asking.'

'Never heard his name. I asks Jacko but he just gives me this look.'

'What'd he look like?'

'You've some neck on you, do you know that, Agnew? There's many a man would stop asking questions, if you get me. There's many a man would get up off that bar stool and head for the door and get away on to fuck out of this town.'

'What are you going to do, Hoppy, shoot me or what?'

'You know me, Agnew. I'm the happy-go-lucky type.'

'There's a relief.'

'There's one or two boys sitting in this room right this minute who's maybe not got the patience that I've got.'

'They likely to top me in the next ten minutes?'

'Not if you mind yourself.'

'That's good. I'll get to finish this drink, then.'

'You taking a hand out of me, Agnew?'

'God forbid. What captain, Hoppy?'

'Captain fucking America.'

'Was he wearing a donkey jacket?'

'Could of been.'

'Black hair. Was his nose broke?'

'Broke to fuck. Somebody must have give him a good booting.'

'He was a boxer.'

'I tell you something about him. He was brave, I'll give him that. Just marches into Jacko's house, so he does, like it was his own ma's house.'

'Did he?'

'Here comes the cavalry now, by fuck.'

Agnew looked up. Harris Boyle and Wesley Somerville were standing at the top end of the counter, under the television. Hoppy waved at the two men. They walked slowly towards Agnew and Hoppy. They were wearing black zip-up leather jackets and were working at the projection of a sequenced menace. Agnew knew that Boyle had just been acquitted on charges of possessing two .38 revolvers and ammunition and that Boyle had been questioned with relation to attempted murder.

'What're you doing with thon fucker, Agnew?' Somerville said.

'Take her handy there, Somerville,' Agnew said, 'I'm an officer of the court.'

'You could be a former officer of the court pretty easy,' Somerville said.

He put his hands between his knees and mimed working the slide of a pistol, then raised it slowly until it was pointed at Agnew.

'You looking to get lifted again, Somerville?' Agnew said. 'Because I'm the boy to do it.'

'You can lift all you want,' Somerville said, 'I'll be out in a day or two. Me and Boyle's looked after, so we are. Tell you something, Agnew, you get in my road, you'll be for the heavy dint, the heavy fucking dint.'

Boyle stood there, saying nothing. He seemed to have acquired gravitas since the last time Agnew had seen him. He was able to project an air of effortless foreboding that was normally perfected only by men older than him, grizzled veterans with serious gaol time and a long-term criminal's range of sentimental regard for small children, domestic pets. Boyle knew he was doing exactly the right thing by standing there without speaking. Agnew found himself shifting uneasily on his stool, running a finger around the inside of his collar, glancing at the door. He felt like a parodic accused, a weasel-faced con with a bad conscience. Somerville and Boyle were standing too close. Even Hoppy seemed to be in possession of dangerous knowledge.

Afterwards he knew that they were all far more deeply involved than he realized. It was there in the quiet way they watched him leave the bar. He glanced back from the doorway and saw them gathered at the end of the counter. Somerville raised his right hand mockingly to his temple, so that Agnew felt he was taking salute from some hellish militia raised for the purpose of butchery and pogrom.

8

Robert built Airfix models of the Tirpitz. He constructed Panzer Tigers and Soviet T-20s, working in miniature, trimming the pieces with a modelling knife, manoeuvring the elements into position with tweezers. A Stuka hung from the ceiling. He removed excess glue with a petrol-soaked rag. At odd moments the smell of modelling glue would come back to him, a sweetish acetone smell, faintly toxic, like an industrial lacquer with overtones of deep cell damage, creeping malignancy. He liked to build German military vehicles. He liked the harsh symmetry of them, a kind of brutal grace. There was a sense of countries going under about the German military vehicles, of nationhood being obliterated. He bought a German coal-scuttle helmet from a market stall dealing in military memorabilia. He liked to hold it in his hands. The interior webbing was intact, although frayed and sweat-stained. The grey paint was chipped. It was heavier than he had thought it would be, a weighty object in sombre iron. There was a swastika decal on one side of it and stencilled lettering on the inside. He traced the shape of the words with his finger, their guttural angularity. He imagined the words being shouted, an argot of empty boulevards and small terrorized towns, jagged and brutish.

He kept war comics on two shelves above his bed. The Victor, the Hornet, the Hotspur on the top shelf, Commando books on the bottom. The ink came off the Hornet on to your hands. He liked the symbol for the Commando books, which was a dagger with a laurel wreath around it. He liked the sense of continuity about the stories. There were small cockney soldiers with names like Sparrow and East End accents and overtones of malnutrition, low birth-weight.

There was a theme of defiance of authority to many of the stories that he liked.

When Robert was eleven he was sent to Ampleforth. Ampleforth was a Roman Catholic public school. It had red-brick buildings and quadrangles and was subject to reverent evening hushes, a sense of historical continuity. Oak panels recorded the names of former pupils who had died at Verdun, at Rorke's Drift. There was an undercurrent of Jesuitical guile, men in ornate church robes with hooked noses and burning, deep-set eyes. On parents' days former pupils came, bluff white-haired men with firm handshakes and a high colour who referred to themselves as Old Amplefordians.

Mother sewed name-tags into his clothing. She fussed over him, put things in his case and then took them out again. Robert's father told her to stop fussing. Robert's father said, 'For heaven's sake.' They took him to school on a Sunday evening. His father drove the car, asking him the meaning of school words. The meaning of dormitory. The meaning of rec. Robert looked at his hands on the wheel. A surgeon's hands, fine and white and hairless. You thought of the hand holding a scalpel, reaching down to cut. Almost a blow, was what he had read in Gray's Anatomy. A deft brutality to the act which scared him.

'Fix your tie, Robert,' Mother said.

'There won't be anyone to tell you to fix your tie from now on, Robert,' his father said. 'You'll have to learn self-sufficiency.'

The gates and driveway of the school looked familiar. They belonged with the family's world of tree-lined avenues, well-kept lawns. The driveway was gravelled and their car swept up to the front of the school with a rich, textured sound. They were met by the dean. He was a small man with cropped grey hair who projected an air of shrewd kindliness. Robert sat in a parlour while his parents had tea with him. A girl poured the tea into bone china cups. Robert noticed that the Dean did not look at her or thank her. He saw that her knuckles were raw and skinned and the skin on her face was chapped.

'The nuns send them up to us,' the Dean said, nodding in her direction. 'No better than they should be, but we make sure they don't talk to the boys.'

As the girl picked up the tray and left, she glanced up and Robert found her eyes locked on to his. Her face was completely immobile, her lack of expression exaggerated by the chapped skin. Robert had the impression of being watched from an opening in an ancient gate, a sense of vows taken, of long vigil.

After half an hour the priest told him to take his bags to the dormitory. The floors were linoleum polished with beeswax. The beds were steel-framed with lockers beside each one. There was a sense of exile, of male solitude despite the proximity of the beds to each other. At the end of the dormitory there was a row of sinks. The porcelain was cracked and rust-spotted. The chromium on the taps had peeled off. A faulty washer leaked continuously. There was a smell of drains. Robert compared it to the neatness of the rest of the dormitory, the studied dereliction and felt that there was a methodology at work here, a theology of ruin.

The Dean had told him to explore the college since most of the other boys were in the study hall. He walked alongside the tennis courts and down a hill towards the playing fields. He met two older boys. They were carrying cricket stumps and pads. One boy's face was covered in acne. It seemed to be something he wore. A mask of affliction. The other boy was tall and blond with pale blue eyes. When they saw Robert coming, they stopped and placed the cricket gear carefully by the side of the path. They waited until Robert drew level with them. One of them pushed him.

'The new boy.'

'An overly fresh boy.'

'He looks a bit green to me.'

'He'll have to learn his lessons. Then he won't look so green.'

'He'll learn his grammar.'

'The verb to beat.'

'The verb to ride.'

They pushed him back and forth between them. He knew that you did not show fear. His father said that fear was glandular in origin. Fear led to flight, he said. It had no other purpose. The mind could conquer the primitive impulse. He held his breath. He felt a blow on the side of his head. He went down on the mud of the path. His uniform was grey flannel trousers with a white shirt and striped tie. He felt the mud coming through the trousers on to his knees. He remembered the boots that they were wearing. Black square-toed boots that made them look as if there was something wrong with their feet. They looked as if they would limp badly when walking. They kept on kicking him. They kicked him in the kidneys. They kicked him at the base of his spine. Robert looked at the boots. He kept thinking about spinal deformities, calipers, about white-faced slum children with dragging walks.

Robert used to see the girl with the chapped face. She worked in the school kitchen. The other boys referred to her as Scabby. They made uncalled-for sexual remarks about her. Sometimes they made them to her face as she served meals in the refectory. She didn't appear to hear them. Robert could see the face behind the skin. When she was serving meals, she sometimes lifted her eyes and looked at him. The same unreadable look, covert and allusive. He imagined her asleep in an attic room, wearing a worn nightdress fastened tightly at the neck. He wondered if the scales of skin on her face continued past her throat. He wondered if her body showed signs of the transgression which had consigned her to the care of the laundry. He imagined a pale freckled torso, something broad-hipped, something wan and coveted.

Robert was good at sailing. He was good at archery and fencing. He played rugby. He went on climbing expeditions to the Lake District. Robert knew how to take a bird's egg from a nest and keep it warm underneath his shirt. He was a member of the school rowing team. He owned a Hardy split-cane rod and a brass Mitchel reel made in France. Robert befriended the mechanic in the local garage. He competed in motocross on a Matchless 125. He was junior champion in the boxing club. He would talk other boys into fighting without headgear. You would be sparring with Robert, trading punches, and you would find your face laid open to the bone, the nose broken with the first punch, and then he'd hit you again as you stood with the gloves by your sides, feeling the cartilage being driven back into the nasal cavity. You had a sense of bone splinters being driven into the brain. You would look up to see Robert watching you from behind his gloves, his face blood-flecked, the eyes holding you, something feral in them, steady and unblinking and remorseless, watching you from a covert.

During the school holidays Robert would go into town to Clark's Gym. Just saunter in, his hands in his pockets. It was the kind of place that he had been looking for: the peeling posters, the hangers-on in the shadows, the sluggers, the brain-damaged, the wiry young men boxing and watching their moves in full-length mirrors. There was the smell of cigarette smoke, of wintergreen-based liniment, of old blood. Bill Clark owned the gym. He was a small man with a boxer's face. He wore a white shirt with the sleeves rolled up and kept an unlit cigarette in his mouth. He felt that he had to smoke something, that there was a responsibility on him to cultivate character. When he wanted to talk to someone, he had to take it out of his mouth. The first time Robert went to the club he stood by the door, watching. Men skipping, men hitting the bag, men sparring, the low, grunted sounds. The second time he went to the club Clark motioned him over, Clarke took the cigarette out of his mouth.

'College boy?' he said, looking Robert up and down. Robert nodded. Clark took him by the shoulders and put him against the wall. He stood back and looked at him. Robert knew he had a boxer's physique, that he had a good chin, that he had reach and a good jab. But Clark seemed to be looking for something else. He got him to strip down and put on gloves and get into the ring. He made Robert take up positions, archaic stances with a bare-knuckle feel to them. He felt like a figure from an old photograph, a bare-chested figure with a moustache.

'Can I join?' Robert asked.

Clark waited a long time before he answered.

'You can join,' he said. 'You can join the club. But if you fucking hurt anybody here I'll make sure you never box again, you hear me? You hear me?' He felt an obligation to talk to his fighters like that, in short clipped sentences with multiple repetitions.

He told people about Nairac.

'You get these boys, they're not interested in boxing, getting in a ring and winning a fight. You get these boys, I got a few over the years, all they're interested in is pain. How much fucking pain you can hand out, how much pain you can take. Pain merchants. Sooner or later they go over the top, give somebody a doing.'

He was asked why he took Robert on if that was the case.

'See, somebody like that is useful in a gym. You take your eye off a fucker like that, he'll hit you and burst your fucking eye socket or something. That's a lesson you only need to learn the one time.'

It was over a month before Robert got into the ring to spar. Clark had him doing weights, working with the bag, skipping, working in front of the mirror. He made him weigh himself every day, made him feel his own muscles to ascertain their tone. He made him strip naked and stand in front of the mirror in the changing rooms and look at the actual muscle. The pectoral. The dorsal. It wasn't about boxing at this stage, Clark believed, it was about cultivating the way the fighters saw themselves, how they inhabited their body. It was important to cultivate a murderous narcissism.

'See, all the best fighters,' Clark said, 'they fucking loved themselves. What they seen when they looked in the mirror they loved.'

Robert watched himself in the mirror, an old mirror with the silvering gone that gave a reddish tint to everything. He practised his feint, his hook, his jab. He worked at not giving away his emotions, his eyes steady and unblinking. He practised until his gymwork seemed almost robotic. You looked in the old glass of the mirror and you saw a less than human figure, a coppery automaton. Clark watched him, corrected his posture by reaching in and adjusting the angle of an elbow.

'Most toffs ain't worth a fuck in the gym,' he said, 'won't take advice. But Nairac was a game little fucker and he never gave you no guff or backchat neither. Too fucking busy getting ready to knock somebody's pan in.'

9

In January 1972 Knox came to Erskine's office in the corridor. He was looking for a way to spread unease in the civilian population. He felt that they had settled into low-intensity urban warfare, random house searches, arbitrary arrests. He felt that their fears needed to be awakened on a deeper level. He thought that there was a complacency abroad. Acts of brutality were referred to on the evening news as senseless and people drew solace from this, random death stripped of meaning. There was a duty to return depth and resonance to the situation. He wanted the civilians to fall victim to premonitory dreads. David suggested that they set up a small publishing company. Knox liked the idea. He thought the title of the company would be important. He suggested a name derived from classic texts. Omega. Minerva. Names that had a shadowy authority, the cachet of arcane usage. The books would be printed and published with spurious academic titles, but there would be no information about author or publisher on the title-page. The books were to consist of photographs of the maimed, of the shot, of percussive-type high-explosive injuries. Knox obtained the pictures from military photographers who had attended bomb scenes and from the morgue at the city hospital. He had them printed by a printer of pamphlets for the government. The plates were in colour, badly printed, which lent an air of unreality to them, the vivid impacted mass in sickly technicolor.

'It's a good idea,' David said. 'Let people see the real effect of these things. Stoke the hatred and the fear.'

'Not where I'm coming from, I'm afraid, chum. We want to work a bit deeper than that, put them on the edge.'

Knox knew that people would buy these books. He distributed them through small traders in the Markets, at Nutts Corner. The sellers of erotic postcards turned up at the edges, the sellers of second-hand pornographic novels. He wanted people to feel furtive buying them, to give in to a shameful curiosity, to bring the books home and hide them in the garage, in the shed, in the hidden places. They would bring them out at night, when everyone else in the house had gone to bed, the photographs lingered over, the loathsome secret thing.

Covert operations had started to proliferate. A laundry van appeared in the Q-car compound at Theipval. It was a Commer van with the words Four Square Laundry stencilled on the side. There was a hidden compartment in the roof where an MRF operative lay on his belly and took photographs of men standing in doorways, on street corners. The film was brought to Theipval, developed and P-carded. They collected clothes door to door, brought them to Theipval where they were examined by forensic techs, men in white overalls sweeping fibres into brown paper bags, scraping sleeves for firearms' residue. David went down to watch them going through pockets and trouser turn-ups. They flew a photo-electron microscope into Aldegrove and set it up in Theipval. Silent men in white coats and heavy-framed glasses moved around the big machine. The ordinary soldiers gave them a wide berth in the canteen. The lights stayed on in the laboratory late at night. The bulbs in the Orlitt hut would momentarily dim at night. There was a sense of things being calculated to infinite tolerances. Of dread process. When the lab work was done, the clothes were handed over to a group of Korean women who had been brought over with the machine. They washed and ironed the clothes so that they could be returned to the suspects. The air in the car park at Theipval smelt of starch. David found himself opening doors only to be faced with one of the Korean women carrying a basket of laundry. The women were unsmiling and formal. They looked at the

62

ground in front of them when they walked, refusing to meet your eye, so that David felt their desire to erase any trace of themselves from the barracks.

On slow afternoons in Gemini, David would meet Joyce in a small hotel ten miles up the coast. There were no tourists any more and few day-trippers from the city. There were salt-stained palm trees at the entrance to the hotel. David paid for the room with cash and allowed the owner to see the warrant card in his wallet when he opened it. He used clipped military tones when he talked. It was intended to convey a sense of wartime exigencies, the sexual urgencies of men on leave. This was not a middle-aged man in civvies leading a woman up a staircase with worn carpet. When they got to the room Joyce would wander about, lifting things and touching them. David had to lead her to the bed. She sat on the edge of it with her hands in her lap while he undid the buttons on her blouse, her clothing a thing of nylon and Draylon, fine-textured synthetics. She kept talking as he did it, his hands working at pearl buttons, at zips and fasteners, her skin patterned with strap marks, with small chaffed areas, tiny ridges felt through polyester.

'This soldier come into the club yesterday.'

'What soldier?'

'An officer I would have said, except he weren't dressed like one.'

He liked to get her blouse off, stretch her out on the bed, still marked by her clothing. She kept talking, looking off into the distance, lifting her arms so that he could remove her blouse but otherwise disregarding him, the words coming fast and dense as though they formed part of an office she was compelled to relate.

'Went in, talking to all the girls, told them they were doing a good job. Had this shotgun with him. Next minute he just walks out the door, shotgun under his arm, like he was safe as houses.'

63

David pulled back the bedclothes. Her nylons were on the floor at her feet. She picked them up and smoothed them between her fingers, touching a small defect in the weave of them.

'Let me guess,' David said. 'Let me guess. His name was Robert.'

'He never gave any name.'

'Big bloke, broken nose.'

'That's him. Spot on. Girls were mad for him. You'd of swore they were convent girls, pure as the driven. All giggles and all. That Polish bitch near wet herself.'

David had an image of the girl standing apart from the others, heavy-lidded, slovenly.

He took her by the arm. She got under the bedclothes beside him. The edge of the bedspread was frayed. Her hair smelt of cigarette smoke.

'He called me ma'am,' Joyce said, 'the soldier, he called me ma'am. Dead serious and all. "Thank you, ma'am," he says.' She laughed softly.

David didn't want to think about Robert in Gemini, or why he was there. He felt that the operation had somehow been altered by the fact of Robert being there, something in the fabric of the building itself, a feral presence in the rooms now, a prowled-through feeling. Joyce asking him what he wanted now. She had a formal terminology, a sex-manual idiom. Oral. Intercourse. He put his hand between her legs, the afternoon filling with sexual commonplaces, the perfunctory rhythms. Sheath. Stimulation.

Agnew knew that he was being protected. He turned up late. He turned up drunk. His superintendent looked past him when he was talking to him. The older policemen in the station ignored him, but the younger men looked up to him. He was aware of the way they watched him crossing the compound, shambling and depraved. They sat in a circle around him in the canteen. One of them told him that he had been

64

seen talking to Jackson. He suspected that Knox was the source of this piece of information.

Agnew was stood down from normal duty and attached to a Para brick tasked with carrying out house raids. They entered small streets in Saracen APCs. They fired tear-gas canisters into hostile crowds. There was a sense of things being done on the run, boots pounding on the pavement, hitting the rhythm, the tempo, rifle butts crashing through doors, boots pounding up narrow stairs, ashen women in nightclothes. Agnew liked the pre-dawn aspect of things. Sitting in APCs, your eyes streaming with cold, waiting to move off, the shouted order, the brutal NCO squawk. The Para-troopers smashed through floors to search foundation cavities. Wardrobes and drawers were emptied out of windows into the street. Terms of sexual abuse were used in relation to females. Agnew stayed in the background during the first part of the searches. He was wary of the soldiers' aptitude for brutal self-pity. He would wander round the houses after they had been searched. The scattered clothing, the overturned furniture. He started to take photographs from the houses. When he got home he would spread them out on the kitchen table. One night Janet came, saw them and asked about them. He said that they were relations. She sat down beside him, picking out photographs, dwelling on the mothers, the children. He gave them histories, devised small, poignant events occurring in childhood. He ascribed qualities of quiet heroism to the women, cited examples of selflessness. He found that he couldn't stop adding incident to their lives. Janet picked up a photograph of a small boy wearing shorts.

'That's you, isn't it?' she said.

'That's me,' he said. 'I was in the Scouts. Five years old.'

She nodded. She placed the photograph on the table and smoothed it gently. There was a faint chemical smell from the prints.

He picked out a photograph of a small girl.

'Who's that?'

'My younger sister. She died of meningitis.'

He was aware that he was violating fundamental principles here. He could see that Janet had tears in her eyes. He wanted to stop. He told her that his father had wept throughout the funeral, that the death had broken his mother. He evoked a country graveyard, rain-blurred scenes of quiet grief. Janet held his hand as he told the story. Later, when she had gone to bed, he sat alone at the kitchen table, going through the photographs again and trying to fix each person's narrative in his mind. The unsmiling children. The workworn adults. They seemed prone to introspection, trying to come to terms with the stony fictions he had created for them, tasked with the sombre detail of surrogate lives.

Knox arranged to meet Agnew at a furniture and carpet store on the Boucher Road. Agnew parked outside in the rain. He had to climb over piled-up carpets to get into the building. There were leatherette sofas, Parker Knoll armchairs, Formica-topped kitchen tables. You had to squeeze between tallboys and wardrobes and chests of drawers. There was a rubbery unwholesome smell from the rolls of carpet.

You got the impression of domestic catastrophe, a drastic jumble of household effects. He saw a small office at the back of the building and made his way towards it. Knox opened the door as he reached it. Agnew entered the office. There was another man present, bald with black-rimmed glasses. A desk in the centre of the office took up most of the room. David had to stand with his back against the wall and the edge of the desk pressing against his thighs. Knox introduced the small man as William McGrath. Agnew had heard of McGrath. His name was linked with shadowy groupings. TARA, the Emancipation Crusade. Agnew noticed pamphlets for the British Israelites on the desktop, pamphlets for the Unison Committee for Action.

'Now, Mr Agnew,' McGrath said. 'Now.' He rubbed his hands together, then sat down at the desk and began opening and closing drawers. 'What do you consider the real peril in this conflict of ours, Mr Agnew?'

Agnew shrugged.

'The red menace is every bit as alive in this province as it is elsewhere. It reaches into every corner. With vile tentacles, Mr Agnew. It is insidious and not unconnected to the Roman heresies.'

Agnew looked across the desk at Knox, who was doubled up between the desk and the door. He looked uncomfortable. I hope he gets a backache for bringing me here, Agnew thought. I hope he slips a fucking disc. He noticed that Knox was oddly intent on what the man was saying. McGrath moved some of the papers around his desk. Agnew thought that he looked like a minor trade union official, a small-time functionary with a disposition towards domestic violence.

'I think Mr Knox here is aware of the proven links between Comintern and violent civil disorder in this city. By right of Calvary, this land belongs to Christ, Mr Agnew. Are you saved in Christ?'

'Spare us the fucking sermons, McGrath,' Agnew said. 'I know what you are. What I want to know is what the fuck I'm doing here.'

'It's important that you are familiar with key players, that you have a personal acquaintance,' Knox said.

Knox liked to talk about background, about picking up the figures on the periphery. He liked to broaden an operation beyond its immediate confines, open it out. He spent time on the details. It was the details that gave an operation texture. Dealing with the Russians in the eastern sector, he had learned to think of covert work as a language, subtle, inflected, at rare times building to a clamour, moments of terrible allegory.

'The sword of Jehovah smiteth his enemies,' McGrath said.

'Hold on, hold your fucking horses here,' Agnew said. 'I know where I heard your name before. I know you now.' Agnew held up his hand and closed his eyes. Then he started to quote, hesitantly at first, building in confidence.

'I was in . . . my bedroom packing my clothes when Mr McGrath came into the room . . .'

'I told him never to do that again . . .'

'He got up on to the bed on his knees, took his cock out . . .'

'I was scared and didn't know what to do . . .'

'There was blood on my legs . . .'

Knox watched Agnew carefully.

'I'm impressed with the feat of memory, Mr Agnew. I trust you're not inventing any of this.'

'Statement of William Moggs, not his real name. Statement of Ronald Walmsley, not his real name. Statement of John Flaherty, not his real name. Statements transcribed 30 June 1973 re complaints concerning Joseph Mains, William McGrath, Raymond Semple, employees of Kincora Boys' Home, at time of alleged offences. Boys' statements judged unreliable. No further action taken.'

'The scion of Judah is awakened in the street,' McGrath said.

Agnew realized later that Knox had been leading him along the perimeter of shadowy events, putting him in the vicinity of significant incidents, placing him in the ambit of key treacheries. When they emerged on to the Newtonards Road it was raining and dusk had started to fall. The pavements were crowded with shipyard workers returning home, men from Mackies, women from Gallaghers, from the Swastika Laundry, workers from Shorts, from Wallaces, from the Co-op, rain-soaked, gleaming, a crowd that seemed to grow vast as he watched, the night's swarming tenantry dispatched in occupation of these rain-swept streets that they might enter and abide there.

10

Agnew worked at the back of the caravan. There was a mal-functioning gas heater in the caravan which covered the inside of the aluminium panelling in condensation, so he worked wrapped in a blanket instead. He liked the sense of dedication in the face of overwhelming odds that it gave him. He thought about developing a racking cough. He thought that his eyes were damaged. He asked Lorna to look at them.

'Tell me truthfully what you see.'

'I can see yellow in the whites of your eyes.'

'Where? I don't want you to hold anything back.'

'Everywhere. Yellow with darker-coloured flecks. It's a sign of liver damage. In certain lights your skin has a yellow tint.'

'What does that mean?'

'Jaundice maybe. Cirrhosis. It's hard to tell.'

'Does it mean I need glasses?'

'I don't know. I don't know if there's a connection between failing eyesight and liver damage. I can check.'

Agnew kept adding to the material. He went to public libraries and removed text from restricted books. He wrote to the MOD, asking them for specific details in relation to regimental postings in the aftermath of Robert's death. He wrote to foreign intelligence agencies in several countries seemingly unconnected to the events that surrounded Robert's disappearance. He faxed watchdog bodies, select committees, citizens' advice bureaux. He tried to arrange access to emerging intelligence assets in the Eastern Bloc countries. He envisaged vast archives of material, a great swathe of human mystery, of endless reportage, minute observation.

One night he fell asleep on the couchette under the window. A draught of air and the soft click of the door opening wakened him. He saw Lorna close the door gently behind her. She went to the sink and poured herself a glass of water and then another. It was one of the things he had been told to look out for. He didn't know if she knew he was there. She took off her coat. She was wearing a man's shirt underneath. Something she had bought in a second-hand shop. She bought all her clothes in thrift shops. It seemed important to her that her clothes were worn-out, that they had a sheen of worked-in dirt, that they came into her hands with a patina of hopelessness. He had seen her once going through baskets of clothes, holding garments up to the light looking for the darns, the threadbare places.

She took off the shirt and went to the sink again, where she poured herself another glass of water. Agnew had never seen anyone so thin. You could see each rib, the actual operation of the skeleton, its articulate motion under the skin. The area under her shoulder blades was deeply shadowed. The bones on her shoulder were raised, complex, so that she looked as if she was wearing epaulettes, the insignia of some pale and melancholy corps. As he watched, she slipped silently into the bedroom, a sense that she had not physically left the room as such but had worked a denial of her own presence there.

Next morning he was awakened by knocking at the door. When he opened it Mallon was standing there, wearing a sheepskin coat. Agnew dressed and they walked along the beach. It was early and there were few others around. A small freighter laboured up the estuary. You could hear the thin piping of birds coming across the water. On days like this, with your back to the expanse of caravans, Agnew felt isolation seeping into the air, as if he had somehow found himself in a melancholy Baltic inlet, a salt-marsh bight.

'How's the search for the lost captain coming on?' Mallon asked. He was looking for inflections of hearty scorn.

'The paper keeps coming in. I get letters which use the word restricted more than once.'

'You don't want to draw too much attention to yourself from them boys. Next thing you'll get the knock on the door, some DI sticking the warrant card in your face, we require you to answer enquiries regarding breaches of the Official Secrets Act.'

'I haven't breached anything. Did you know that, in answer to a parliamentary question in 1987, it was stated that all records relating to 14th Int had been destroyed? MRF became 4 Field Survey Troop, became 14th Int, became FRU.'

'Commanded by Gordon Kerr, I wouldn't get too worked up about it. Records get destroyed, files get misplaced. It's standard practice when anybody gets too nosy. Arguable whether 14th Int ever really existed anyhow. They say it was a cover name for MRF, invented after the fact. But I still think you're in deeper waters than you think.'

'Look at me, Mallon. For fuck's sakes, what sort of danger am I to anybody?'

'You never know. Do you mind RJ Kerr?'

'Portadown?'

'That's the boy. Mate of Robin Jackson and the rest of that crew. You hear tell that he used to cross the border with Nairac, although I don't credit them stories much. Anyhow, Bob's retired from all thon stuff. All he's interested in is this boat of his, twenty-five-foot yacht.'

'I'm losing relevance here, Mallon.'

'Bear with us. Anyway, Bob had this boat on a trailer, he's towing it to the sea. The police find it parked up in a lay-by, nobody at the wheel. So next thing they climb on to the trailer and look into the boat. Lo and behold, there's our Bob with the shite blew out of him.'

'What happened?'

'The inquest comes in. Forensics say it looks like our Bob is the victim of a gas explosion, but the injuries are too extensive to tell. The whole thing stinks to high heaven. There's Bob driving along, decides he wants a cup of, stops the car, climbs into the boat and starts to make tea on the gas cooker, wherefore he blows himself up, without blowing up the boat or setting it on fire. Bob was took out – you'd get no odds any other way.'

'What's the point, Mallon?'

'The point is that Bob wasn't much danger to nobody either.'

'It's all a bit far from here.'

'That's the point, Agnew. It wasn't far away. The unfortunate demise of RJ, otherwise known as Bob Kerr, took place nine miles from where we're standing, and this caravan site is the very place that Bob was heading for when he met his end.'

Lorna watched the two men from the dunes. She had an old pair of Leicas belonging to Agnew. The coating had worn off the barrels of the lens in places, so that the metal beneath was visible, and the binoculars were dented in places. She knew that Agnew had kept them from his days in the police. They were in a case under the bed, along with the Webley revolver and the lanyard belonging to it. The revolver had a sheen of gun oil. Agnew kept a fine cloth to polish the lenses. You could tell that he respected both objects. They had the authority of the well made thing, a seriousness of purpose. They made you think about the men who made them. Men with a stalwart grasp of the physical nature of an object. Men in clean overalls, sturdy utilitarians.

Agnew looked small and shambling beside Mallon, as though he had been taken into a forlorn custody. She thought he looked like one of those men who run away from their own countries, defector was the word. Who people feel a bit sorry for because of having no country any more, even though they are spies and betrayers and have sold out all friendship. It was still better to be with him than with a mother who goes through your things when she thinks you are not alert. But you are alert. And you know that, when she is not drinking, she lies awake in nights of lonely envy of girls who are young. And you know that she wants to keep you all in a prison that is your body so you do not grow up. Anorexia nervosa she says but she is a little bit nervosa herself when her sinister new husband does not come home at night she thinks you can't see. But she cannot take you when you had the hungry pain. The hungry pain in the middle of you. Talk about education what would they know the things that you learn in school bathrooms in among the drippy taps the girls whispering.

Agnew travelled to distant government buildings to obtain inquest reports. The inquest into the death of Wesley Somerville. The coroners report in relation to the death of Harris Boyle. The inquest into the death of Sapper Ted Stuart, killed in gunfire related to the Four Square Laundry operation. He obtained original handwritten copies of witness statements, although he already possessed the typed versions, the official court record, the inky thing with the smell of copying fluid and the look of a confession about it. He was surprised to see that the handwritten statements were less immediate than the typed ones. There seemed to be a buzz of rumour and hearsay about the typed sheets. They seemed more open to interpretation and to implication. They could be subjected to electrostatic tests. Ink could be analysed, paper batch numbers identified. The actual typewriter could be identified, an expert standing in a darkened courtroom pointing out the detail of broken keys on a blow-up of the page, each individual letter rendered vast and flawed and monumental. Against these statements the handwritten page seemed a bare text. You were left with the words themselves, plain and graved in a policeman's careful, unencrypted hand. Agnew knew that the words alone were no good. You had to go outside the words. The meanings were unspoken, had not been formed into words. There were nights when he took out the plain brown file that contained the actual inquest into

Robert's death and sat with it on his knee, unopened, the brown cover slightly damp-stained, smelling of old cardboard, wrapped in brown twine, a feeling of trove about it. He did not open it. He weighed it in his hand, the signifying heft of it.

The material kept coming. Duplicate birth certificates. Clippings from small local papers. Hand-printed political tracts. Copies of Falconer magazine. A Grenadier Guards mess list *c*. 1968. It was important to accumulate as much as possible. That was the meaning of the vast clutter in the caravan. That was the purpose of the lonely blizzard of paper.

11

In the third year Robert would go out shooting in the woods at the college perimeter. He used an old .22 with a rusty trigger guard. He liked to spend time in the woods, which were oak and then a long drift of pine trees, very old, with a storybook darkness at the heart, something lightfooted out there, just at the edge of your vision. In the early spring Robert would go out shooting foxes for the local farmers. There was a scrubby plantation of ridgepole spruce on the eastern edge of the forest and Robert would wait there for the foxes on nights when the sheep were lambing, the foxes smelling the afterbirth, the parturient reek of it, to be drawn from the darkness under the trees. Robert did not know the meaning of the word slink until he saw them although slink barely described their motion, you could just make them out, moving forward on their bellies, a seeming reluctance to their creeping, as though some resistance attended them, some swirling atmospheric pressure that pressed them to the ground and flattened their ears to their skulls and dragged on them, their lips pushed back from their teeth and their eyes at the corners, a terrible shuddering G-force that they exerted themselves against, the tension of congenital hunger. Once or twice one of the men attending the sheep would shine a torch at the foxes and they would edge backwards without turning, their hindquarters and tails moving in some sort of obscene ingratiation, but as soon as the torch beam left them they started to move forward again, one of them sometimes lifting its muzzle as Robert rested the sights of the .22 on it, smelling the air and turning towards him its mute, larcenous stare.

* * *

In spring Robert took the rifle to shoot hares on a piece of moorland that opened out at the other side of the forest. It was a landscape that he liked, heather strewn with black rocks and shallow icy pools. He would construct a hide from dried fronds of bracken and whin and hunch in it against the wind and sleety rain and wait for the yearling hares to come, their eyes unlike anything he had seen before, vast silvery-carbon discs from a distant machine age, futurist prototypes.

In March 1963 he targeted a hare which had silhouetted itself against the morning skyline. As his finger squeezed the trigger he sensed movement along the ridge to the east of the hare. He pulled away from the eyepiece and saw a hawk hovering over two leverets. The leverets were feeding on heather shoots. He thought that there was a busyness about the way they were eating, a staged feel to it, as if they knew on some level that the peregrine was there, the bleak-eyed raptor, hovering forty feet above and behind them, and that they were affixed in its vehement regard. Robert estimated a forty-knot wind but the bird maintained its position precisely, swooping a few feet lower in a dipping movement every ten seconds or so until it was barely twenty feet above the hare and Robert could see the yellow eyes and beak, the falcon like a hooded actuary come to exact a predetermined tariff from the yearling hare. As he watched, the hawk folded its wings and descended on the hare, dark accelerant, the hare killed at first impact, the falcon resting on top of the corpse for a moment, shrugging to correct the nap of its feathers.

There was a falconry club at Ampleforth, run by a man called Walmsley. You went through the kitchen courtyard and past the fuel bunkers, where there was an old barn where tractors were kept. The falcons were housed in the loft above the barn. Robert climbed a wooden staircase pocked with woodworm, dust rising on every footfall. He unlatched the door at the top and stepped inside. The only light in the loft filtered up through the eaves but he could see the birds sitting on their perches, arranged around the room. The merlins. The peregrines. The sparrowhawks. The buzzards. The goshawks. Raptors. Robert moved closer. The birds did not recognize him. They were restless, the stillness of the loft disturbed by feathery shiftings. Robert heard a voice behind him. He had not heard anyone enter.

'What are you doing here, boy?'

He turned to see Walmsley standing in the doorway.

'I would like to learn about the birds, sir.'

'I like to hear them referred to as falcons.'

'Falcons, sir.'

'What is your name?'

'Nairac, sir.'

Walmsley stepped forward into the light. He was not the kind of man who kept falcons, Robert thought. He was wearing worn carpet slippers and he shuffled like an old man. His skin was very pale, almost translucent, and you could hear his breath coming with a hissing sound. Moving rapidly to one of the perches occupied by a buzzard, he held out his forearm. The bird moved sideways along the perch and stepped on to his arm with an odd delicacy, something Robert would come to notice in the birds, the way they displayed what seemed like a murderous fastidiousness. Walmsley motioned the boy to stand beside him. Robert moved over beside the man and held out his arm. Walmsley placed his hand over Robert's. He smelt of wintergreen. His hand rested on Robert's with a light, dry touch. Walmsley tilted his arm slightly and then a little more, so that the bird was forced to edge down his arm.

'They like their perch to be horizontal,' Walmsley said.

Robert was aware of the man's eyes on him in the gloom. Walmsley tilted his arm once more and the buzzard stepped off his arm and on to Robert's. Robert felt the talons through the sleeve of his jacket. He realized that he had tensed his arm, waiting for the bird to step on to it, then realized that the bird was almost weightless, all hollow bones and minute balancing mechanisms. Which made you wonder where the strength in the talons came from, almost circling his arm, the feet with the look of something ancient about them, nude and vile with small, polished nails. You could feel the power in them, tensile, sinewy. There was a faint bird smell from the feathers, a mealy odour. Robert moved his arm slightly and the bird moved to regain its balance.

'Don't do it too often,' Walmsley said. 'They are easily irritated.'

'What do they do if they get cross?' Robert asked.

'They would peck the eye out of its socket if they wanted,' Walmsley said, 'but that isn't likely. You really have to guard against their becoming discontented and bored. Then they become untrainable. They are likely to fly off and not come back.'

Walmsley lifted the jesses which dangled from the bird's leg. He opened Robert's hand gently, placed the jesses in his palm and closed his hand. Robert was to learn that about Walmsley. He liked to handle you when he was demonstrating something. He would hold your shoulders to demonstrate a stance. Something that made you uneasy. The way he would open your hand and close it again in a subtly different way, a wrongness to it. The older boys said that Walmsley had been shell-shocked during the war. They said that he had fought at Monte Casino. They said that he did not sleep and walked the corridors of the school at night. Boys who misbehaved in the dormitories were put outside the door to await Walmsley. Robert would shiver at the thought of him, the sleepless patrol on the cold linoleum, the waiting boy rubbing spit into the palms of his hands against the sting of the cane. Walmsley's eyes were always red-rimmed. He wore rubber-soled shoes when he walked the corridors at night. The boys looked at him and they imagined the cacophony in his head. The buzz bombs, the thousand-pounders, the 12-inch mortars, the howitzer shells. That was what shell-shocked meant to them. The boys knew that he could not shut his eyes because that was when the noise was unbearable.

Robert looked after the birds for two months before Walmsley would permit him to fly one. He rubbed polish into the leather jesses and hoods and gauntlets. He fed gobbets of meat to the birds. He prepared the lures when Walmsley was taking them out. He became used to handling the birds. He learned their personalities, their aptitude to slaughter, their tendency to murderous pique. The Dutch hood. The Arab hood.

'You are not a falconer unless you are hunting in the field. You are a hawk pet owner,' Walmsley said.

Later in 1963 Robert travelled to Germany with the school Cadet Corps. They crossed the Channel at Ostend and drove across the Low Countries in a Leyland bus. Outside Bonn they drove through a NATO exercise. Outside Essen two Vulcan bombers flew low over the bus so that it was buffeted with jet wash. In early-morning mist they saw a tank squadron lined up across a ploughed ridge. Walmsley told them that the area contained six missile silos. Robert thought of the silvery missiles, sombre with kilotonnage, the silent threat of fallout, the radiation sores, the creeping cell damage. The landscape dissolving in mystic spume. At a hostel they watched footage of Chinese soldiers in protective clothing racing into the radiation zone. Across the border Walmsley said the Soviets were lined up in their tanks, the massed divisions. The Soviets did not care about the men under their command. The officers waited behind the lines in machine-gun nests to gun down those who threw away their weapons and ran. They were prepared to sacrifice millions to achieve a minor objective. That was the threat. To unnerve you with mass dying. It was a country of zones. Zones of occupation. Free-fire zones.

Industrial zones. Currency zones. The French zone. The Soviet zone. Robert liked it when the bus got on to the autobahn. He had expected a notional road, something with a hard aspirant gleam. He had not thought of this dark thrilling place, car headlights going past in the outside at 130, 140 miles an hour, the road surface cracked in places, scrubby weeds on the hard shoulder. The autobahn was road as epic, Robert knew this. There were elaborate histories. The autobahn skirted the border and you could see the watchtowers, the miles of fencing running eastward, the incendiary flare of searchlights over the mined strips. Every so often you passed a military convoy lumbering in the slow lane – 150, 200 trucks with canvas backs. The boys were silent. They knew the real meaning of the landscape they were passing through. Walmsley got to his feet at the front of the bus and stressed the importance of conducting themselves well when they got to the camp. He referred to their location as the European theatre. He advised the boys not to leave the camp unaccompanied. The Stasi were everywhere. The East Germans employed cleaners, shop assistants, loiterers in bars. There are friendly men who ingratiate. There are women who tempt.

Happy Valley was a sprawling base on the outskirts of Berlin. There was an atmosphere of echoing parade grounds, empty barracks, cloud massing in the east. Walmsley said that most of the men were taking part in the NATO exercise. The cadets were billeted in green canvas tents. They slept in cots with green army blankets wrapped around them. There was a sense of an army on the move. They queued with aluminium mess tins for food. During the day there was rifle practice on the range, unarmed combat. At night they played cards in the tents. A boy called Chichester rigged up a short-wave radio and they listened to the radio traffic generated by the exercise, routine stuff mainly but given urgent syntax by the way it came in on static bursts. It gave the boys the feeling of being on the edge of great events. Charlie Tango Bravo.

After a few days they were taken by bus to HQ 7th Armour. A lance-corporal, Supplies, explained that most of the heavy armour was on exercise on the East German border.

'For the purposes of familiarization,' he said, 'we have provided a scout car, Ferret, Leyland in origin.' He kicked the large tyres. 'The point of the scout car is battlefield manoeuvrability,' he said.

They were allowed to climb into the Ferret and sit at the controls. The levers were worn smooth from handling. The leather seat was cracked and torn. The lance-corporal pointed out the size of the controls, the solidity of them, the emphasis on function. The turret moved on silent bearings. Robert handled the browning 9mm cannon, tilted it on its axis, the gun perfectly weighted between the breech and the long perforated barrel. He wanted to fire it. He wanted to see the impact of the heavy copper-jacketed bullets. The lance-corporal started the engine of the scout car. The interior smelt of diesel. Robert closed the flap and looked through the slit. He remembered his father talking about the loss of peripheral vision, the way you couldn't see to either side. There was something different about looking out on the neat rows of chalets and trimmed lawns of the base when what you saw was framed by the driver's slit. A note of threat was introduced. The suburban feel of the place flooded with wary apprehension.

It had been cold all day and it started to snow that evening. Walmsley said that the winds blew from the north, from Siberia, falling silently into the Barents Sea, the Caspian Sea, the Baltic, the frozen dream seas, submarine-patrolled. The darkness came and the wind drove snow across the camp, and when Robert went to tie the tent door closed he found the tags stiff and frozen.

Walmsley came to the tent that night and sat on the edge of Robert's cot.

'You are an adolescent. Adolescent boys must be conscious of hygiene at all times.' Hygiene. The man almost whispering the word. 'You must be careful of leanings if you intend to join the armed forces. The barrack room can be a cruel place.'

'Leanings?' Robert said, thinking to himself that here right in front of him was a queer. Queer meaning odd, singular, quaint.

'Service to one's country is not a joke,' Walmsley said. 'Particularly overseas, a young man can be suborned by clever outsiders. The use of homosexual blackmail is a common thread. They are cunning. They wait in the long grass. The NKVD. The Stasi.'

Walmsley was breathing fast. He looked as if he was trying hard to remember something. His brow was knitted. Robert kept his eyes fixed on the man's face. He knew that Walmsley's hands were working at something below his waist, as though he was trying to perform a complex task from memory, trying to reconstruct some fragile, dismantled thing. Robert recalled what they had learned in unarmed combat that day. Drive the heel of the hand forcefully into the underside of the assailant's nose. With force sufficient to drive shards of bone from the nasal cavity and the septum into the base of the cranial cavity and thus into the brain.

'You're thinking homosexual, aren't you, Nairac? You're thinking men who hang around public toilets. A fruit. Isn't that what is on your mind? I know the words that boys use.'

Walmsley's lips were flecked with spittle. The verb to ride. His hands were working at the bedclothes.

'What did you learn today? Tell me, boy, what did you learn today?'

Robert knew that the other boys were awake, listening in the darkness. He felt cold air on his legs as the bedclothes were lifted back. Robert closed his eyes. When you closed your eyes you saw flecks drifting around in the darkness. He heard his father's voice say the words cellular debris, the damage that accrues to the body, the pieces that slough off and are left to drift. He did drill in his head. Underwear two pairs folded. Cadet to stand by bed hands in line with trouser seam. The canvas of the tent cracked in the cold wind. The wind carrying snow across the East Prussian plain.

Stasi. The bone-splinter word.

12

David set up an information office in the annexe to the corridor. He put army recruitment posters on the wall. He stocked literature promoting physical fitness. There was a chart detailing arrests of PIRA suspects by army units, explosive finds indexed by location and quantity. He asked for a civilian secretary. He put a sign with his name on the desk. He wanted the room to resemble a pensions office, a branch office of civil administration, open and guileless. The word PsyOps wasn't mentioned. Popular local charities were supported. Cancer research. Heart disease. He held drinks receptions for local journalists and local Special Branch men. He thought that the army displayed a certain arrogance in their dealings with the locals. It was a question of building up their trust. You gave stories to the journalists. You gave the Special Branch men what they wanted. Two Branch men from Castlereagh started coming to see him on a regular basis. Cooper and Mahood liked to project an air of hearty brutality, of skilful beatings administered. Cooper was short and blocky and livid. David looked at him and thought fatty liver deposits, coronary blockage. Mahood was stooped and almost hairless, his skin stretched tight over his face. He was prone to a sepulchral drollness. He told David straight away that he suffered from alopecia. They fed information to David and he passed it on to the press pool. Much of the information was unreliable. They all knew that was not important. They were looking for narrative qualities. The veracity of the story was a secondary consideration.

'I hear tell your boy Knox is one of them Ultras.'

'See that, Mahood. The expression never changes when you say the word, Ultra. Not a flicker. I like that in a man.'

'Now, gentlemen,' David said, 'this Ultra story is just that. A story. There's no truth in it.'

'Like fuck it's a story.'

'Tell us a story Jackanory. It's a fucking good yarn if it's not true.'

'What's your interest in it, gentlemen, if you don't mind my asking. It seems a little off the circuit, so to speak.'

'That's the problem. It's not off our circuit no more. There's been a bit of talk, so there has, that the Ultras is running round over here now.'

'Ultra,' Mahood said. 'Sounds like something to do with washing powder.'

'You know the problem?' Cooper said. 'You got far too many security services. Too many people involved. You got MI5, MI6, you got 14th Int, G2, Unit 216, Group 13, MRF.'

'Gen 42,' Mahood said.

'Gen 42. You get my drift? All of a sudden you have this little bit of civil unrest in a place like this, some internal dissent, and they're all piled in all of a sudden, looking to make a name for themselves. Makes things a bit difficult for the natives.'

'For the locals,' Mahood said.

'I'm still not with you,' David said.

'The way I see it, what's happening is that security services are getting themselves involved with local paramilitaries for reasons known to themselves and we get caught in the middle.'

'If you have any examples of this, gentlemen, I'm sure I can look into it.' David being urbane, the middle-ranking civil servant, slightly bored.

'You still running the brothel, David?' Mahood said. 'Maybe we'll call up there some day, get a ride off one of them girls. Maybe get discount, friends of the owner and all that.'

'You got a happy hour in that place? Two fucks for the price of one?' Cooper said.

'You just taking still pictures up there or you got an eight-millimetre? I always wanted to be in the films,' Mahood said.

'That's enough of that, Mahood. As true as I'm sat here, you never want to see Mahood in the raw.'

'Bald as a nut,' Mahood said.

'A fright to the world,' Cooper said.

'The point is taken, gentlemen,' David said.

'He's very smooth, this boy,' Cooper said, 'but I'm not too sure that the point is in fact took. I'm not sure that the point is took at all. We're talking widespread illegality here.'

'A total disregard for the law.'

'What do you want?' David said.

'We want to keep an eye on them Ultras. We want to know what the fuck they're up to and when.'

'The city is the city. The province is the province. There are no communists here, David. This is the least communist place in the whole wide fucking world, so if these Ultra boys want to resist communism let them fuck away off to Moscow to do it.'

'Peking,' Mahood said.

'Peking, where they can do what they fucking well like with the red peril or the yellow menace or whatever.'

'I think I follow you. I think I'm with you,' David said.

David wondered if the two policemen knew what they were talking about. The Ultras were like something you dreamed about David thought. If they existed, then it was beyond the sphere of deniability, they were subject to higher principles. The words right-wing conspiracy did not apply to them. David saw right-wing coups of the period following broad theatrical principles. Men in ornate uniforms brandishing pistols. Smoke coming from the presidential palace. Prisoners massed in football stadiums. Events were played out according to certain paradigms that were generally understood. Scenes of pity and cruelty. None of these things applied to the Ultras. There was an air of the sublime about the Ultras. Of men dreaming alone in rooms. There was none of the information about the Ultras arriving along the normal channels,

86

the standard psychic clutter at the edge of things. In fact, David could not recall where he had heard the name first. They saw themselves in visionary terms. Men who dealt in allegories. No one could name them, but people at Theipval believed in them. David thought that once you were in the field it was necessary to believe in them. That in the middle of chaotic events, bombing, sudden and inexplicable death, there was a calm centre, a dark, ordering artifice.

David remembered what the two Special Branch men had said about Knox when the older man called David to his office.

'What do you know about the Ultras?'

'Nothing much.'

'It doesn't matter. You've met Captain Robert Nairac?'

'Yes.'

'I hear he paid a visit to your bordello a few days ago.'

'That has come to my attention.'

'Did he sample the wares, David? Was he tempted?'

'Not as far as I know.'

'I didn't think so. Far too much the Guardsman, Captain Nairac. Any idea what he was doing there?'

'No idea at all. Nosing around, I would expect.'

'Nairac does too much nosing around. He's too inclined to get into other people's business.'

David started a policy of debriefing street patrols, troops who thought of themselves as frontline. He felt that many of the patrols were unnecessary and that actions were frequently duplicated. He knew that much of the advice in this regard that was supplied to GOC came from Knox. David wondered if the policy was deliberate. The troops he interviewed were unshaven, red-eyed with fatigue. They talked about street battles, about single-shot snipers, booby traps exploding at waist level. There was an atmosphere of barely contained psychosis. It seemed to be policy to keep the troops edgy and unpredictable. Each time they returned to base they were presented with another Daily IntSum setting out new threats. The IntSums were generated at Theipval. The documents tended to be themed. That December there was a theme of honey traps. Of women who would lure soldiers with promises of sex. There were descriptions of how PIRA women would smuggle explosives strapped to their thighs underneath their skirts, gun parts hidden internally. The reports were entirely spurious, but Knox liked the atmosphere of aberrant erotics that was introduced. He read accounts of the Baader-Meinhof grouping and their operations in Germany involving bomb attacks, kidnapping of industrialists. He was appreciative of the kind of fear that was generated by the presence of women in Baader-Meinhof. There was an inflow of SigInt from BND which stated that in armed situations the women were to be killed first. He could see that the fact that the women were educated was truly terrifying.

He could see the remoteness of them, pinch-faced, small-breasted, set apart. Their unsmiling faces. Their doctrinaire views. Their utilitarian sexual activity. Knox thought that they could bring a new level to events in the city if they could suggest the presence of such women on the streets. He pointed to Patti Hearst and the Symbionese Liberation Army. What strangeness, he seemed to be saying.

Throughout that winter GOC maintained saturation patrolling of key areas. Troop morale was low. They were permitted four or five hours sleep, then redeployed. Amphetamine use was widespread. Officers in the field reported units running amok in civilian areas. Whole battalions were redeployed with only hours' notice. That was when Robert's name started to come up in the debrief. Soldiers talked about a tall officer carrying a shotgun who would come out of a side street or step from a doorway. He seemed to have extensive local knowledge. He would go through streets, house by house, reciting the names, the political allegiance. He spoke in clear and resonant tones. He took their street maps from them and explained the geographical context. He seemed to be able to trace lines on the maps that no one else could see. He was able to establish strange but credible contexts. He crouched in the lee of burnt-out buildings and related self-deprecating anecdotes. He led lost patrols home.

Knox pointed out to David that this could be useful in the overall perception of things. The appearance of an emissary among weary and frightened troops. Men who were almost ready to believe anything. Nairac talked to them as equals. He told them to call him Bob. He wasn't a crap hat.

As the end of their tour approached the soldiers became quieter, less aggressive. They sat in exhausted knots when they came in off patrol, talking quietly. There were transcendent episodes. A soldier claimed to have seen a boy he had shot during a riot. His chest had been blown open and he held his hands out to the soldier, pale and wordless. At the scene of a convoy ambush with multiple casualties on a lonely dual carriageway, motorists reported a phantom truck, its headlights blazing, that appeared in their rear-view mirror, bearing down on them and then suddenly disappearing as they reached the junction at the end of the road. NCOs reported an increase in religious observance among the troops. David could see that Knox was more comfortable with the idea of Robert in this context. David wanted to leak it to the papers – the brave young captain taken to the public's heart – but Knox vetoed the idea.

David realized afterwards that Knox had different outcomes in mind. Knox had detected a potential for larger themes in Robert, something classical, the stark, fatalist outlines of blood narrative.

13

Agnew was encouraged by Knox to cultivate the relationships in Portadown. He rarely saw Jackson. It seemed to be understood that Jackson operated on a different level. He played pool with Bob Kerr and Hoppy in the Blues Bar. He drank with other minor figures. For the time being, he did not mention the British captain. When Jackson did appear, he was flanked by Somerville and Boyle. Agnew told Knox that they had that thing about them again, the hint of lethal swagger barely there, the low-key malignancy. Agnew told Knox that he didn't think much of Somerville and Boyle, but that it seemed that Jackson had elevated their small-town souls.

Knox got Agnew to remove ammunition from a PIRA dump and replace the gunpowder with blasting powder, then put the ammunition in the dump. When the PIRA operative tried to use the bullets, the gun would explode in his face.

One Sunday evening he was drinking in the Blues Bar when he was told that Jackson was waiting for him in the street. Outside, Jackson was in the driving seat of a Humber. Somerville and Boyle were in the back seat.

'Get in,' Jackson said. 'We're off for a bit of a drive.'

'Where are we going?' Agnew said.

'Get in, to fuck, and never mind the questions,' Boyle said.

Agnew sat in the passenger seat, shifting the Webley around to the front of his belt and slipping off the holster catch.

'You'd never get it out in time,' Jackson said quietly.

'The peeler and his big gun,' Boyle said.

'Boom, boom,' Somerville said.

'Please don't shoot us we done nothing wrong,' Boyle said.

'Cut it out, boys,' Jackson said.

They drove for forty-five minutes. Perry Como on the eight-track. George Jones. Some time after nine they turned on to a rutted lane. There was a farmhouse at the end of the lane. The house was in darkness and rainwater spilled from broken guttering. Archetypes of semi-derelict farmhouses, rained on and bleak. Broken-down farm machinery lay at angles in a muddy yard. Rusting sheets of galvanized stood against a wall. Jackson parked the car behind the house. Agnew noticed that there were several other cars in a small barn which stood at right angles to the house. Agnew thought that they looked like Q-cars. A Datsun. A Vauxhall. Used cars with that faint air of contrivance about them. Jackson leaned on the latch of the back door and pushed it open. It led into a scullery. There was a strong smell of marzipan, which Agnew knew to be the smell of gelignite. Agnew went through the scullery into a small kitchen. He turned on the light. There was an oil-fired stove in the room, an oilcloth-covered table with four wooden chairs. You got the feeling of makeshift habitation, of wartime privation. Agnew saw ammunition boxes stacked against the wall opposite the stove. He lifted a small unmarked cardboard box from the shelf above the stove. He opened it and saw the firing pin, extractor and barrel of a 9mm pistol, the head of the pin worn smooth with use.

'Army issue,' Boyle said. 'Sent for destruction last year. You fit them to a pistol, then when you fire them, there's no way they can be traced to an extant weapon.'

Extant weapon. Agnew noted the training-manual jargon. Jackson lifted a package from the table, a rifle wrapped in brown paper. He stripped away the wrapping, turned the weapon over in his hands. He worked the action. SLR. Agnew thought, US-made Armalite, lightweight infantry rifle. PIRA standard weapon. Somerville was taking ammunition clips for the rifle from one of the boxes. Boyle lifted a phone from the table and dialled a number. He spoke into it in low tones. He felt the three men moving within prearranged parameters, things happening with precision. Agnew realized that they were on an op. Jackson inserted a magazine into the Armalite and worked a round into the chamber. Agnew could smell the gun oil. He sat down at the table. He noted signs of male habitation. There were open tins of food on the draining board, a half-empty whiskey bottle, a full ashtray. Jackson, Somerville and Boyle were checking small arms, speaking to each other in terse, half-heard bursts. Jackson worked a rag along the barrel of the Armalite, wiping off the excess oil. He placed the gun on the table and sat down. Boyle put a 9mm in his pocket and leaned against the sink. Somerville sat down.

'What are we waiting for?' Agnew asked.

Boyle nodded towards the phone. Agnew had a feeling that he knew what was going to ensue. That they would sit there in silence, waiting for the phone to ring. That the very substance of the phone itself, the weighty bakelite handset, would acquire unforeseen and dread authority. That there would be a growing sense of attendance upon summons. Jackson sat without moving, his hands resting gently on the table, as if he possessed within him a plenitude of depraved forbearance.

They waited for forty-five minutes. Agnew smoked. He made an ashtray from the cellophane of the packet. You felt that the thing was being taken to its limits. That Jackson, motionless in his chair, was drawing on reserves of malignant poise. Agnew could see the strain on Somerville's face, the development of infinitesimal tics and twitches under the skin, as if the control of the muscles was subject to minute neural misfires. He thought that he could break himself, give in to the impulse to rant, to plead in a semi-hysteric manner, to surrender to spittle-flecked raving.

When the phone rang it seemed a calm, civilized sound. Agnew realized that they had got beyond the madness. Jackson stood up.

'Me and Somerville got a job to do. You sit here, Boyle, and keep an eye on this cunt.'

'You going to tell him to shoot me if I move?' Agnew said.

'A funny cunt,' Somerville said.

Jackson turned to look at Agnew. 'I tell you what, Agnew,' he said, 'you want to come with us, get the mitts dirty for a change?'

'Come on, to fuck, Agnew,' Somerville said. 'About time you seen some blood, so it is.'

Agnew looked at the floor and shook his head. He could feel the presence of Boyle and Somerville, standing over him, ugly grins on their faces, looming, derisive. He made small apologetic movements with his hands. There was a vocabulary for the place he was in now. Yellow. Chicken. He could feel tears starting in his eyes. He started to count nail heads in the linoleum floor. He coughed and cleared his throat, a brisk, womanly sound.

'Come on, to fuck, Somerville,' Jackson said.

He heard feet moving, the flat metallic sound of a firearm knocking against a chair. When he looked up, Boyle was sitting alone at the other side of the table. There was a pistol on the table in front of him. Boyle wasn't looking at him and his face was blank, with a kind of lethal disinterestedness that made Agnew think he shouldn't make any sudden movements. He cleared his throat and scraped his chair on the ground a little. He thought it was a good idea to introduce some sound to the situation. He was aware of the nature of the silence that was closing in on them in the cold, empty room, something glacial and impersonal about it. Something of explorers frozen to death in tents, unmoving over decades.

'Don't get me wrong,' he said.

'I never got you wrong, Agnew,' Boyle said. 'I got you fucking right, for a man who lets everybody else do the dirty work for them, that's what I got you for.'

'Where did they go, anyway, Boyle?'

'Shut your beak, Agnew.'

'I'm only asking.'

'This here's a wet job situation, Agnew. You've no foot to stand on, asking members of this unit what they're at.'

Wet job. Unit. Boyle had the gun in his hand now, moving it in vague circles, suggesting that he might have found himself uncoupled from the moment and open to spontaneity of the worst kind, making Agnew think that he might in fact open fire. He saw himself sprawled on the floor. The dark pool spreading. The matted hair.

'The gun,' he said.

'What about it?' Boyle said.

'The gun that Jackson was carrying, it's a PIRA gun.'

'What are you talking about?'

'You shoot somebody with an Armalite, everybody thinks PIRA involvement. It's perfect cover.'

'If I was you, Agnew, I wouldn't go talking like this around Jackson.'

'Where'd the gun come from, Boyle? Some evidence locker somewhere? Lifted from a dump? Rub her down for prints, put her back in the dump, nobody's any the wiser.'

'I don't know nothing about no weapon, but I'll tell you something for nothing, Agnew, you do anything to fuck up this op, you'll be going for a fucking ride with me and Somerville and we'll give you another hole in your head to go along with thon big mouth of yours, so we will.'

Weapon. Op. Agnew noticed the accumulation of succinct operational terminology.

He noticed that Boyle had clicked a round into the chamber of the pistol and was holding it cocked by his head. Agnew read the writing on the underneath of the butt. Star SA 47320-N360.

Jackson and Somerville had been gone for less than an hour. Considering margin for error, Agnew reckoned on an operational range of less than ten miles. You could feel Somerville's presence when he came into the room. His elation. His eyes burning with it. You knew he had killed. Jackson seemed to obtain satisfaction on some other level. It was about the forfeiture of self. To kill was an act of fearsome and depraved introspection. About finding a place in the hierarchies of ruin.

'Who'd you kill?' Agnew said.

'A better man nor you,' Jackson said.

'A fucking big-mouthed peeler,' Somerville said. He ejected the magazine from the Armalite and cleared the breech. He carefully wiped the weapon with a gun cloth, starting at the stock and working his way towards the barrel.

'I want you and Boyle to take the car and burn it,' Jackson said. 'Are you fit to do that at least, Agnew?'

'He kept asking questions about what you were doing,' Boyle said.

'You should have shot him, then,' Jackson said. 'Come on, to fuck, we got to get going now.'

Jackson placed the Armalite carefully in the middle of the kitchen table. There was a faint odour of gunsmoke from it, sulphurous, rank and oily.

Boyle and Agnew drove the car to the Hillhead Estate outside Portadown. They did not meet any checkpoints on the way. Agnew thought that the area had been disinfected. That was the word they used. Boyle drove the Hillman on to the grass and they got out. Boyle took a jerry can of petrol from the boot and spilled it over the back seats. Agnew was aware of teenage boys coming up behind them. The boys took tartan scarves from their pockets and tied them over their faces. Agnew knew that there was no chance of them being recognized but that there were solemn observances to be performed. The boys arranged themselves in a semicircle just behind Agnew. There was some shuffling and coughing. Boyle poured a trail of petrol across the thin grass and lit it. They watched as flames ran across the grass to the car. Agnew noted the way Boyle had stopped the car. It was part of the thing that the car be slewed sideways, doors lying open. The petrol in the back of the car ignited with an abrupt sound like something being folded in on itself. For a few moments the petrol burned silently, with a blue light, the seat fabric remaining untouched, a sense of eerie marsh light about it. Agnew looked across to the other side of the car. A moment ago there had been no one, but now he could see more boys. They were wearing parallels and bomber jackets, Oxford brogues. They adopted stylized poses, slouched, hands in pockets, cigarettes cupped in the palm of the hand and brought to the mouth in a mannered way. You had a feeling of wary-eyed tribesmen appearing in forest clearings. You expected communication using rudimentary gestures. Agnew saw the way they were absorbed by fire. They appreciated the wantonness of the gesture, the destruction of a car, but they were more than that drawn to the manner in which the fire was spreading in the car, the incendiary mechanics involved.

The seat covers and the rubber floor mats caught first. Thick black smoke with suspended particulate matter common to the burning of manmade fibres. There was a gratifying sense of unidentified toxins being released.

'I'm away,' Boyle said.

'How am I supposed to get out of here?'

'Do I look like I give a fuck?'

Boyle walked away and the boys parted to let him through. Agnew was glad to see him go. He could give himself over to appreciation of the burning car. He knew it was not an opportunity that arose often. The dashboard was on fire now and smoke was pouring from the wheel arches. In minutes the whole car would be consumed. Agnew knew that this was the thing they were meant to draw from the experience, the thing they had not known, the speed with which a car burned. There was a soft thud and the car rocked gently on its springs as the petrol tank went up. There were jets of flame from air vents. The interior of the car was dense with amassed combustions. The boys registered the paint blisters, the white flame of material burning at impossible temperatures. The heat intense as the entire car was consumed, but it was important that you did not step back. The car an orange mass of flame with the impression of higher processes taking place, muffled implosions.

The other thing you learned was the speed with which the flames died away. The way they guttered and died and you became aware of the drizzle again. The boys still standing there, waiting for something, a despondency with global dimensions. The air smelt of burnt rubber, of spent polycarbons. This was the point of their social deprivation and their limited horizons. They were attuned to feelings of inarticulate hopelessness, the crushing weight of human disappointment.

14

There was more snow. The Rheindalen base was snowed in. Ice formed on the aluminium ridgepoles of the tents. News reports in German were translated to the boys. River transport was suspended because of ice. Robert stood on the bridge and watched floes of ice which had broken off from the main as they crashed into the infrastructure of the bridge and off the steel hulls of moored barges. He tried the names of the rivers in his head. The Oder. The Elbe. Flowing from the east. You could see the remains of the old bridge under the water, the twisted wartime girders. The water was black and often concealed by snow flurries blown off the ice, freezing vapours, unexpected hazes, so that you felt the presence of a phantom traffic.

Robert went walking in the forest above the town. The trees were different from the ones at Ampleforth. Old growth spruce, forty and fifty feet tall. He liked the way you could disappear into them. The forest seemed to offer possibilities of concealment that went beyond the physical. He met one of the cooks from the camp in the forest. He was a stocky man from Lancashire called Fulbright. Robert came up behind him in the snow as he was setting a snare. Robert stood in the shadow of a copse of blue spruce, watching as Fulbright knelt with his back to him.

'How'd you know there was somebody here?' Fulbright said without turning around.

'I followed your footprints in the snow,' Robert said.

'Followed my footprints in the snow. Now there's a thing. I was tracked. I never reckoned to be tracked,' Fulbright said. 'Come over here, if you want to see how to set a snare.'

Robert didn't move. Fulbright held out his hands. They

were small and fine and made Robert think of small wild things struggling.

'Come on, lad, I won't touch a hair on your head. Ain't you the wary one? I bet that head is full of secrets. Have you done trapping before?'

Robert shook his head.

'What then?'

'Hawking.'

'Done a bit of hawking in my time, not much though. Need room to keep a hawk.' Fulbright's head was shaved and he had prominent eyebrows. 'Never had much room. What is it you call a place where you keep a hawk?'

'A falconry.'

'That's right, a falconry. Well, I suppose you got your way of catching conies, I got mine. What kind of hawk do you use?'

'Kestrels mostly.'

'Aye, a kestrel. That would be it all right. Small and vicious. A right little killer is a kestrel. A right wicked little bastard.'

'Show me,' Robert said.

'What's that?'

'Show me how to set the snare.'

'Aye, I thought that. A sportsman. I thought that when I seen you following my tracks.'

'I thought you said you didn't see me.'

Fulbright didn't say anything. He knelt in the snow and showed Robert how to set the peg, how to fit the noose to the entrance of the burrow, the shining steel wire, and how to construct the slipknot so that it would close and tighten each time the animal struggled.

'By rights you need a ferret. Send ferret into hole, the bloody rabbit bolts out of the burrow, breaks its bloody neck straight off.'

Kneeling in the snow, Fulbright told him about traps. The hair-trigger mink traps, the heavy-jawed wolf traps. He elucidated upon principles of concealment and stealth. The use of

99

stakes, drags and earth-hold anchors. The use of leg-hold traps. Fulbright gave him to understand that there were theorems relative to the practice of trapping. That an animal would gnaw its own leg off to escape and in that fact there was something to be learned in the matter of doing what was required. Fulbright said that he had been to a bear-baiting in a forest adjacent to the Czech border. He said that was an event of terrible majesty. As he described it, Fulbright's speech began to slip back into archaic forms, a richness and texture in the way he spoke. There was a need for language that could encompass the bestial tableaux played out in a forest clearing. The unfolding of it represented in wording that was rich, textured, prone to hyperbole. The swart beast chained and muzzled. It seemed that Fulbright summoned the bear, saliva running from its jaws as it turned and turned again in its lurching burlesque. 'Man pities the bear,' Fulbright said, 'it is certain he does, for there would be no sport forby the man pitiest the bear.' Fulbright did not know the nationality of the men who brought the bear, manacled in a box. Ukrainians perhaps, or Belorussians. Local men with dogs lined the clearing and the men with the bear took wagers, the bear beset on each side by a dog, blood running from its flanks and a broken-backed cur in rictus in the trampled snow. 'Old Ursa, he don't die too easy,' Fulbright murmured. And when the bear found a corner to defend, the men would take a steel goad on a long pole and drive him from the shelter. Goad meaning to antagonize. Ursa meaning bear. It felt to Robert that he had been kneeling there for a long time and that winter darkness was stealing over the forest. 'In thy daylight heart thou sidest with the bear,' Fulbright whispered, 'but in thy thought thou sidest with the mastiff.'

15

Mallon had started to call on Agnew every week. Agnew wondered if he was acting on his own. He noticed that Mallon would edge closer to him, as though he were wearing a wire. He thought that he was entitled to a certain level of suspicion. Part of him hoped that Mallon had betrayed their friendship, that somewhere there was a room with serious-minded people scrutinizing his account of events, men who were engaged in evidence-gathering activity. Men who believed in conspiracies. He imagined Mallon talking to them, recounting their conversations, offering opinions as to Agnew's mental state. The account sometimes halting, stumbled over, the man who is betraying his friend. Agnew wanted to believe that material was being generated. Statements, affidavits, witness summonses. That what he said stood as stony testament to Robert's life.

He thought that Mallon had become more attentive lately. He would go through Agnew's account of events with detailed, sceptical questioning. Agnew thought that he had started to detect false bonhomie, hollow protestations of friendship. Mallon had begun to bring a half-bottle of whiskey, which he kept in his inside pocket. Mallon insisted that they fill the lid of the whiskey bottle and drink it that way. He said it was different to drinking from the bottle. There was an improvised feeling to drinking that way, a gesture in the direction of spontaneous out-of-doors activity. They had taken to walking as far as the pilot jetty. They sat on a rotted piling. There was a run-down boatyard beside the jetty. The area was littered with rusted boat parts, snapped hawsers, fused winch gears, rotted hulks. There was an understanding that the atmosphere of marine dereliction was important to Mallon's view of himself as the possessor of a corrosive heartiness. On rainy days they stood in the wheelhouse of an abandoned trawler, staring across the lough through windowpanes streaked with salt. There were dangerous currents in the lough, unnavigable bars, tidal surges. There were buoys, navigation towers, pilot boats. A deep-sea infrastructure based on principles of simple guidance which Agnew found hard to fault. He would have liked to cultivate an attitude of mellow competence, that when it came to it you could rise above wistful companionship and indulge in the exchange of ruddy confidences. He saw other men of his age on the dock. Retired men who spent their days working on small boats. Men who wore sailors' caps and were capable of medicating themselves for minor heart problems without succumbing to dread. Men who recognized fatalism as part of the slippery slope. He envied them their good husbandry, their bluff narratives. Agnew wanted what he saw in them, the sense that throughout a difficult life they had reserved a little goodheartedness to see them through bleak midwinter days.

'You never told me you were with Jackson when he done your man,' Mallon said.

'I wasn't with him. I was sitting in the farmhouse with Boyle. I never saw what happened.'

'That's what you say. I'd say the same.'

'I was with Boyle.'

'The soon-to-be deceased Mr Boyle. It was an RUC man that Jackson shot that night, you know that. Shot him with a PIRA weapon to cover his tracks.'

'A Sergeant.'

'This Sergeant knew that there was collusion going on. That's why Jackson done him. Called him at home and told him to come to the barracks, then blew his head off when he was opening the gates.'

'The only thing is that Jackson never made any call that night. Someone else called the Sergeant.'

'The call come from a phone box in Armagh.'

'Nairac was based in Armagh, in Bessbrook.'

'You got Nairac on the brain. You can't tie him in to this just because he was in Armagh at the time. That doesn't work.'

Agnew had a mental image of Boyle looking at him across the table in the farmhouse with the gun held barrel-up at the side of his head, a gesture which seemed self-mocking now, in parody of an arcane duellist, as though he was about to lower the barrel to the horizontal and sight along it. But it was the serial number which Agnew remembered. Star SA 47320-N360. According to the information available to him, the pistol which was manufactured in Galicia in 1972 and imported by PIRA as part of a weapons shipment in 1972, was known to have been in the possession of Robert Nairac.

'They were assembling devices in that farmhouse,' Mallon said.

He took a deliberate sip from the lid of whiskey and fixed his gaze on a distant object. Each word was deliberated over and he delivered them like objects he had crafted himself.

'Who was?'

'That's the question, isn't it?'

'Jackson and them boys didn't know how to build bombs. They must have had help.'

'Who was helping them? 14th Int? MI5? You told me you smelt gelignite when you were there.'

'I did.'

'They were robbing it from quarries and using it as a booster in anfo devices.'

Ammonium nitrate and fuel oil. The improvised explosive smelt strongly of diesel. Agnew tried to remember if there had been an odour of diesel around the farm.

Anfo. Device. Agnew noticed the way the conversation had started to gather euphemisms to itself. The way that meaning devised concealed positions for itself. The fact that devices were assembled implied that devices were used. In 1976 he had been called out to a small country road. A farmer had found a bomb concealed in a culvert under the road. The device was contained in an aluminium beer keg and lay half buried in the mud. There were weld marks on the keg. There was a grey coil of det cord around the top of the keg. The detonator was fitted into the top of the keg at the valve opening, with wires protruding from it. Agnew would have been disappointed if there had not been protruding wires. The side of the keg had been partially eaten away from within and you could see the material of the explosive inside, the power gel which had deteriorated and was weeping. You had a sense of dumped chemical waste, compounds of terrible malignancy, dark corrosive processes. The muddy water underneath it glistened with toxic leachate.

When Agnew was not in the caravan Lorna would read through the material he had amassed selecting a document at random. She knew that her mother also kept a file of cuttings concerning Agnew. Her mother knew that Agnew had not told her the full truth about his past when they were married. That he had lied to her and added dark perjury to his crimes. Lorna knew this because her mother talked about it at night saying things that she thought Lorna would not understand. Such as your father is not the man you think he is. Such as you let the heart rule the head you see what happens. Then there would be a lot of sighing and staring off into the distance as if to say why did I marry a betrayer? The file of cuttings was in the back of the wardrobe behind her shoes and the lingerie she kept hidden. Lorna wasn't surprised why. She couldn't believe the colours. Cerise dusky pink. What did she do? Perform sad middle-aged-lady sexy dancing for her new husband? Not that husband number two Mr Sinister in his aftershave was much better than Agnew.

Lorna would take the file to her room and lock the door. The file consisted of newspaper cuttings about Agnew's trial. He was charged with conspiracy to murder though he looked too sad to be a conspirator to murder. He looked like somebody who stole something sorry I wish I hadn't done it I'll never again. He looked as if he was about to start crying max embarrassment to all. You'd have thought a conspirator would be someone with a secret smile on their face nobody knows what they are smiling about. Mr Sinister the new husband looked like one he thought she didn't see him. She couldn't find out anything about the trial because the case was heard in camera which means in secret. And witnesses gave evidence without using their real names being called things like Constable A. She knew that Mallon had given evidence saying that Agnew was a good policeman because she had heard them talking about it one day. And she knew that Agnew received some prison and some suspended sentence which means that you do not go to prison unless you do something bad again. And there was a photograph of Agnew coming out of a courthouse in handcuffs. At least that was what it looked like with big steps and men in wigs and men smoking worried cigarettes as if this was their last smoke for ever. Agnew did not look like a man who had just got off from twenty years or possible life in a prison adrift among the fiendish scum. He looked like a man whose worry had just begun.

It looked like a long time since her mother had touched the things in her wardrobe, intimate garments the words they used in the court case of some heartbroken girl a victim of rape. She looked sad too but maybe the forty-year-old ladies in dusky pink were dancing in her head, the ladies in cerise.

She was going to see that doctor in the hospital week after week, maybe they'd lock her up. It was in the notes that Agnew was put in she wondered if he tried to plead insane please something snapped I couldn't help it. The doctor said that it was only smart people who got eating disorders. Of above-average intelligence was what she said, but Lorna could see it in her eyes what is so smart about starving yourself what did she know. The hospital was full of pale ghost people. Ghost people in the ghost wards. And the doctor was a ghost monitor in a white coat.

She could see that the hospital frightened her mother. She could tell. The way she put on that walk and the cross voice I'll show the scary thoughts in my head who is boss. Then she got angry and told Lorna that she was disappointed. Which is exactly what she was meant to be could she not see that she was meant to be disappointed with her daughter? That she was meant to be angry. That she was meant to not understand and feel to blame. When she blamed herself it showed that things were working. The blame showed that Lorna had control. She knew that they could smell her. That sad starved smell.

He thought Mallon was his friend she saw the way Mallon looked at her. What did he have X-ray eyes? She didn't have any friends so it wasn't right to say anything about Agnew's friends at least he had one.

Agnew watched Mallon drive away. It was always the same. As they walked back from the dock Mallon became distant, dismissive. It made Agnew wonder about their friendship. Mallon's attitude sometimes felt like late-night interrogation-room bonhomie, the air thick with cigarette smoke, the weary, airless complicities of 4 a.m.

Agnew wondered if Mallon was already writing a report of their encounter in his head as he walked away. He realized that he did not know where Mallon was working. For something like this, Agnew thought, they would keep him out of the new buildings. He would be put into an old station earmarked for closure. Agnew saw a typewriter in an office with dirt-streaked windows and cast-iron radiators, a Remington with gunmetal keys, an object with talismanic properties to it. A room that provided you with historical context and a certain vein of dreamy abstraction.

When he got back to the caravan he saw that Lorna had been reading through the material. There was a copy of the

Belfast photograph of Robert lying on her bed. Robert is standing in the middle of a group of children. He is wearing a flak jacket and battledress. The insignia on his beret is indistinct. Robert is half turned towards the camera. The badly broken nose is clearly visible. It is hard to fix the expression. The caption to the photograph describes him as talking to children in the Ardoyne area of Belfast. It is possible the circumstances of the photograph are contrived. You get the impression that Robert is aware of the camera. He is not looking at any of the children or teenagers who surrounded him. There is the impression of a man who had struck a pose for the cameras. At a distance he appears to be smiling, an effect suggested by the slightly undershot jaw. On closer examination, he is not smiling. The caption states that the photograph had been taken three months before Robert's death, but his hair, underneath the beret, is neatly cut. Other accounts said that in the last months of his life Robert grew his hair long as cover. The caption implies that the children and Robert had been engaging in conversation, but closer examination revealed that the children had their attention focused on events in the background. Only the faces of the two teenage boys are visible. One of them is looking at Robert. It is not a friendly look. It is a street look, artful, derisive. The other, short-haired boy is looking at the camera as if he had suddenly become aware of the photographer. His look is one of hostile calculation, working out what threat was posed by the camera.

The photograph was rife with ambiguity. If you framed Robert's face and moved in on it, the print becomes pixilated, the image unresolved, the emulsion scratched and dulled. But it seems that he was lost in thought and that it is not a good thought. He appears to be engaged in a kind of vehement reverie. The eyes are black and hard, and there seems to be an anger there, ire that seems to transcend the time and place.

* * *

Agnew started to put the material away. The phone rang. He had brought the old telephone from his desk at Gough Barracks the night he had left and when he had moved into the caravan he had connected it to the pole running through the site. He liked the tone of it. In the confined space of the caravan, it managed to convey the impression of a phone ringing in an empty house.

'Is Lorna there?' Angela said.

'Not here. Well, here but she's gone out.'

'She could be anywhere. With those boys.'

'Them boys is all right. I'm a policeman, I can tell.'

'You were a policeman. It's good she's not there as it happens. I need to talk to you about her.'

He liked the brusqueness of the way she reminded him of his lost status. The matter-of-fact abrogation of his dignity. He needed to be reminded that his loss of status was important. That being dismissed from the force was a defining event. Not one to be subject to his casual evasions, semi-humorous asides. These things are the beacons in the bleak post-marital landscapes they occupied. They shone a melancholy light.

'What about Lorna?'

'It would seem that her weight loss is progressive. We are approaching the point of irreversible damage. There is oedema to the liver. There is sclerosis to the eye.'

'That what thon buck in a white coat tell you?'

Agnew knew the way that she deferred to professionals. Repeated their words to herself in the car on the way home, finding comfort in the shape of the words themselves, the complex internal structures. Oedema. Sclerosis to the eye. She liked the sense of a hidden order.

'He understands what is happening to her. He says to me that in cases like this the body turns on itself. It starts with the eyes. The body is starved, so it starts to consume the eye.'

He could hear her awe for the doctor in her voice. That a man should possess such knowledge.

'Then the muscles, then the internal organs, then the brain.'

She spoke the words slowly, as though reciting them from a book, a terrible almanac.

'They grow a fine hair on their bodies,' she said.

She was whispering now. He could see her holding the phone, her eyes half closed, trying to keep the words in order, to maintain the sequences. He could hear the tremor in her voice. He could see her face swamped with woe.

'The hair has a name,' she said. 'Its called lanugo I think.'

'I never saw any hair on her body,' Agnew said. 'Honest to god I never. I mean she's thin but nothing like that.'

'A fine downy hair,' she said.

'What do you want me to do?' he said.

'I told you before,' she said. 'Find her diary. It's not in the house. I looked everywhere. It's not at school. So it must be in the caravan somewhere.'

'I see her writing in it sometimes, but I never see where she keeps it.'

'You feel terrible,' she said. 'When I was her age I kept a diary. I would have died if anyone had seen it.' An adolescent note in her voice, an undertone of breathy confidences exchanged.

'I never did.'

'No, I suppose you wouldn't. Somebody might find out what was going on in your head.'

He waited for the discordant laugh, the high divorcee tone of self-mockery, the bitter theatrics. He thought about his daughter. That the body conspires against itself. That the eye consumes itself. She gave the impression of a duty being performed, an act of domestic rigour. She liked to polish silver with an impregnated cloth. She liked to take out boxes, sort things, arrange them. She liked to memorize old wrongs and have them to hand.

'I'll try to find it,' he said.

'It's not that I want to,' she said.

'I know what you're saying.'

'It's an illness she has.'

'She was always highly strung.'

These unwieldy exchanges the best they could manage now. He hung up. He looked in the cupboard where Lorna kept her things. There was a toothbrush, underwear, a pair of men's woollen socks and one of the men's shirts that she wore. He felt the relentlessness of the attention his daughter brought to bear on herself. There was no make-up. There were no small familiar objects on the carefully made bed. There were none of the things that she might regard as impediments to self.

He searched the bathroom. He went outside with a torch and looked at the undercarriage of the caravan, but he could not see anything hidden there. He lay in the darkness for a while. There was a smell of creosote, of anti-rust compounds. The soil was fine and sandy. He had an affinity with hidden spaces. He went back inside. The documents he had taken from Lorna's bed were sitting on the table. He put them back into the cardboard box they had come from and placed it on a shelf. He realized that the light was fading across the lough. He sat on Lorna's bed and thought that he would wait there for his daughter to come home. He thought about what his wife had said. That the body conspires against itself. That the eye devours itself. The edges of his files were picked out in white against the dusk. He took down a file and began to read, starting in the middle of a witness statement and trying to pick out the words, knowing that he needed his glasses but nevertheless able to discern a phrase here and there. Seen the victim lying there. Put my hand on the wound to try to. Said he felt cold. Thinking that this was what made his daughter carry a book and write. That someone would see things for what they were. That someone might give testament.

16

David's office on the corridor had expanded due to new inflows of intelligence. Routine political enquiries from civil servants were directed to him. Knox gave him the names of men he wished to have interned. David compiled documentation on them. He learned that it was more reliable to invent a history for the target. Sightings of targets at known trouble spots by unnamed witnesses. Spurious forensic evidence linking them to explosives finds. He added unnecessary detail for authenticity. He cut out wedding photographs of the target from local newspapers and pasted them to sheets of foolscap in the file. He listed dates of birth, addresses, place of work. The more detail you gave, the more it seemed that guilt accrued. Hair colour. Eye colour. The existence of other documentation elsewhere was implied, fresh revelations, the damning circumstance.

'The army lot go for planting ammo, that kind of thing,' Knox had said. 'We don't do anything crude. What I want you to do leaves no physical trace.'

After a few months working at the files, David found that it wasn't necessary to give any direct evidence of law-breaking. You only had to suggest that transgression lurked somewhere in the information. You created a sense of menace, the feeling that there was something more to be learned. That the target's guilt was a difficult, allusive thing, demanding other proofs, verification in terms of the metaphysic.

David thought that the profiles he created transcended the actual detail of the target's life. The banal accounts they gave of themselves in distempered interrogation rooms. David was tempted to show them what he had done to their lives. To show them the finely wrought thing. The troubled histories he had created, the brooding, overshadowed lives, the terrible symmetry of things preordained coming to pass.

He liked the way that Gemini was going. He was surprised that the operation had endured for so long. He suspected that Knox was protecting it and that he was indulging David in this. Knox said that he preferred homosexual blackmail. That the outlines of terrible necessity were more visible. Less subject to a womanly blurring of things at the edges. David said that there was more room for nuance in a Gemini-type operation. Something that Knox had in fact taught him. The value of the peripheral. He wondered if Knox found women difficult to understand. Sometimes he would see Knox at a mess party in the company of a commissioned officer's wife, a shrill-voiced Home Counties woman with a frail psyche. Women with an aura of unhappy love affairs about them.

It was becoming harder to recruit the type of girl that David preferred. Gemini was seen as dangerous. Joyce was forced to recruit foreign girls, Asians, women with war-zone eyes and a tendency towards drug use and petty theft. There were instances of punters falling in love with the girls, arriving night after night with small gifts. They were useful in a small way, but they were prone to desperate measures. David wondered if the sense of purpose that he had cultivated was being undermined. There were unwanted undertones of erotic possibility.

'That's the problem with the exotics,' Joyce said. 'The men fall for them.'

David thought that Robert was taking on the characteristics of one of these targets. There was the accumulation of detail which led you away from the centre, from the facts of a life. The donkey jacket. The Remington shotgun. The hawking. The prowess at boxing. He dropped Robert's name into conversations and found the same things coming back.

Robert had not been seen in Theipval for several months. Knox told David that he was on the border, operating out of Castledillon. There were rumours of cross-border incursions, extra-judicial assassinations, the beginnings of the ruinous narrative of Robert's activity along the border.

Knox arranged for David to go on a special-operations course in Norway.

'Do you good,' Knox said. 'Get a bit of air in your lungs, metaphorically speaking.'

He gave David the details. Practice of low-level insertion by parachute. Principles of agent extraction. David said that it was nothing to do with the environment they were operating in.

'It's to do with personality,' Knox said. 'How you see yourself.'

It was good to immerse yourself in the day-to-day operational detail, Knox said, that was the way this war was conducted, operating along the edge of the quotidian. But there was also room for something more expansive. Covert operations with a dramatic sweep. Operations with a wartime resonance.

The night before he went to Norway, Robert came to the office. David was working late to finish up paperwork before he left. Everyone else had gone home. He thought afterwards that he had looked up and seen Robert standing in front of him, but he realized that this was not the case. There was always the temptation to mythologize the moment where Robert was concerned. In fact he had heard a polite knock on the glass panel of the door and had looked up to see Robert standing in the doorway. Robert was wearing the donkey jacket with a scarf draped over his shoulders. He seemed a little hesitant, apologetic. There was a Hispanic look to him at times with his dark complexion, a look of minor Iberian nobility, a man who projected a melancholy panache. He apologized for interrupting David's work. David told him to come in. Robert did, closing the door behind him. He sat down at the desk opposite David. David had no idea why he was there.

'I'm dreadfully sorry for the interruption,' Robert said. 'I believe you're off to Norway tomorrow.'

'For my sins.'

'Always fancied Norway. Good rivers. Boxed a Norwegian chap once. Not much of a boxer, but the bugger wouldn't stay down.'

'Afraid I never boxed myself.'

'Not much to it. Keep your guard up. Keep your chin out of the way. Hit the bastard harder and faster than he hits you. What way does a Norwegian speak? Don't know if I can do a Norwegian accent. Expect I could if I tried. I can do most accents. Got a gift for it.'

David realized that Robert had been drinking. The donkey jacket lay open and he could see the handgrip of a Browning in a holster under his arm.

'What are things like up on the border?' David said.

Robert leaned back in his chair and put his chin in his hand in an attitude of exaggerated consideration. David knew that he wasn't going to get the reality. That Robert was formulating an idealized state of affairs. SitInt.

'You know, David, I go into pubs and the locals talk to me. They recognize that I understand the country. I can do accents. Try me on Belfast. Try me on the Ardoyne. I can do Bogside like a native.'

A terse, incomplete feel to Robert's speech when he was talking about the field. Some staccato Com language, abbreviated, compressed for transmission.

'The key to the border is trust, David. I want people to trust me. I bought a black Labrador. Come with me on this, David. These people trust a man with a dog. They don't want PIRA all their lives. They want someone they can trust. Man gets weary of mistrust. These are field-sports people. You don't just ask, "Have you seen any PIRA here?" You go the long way round. You ask, "What the fishing's like here? The shooting?" You direct polite enquiries about topics that the subjects are familiar and comfortable with.'

114

'I have to admit I agree with what you're saying,' David said. 'Your thinking is quite advanced. Have you read Kitson on counter-insurgency?'

'The bible,' Robert said. 'The bloody bible.'

David wondered afterwards about what Robert had said. It didn't fit with what he had heard about the weeks Robert spent in the field, the targeting of suspects, the border incursions, the customized weapons with insulating tape wound around the handgrip. The things that weren't about winning over the local population. The things that were about unequivocal death, the hail of bullets, the single shot to the head. David had been hearing things about that type of activity and about close relationships with local paramilitary leaders.

'Do you know what a pseudo-gang is?' David asked.

Robert stared back at him without answering. It was the dark look, the one people talked about when they talked about Robert. The unfathomable look that made you feel you were subject to terrible reckoning, something amoral and void in the man's expression. Without removing his eyes from David's, Robert leaned across and tapped him lightly on the shoulder.

'Come on,' he said. 'Let's go for a drink.'

Later, David told Joyce that he had been scared that night.

'I've been in many frightening situations,' he said, 'I'm a man of physical courage, but the bugger nearly made me piss myself.'

The fear had a baroque element to it. He thought about his schoolboy idea of Catholics, the flickering votives, black-clad figures moving swiftly across cloisters. The thing you feared on an intuitive level but with doctrinal overtones, subtle and cruel.

They walked across the parade ground to the mess. The mess was in several Orlitt huts joined together. David liked that about the army. The way they named things. Orlitt. Nissen. The names with an improvised aspect to them, like the buildings they described, a bolted-together feel. There were names the army picked up in colonial outposts and brought home. Sangar, dusty and far-flung. Young recruits picking up on the words because these were the words that set them apart from the world.

David had trouble keeping up. He noticed the way Robert fell into a march when he hit the gravel of the parade ground.

'It's a sound I always liked,' he said.

'What's that?'

'The sound of soldiers marching.'

'Are we marching?'

'Well, you are.'

'I don't think so. It's just my walk. If I were to march at the border they would know I was a soldier straight away.'

Robert looked amused. David didn't know why. That was the thing with Robert. You didn't know if he really thought that he wasn't marching or if there was some other meaning to be attached to his amusement. A knowledge of arcane intelligence structures, the practice of bluff and counter-bluff carried out on a higher plane. Or perhaps the assassin's deadpan amusement, the flicker in the eye, the tug at the corner of the mouth. The amusement that comes from knowledge of putting a rifle barrel to a man's head after you've just gunned him down in an ambush and finishing him off and feeling a fine spray of blood and brain matter on your face and hearing laughter in your head, dusty and harsh and windblown.

Robert had to duck his head to get into the Orlitt. The mess was run by the RAF. There were RAF memorabilia on the wall. A wooden Blériot propeller, regimental plaques in the shape of rotor blades, photographs of men standing under nose cones with one hand on an aluminium jet nacelle, grinning and smoking a pipe. The sense of having worked out responses to fiery death in terms of jaunty insouciance.

Around the bar men struck off-duty poses. Some of them were drunk, wearing civvies with the awkward look you saw in men accustomed to wearing uniform, something essential in them destructured. You saw them later on in the married quarters, standing over a wife who was shrinking away, a fist raised, overcome by a murderous gaucheness.

They headed towards the bar, Robert greeting people as they moved through the crowd. The steward came over to Robert, who addressed him by name. Robert ordered a bottle of gin and a tonic siphon. David was surprised to see that Robert had a slate at the bar. He saw Joyce sitting at the bar with two of the Gemini techs. He saw her glance over at Robert in that jaded way she had. He knew that he would ask her about him later. Wait until she was undressing for bed. She would make some vague remark about his height or his broken nose, not looking at him, and he would be expected to find meaning in the remark. He was starting to feel that Joyce had elevated the inconsequential to the status of a court language, a refined and inflected idiom, the bland phrase weighted with nuance. She seemed to be able to navigate the covert world in an effortless way which was not available to him.

Robert left him alone at the bar for a long time. He ordered a beer at first and then started to drink Robert's gin, pouring it into a glass and drinking it straight. He felt the need to adopt a mood to suit the situation he found himself in, left alone at the bar, and felt himself edging towards a position of aggressive self-pity. By the time Robert came back he had finished half the bottle.

'Sorry about that, David,' Robert said. 'Want you to meet a pal. Tony Ball, this is David Erskine. Runs that Gemini op I told you about. He's a good sort. Likes the outdoors. He's no desk jockey.'

David shook hands with Ball. He knew that Ball was regular SAS. He was smaller than Nairac, fair-skinned, and seemed to have a smile on his face all the time. Ball and Nairac started to play drinking games where you had to answer a question and if you didn't you had to drink a finger of Gordon's. David thought it was juvenile. Nairac left them to go to the toilet.

'Bastard Nairac,' Ball said, smiling. 'Every time he comes to Hereford he drinks all my gin.'

Robert at SAS HQ in Hereford. You listened out. You kept every bit of information. You stored all the peripheral data. That was Knox's line.

Robert and Ball started to arm-wrestle on the bar. No one noticed. The tempo of things in the bar had risen now. An officer's wife was lying asleep against a partition, her mouth open. It was the hour of sly gropes under the table. It was the hour of ponderous confidences exchanged. Someone was singing Jim Reeves. David looked over and saw that one of the techs had his hand under Joyce's blouse. He could see the man moving his palm backwards and forwards across the material of her bra. He could imagine it in his own palm. Indented, unyielding. The man had a look of concentration on his face, as though he had his forearm in an engine bay. Joyce was talking to the other tech. He could imagine the talk. Where was he from? What did his mother and father do? The accretion of banalities, Joyce nodding gently to encourage him. The man was the more thoughtful of the two techs. He had high cheekbones, which gave him an ascetic look. David thought he had heard him say he was from Cheltenham, a place of established housing, garden city suburbs, well-kept privet, the shining dominion – the gently custodial aesthetic of the suburb, the tech growing up there with other fine-boned children. His hand stopped moving and held Joyce's breast underneath her blouse with a gentle but insistent air of entitlement, of sexual prerogative.

David found himself slumped up against the partition wall. The mess steward was talking to him. He was a small man with black hair slicked over, wearing a soiled white jacket. David could not understand what the man was saying to him. He was talking urgently into David's face. David realized that someone was singing. He looked up and saw that Robert was standing on a low barstool at the bar. He was singing Danny Boy. Watching the audience as he sang, making eye contact, making sweeping illustrative gestures with his hands. Ball stood with his hand on Robert's shoulder. David realized that this was a necessary part of the whole thing. The fulsome ballad, the eyes glistening with emotion, the way that events were allowed to fade into unwholesome sentiment.

Some time later, David found himself outside. He was leaning up against one of the steel poles of the tennis court behind the mess. He laced his fingers through the frost-hardened netting. Robert and Tony Ball stood in the middle of the court. They were stripped to the waist. David realized that they were going to box. He became aware of Joyce standing beside him.

'He said they done it before. That Ball. He says him and Nairac done it loads of times. You could get brave and hurt at a game like that.'

He felt her shiver.

'Cold,' she said.

The camp was always cold. It was built in a hollow and cold air lay in it. On frosty nights it was several degrees colder than the surrounding area. Robert and Ball had fallen into boxers' crouches and were circling each other.

'They mean it,' he said.

'Course they mean it,' Joyce said.

David had seen prints of bare-knuckle boxers, daguerreotypes. Men wearing knee breeches, broken-knuckled, low-browed. The idea of crude spectacle, itinerant bookmakers, the wagering of vast sums. David could see that bare-knuckle boxing was a public thing, that certain demands were made from it in terms of entertainment, but that this fight would be a private affair. That there was to be an intimate brutality.

Ball punched first, a jab and then a right hand which grazed off the side of Robert's head. Ball making a sound as he did so, the boxer's low, percussive grunt. Robert brought his gloves up to his face and Ball worked his body with three, four punches. David could just see Robert's eyes behind the gloves as he held them up to his face again in a gesture which appeared placatory but was not. There was the feral aspect of Robert. The eyes watching you unblinking from a covert. David could see that Ball's right knuckles were bleeding from the impact to the side of Robert's head. Ball put his head into Robert's shoulder and drove several hard jabs into Robert's stomach. Robert's head rested on Ball's shoulder. His eyes were blank. As David watched, Robert dug his fist into Ball's kidneys, a short twisting punch that made Ball cry out and release him. David became aware of the possibility of real harm being done. The crushed cartilage, the detached retina, pissing blood for weeks from damaged kidneys. Robert clubbed Ball hard on the side of the head and then hit him again on the same spot. The phrase brain lesion came into David's head. The two men circled each other again. David realized that they considered this a necessary adjunct to their profession. That they should abstract combat from every-thing that had gone before. David could see welts on their bare shoulders and ribs. They were breathing hard, their breath hanging in the air around them and trailing behind them when they moved, the camp lights lighting the spume so that it seemed as if they moved within, and were party to some spurious transcendence. Ball hit Robert on the mouth so that blood from his gums welled over his lips and ran down his chin, lending an expression of sanguinary voluptuous-ness to his appearance as he moved forward again, concen-trating in turn on Ball's lower body, both men shuddering with each blow.

'I never seen the like,' Joyce said in a whisper.

David touched his face where it had been sprayed with blood and spittle. Ball's fist glanced off Robert's shoulder. Ball's breathing was laboured, a deep whistle from the chest cavity on the exhale. The men stood toe to toe, their torsos slick with blood and mucus. Making small wordless sounds. Like there was a covert language to the fight. A vernacular of hurt. Welt, gash, lesion. A vocabulary of short, choppy words. Robert began to flail at Ball. Wild, fatigued swings which Ball countered easily with his forearms, Robert sobbing with the effort.

'Like boys in the playground,' Joyce said.

David remembered what that felt like. The flailing arms and the emotion welling up inside you, the terrible pre-adolescent sorrow, fighting on through the tears and the snot. Knowing that you're the one the other children gathered round are watching. That you can beat the other boy into the ground but that you are the one who is weeping.

Joyce took them back to her room in the married women's quarters. Robert and Ball drank whiskey and exchanged shy smiles. Joyce put mercurochrome on their faces. She swabbed deep cuts with cotton buds. She pressed a cold compress to Ball's swollen hand.

'What do you think?' Robert said.

'Of what? The fight? I thought you were going to do some real damage to each other.'

'It's the training. You learn to ignore the pain.'

'In college Robert kept this falcon in his rooms,' Ball said to Joyce. 'Bloody great big bastard. Mad bastard Robert used to put a piece of meat here, right on the bridge of his nose, let the bird peck it off. I thought the bugger would take one of his eyes out.'

'A kite. The bird was a kite,' Robert said.

'It was a bastard. Bird shit everywhere,' Ball said 'I think I broke my hand.'

'It's only bruised,' Joyce said.

David remembered that she had been an auxiliary nurse before she had been a call girl. When he met her she told him that she preferred the term escort. She said that when she told men that she had been a nurse they wanted her to dress up in a nurse's uniform. There was something about the starched hems, the folds, the pleats. The faint odour of antiseptic.

121

'What were you doing,' David said, 'out there?'

'Boxing,' Robert said.

David thought that boxing did not describe what the two men had been doing in the netted shadows of the tennis court. That what was at contest amounted to more than sporting prowess.

David fell asleep on the sofa. When he woke in the pre-dawn, Robert and Ball were gone. There were bloody pieces of tissue on the coffee table, a bloodied handprint on the back of the door. There was an ashtray on the sideboard. The furnishings of the room looked worn and threadbare. It had the look of a cheap hotel room, setting for seamy extramarital adventures, despondent sexual encounters.

17

Agnew told Knox the next day that Jackson and Somerville had used the Armalite to kill the RUC Sergeant.

'I fucking didn't get into this to kill my own people,' he said.

'The Sergeant was a nuisance,' Knox said. 'He'd seen a few things he shouldn't have seen and he was talking about them. Forget about the Sergeant. There are more important things than Sergeant.'

Knox was wearing an old jumper with a hole in the elbow. He had lined the windowsill of his office with cacti and he was watering them as he spoke to Agnew. Knox liked to play with paradigms of Anglo eccentricity. He liked to teeter on the edge of self-parody. He drove an open-top MGB in racing green with a long scarf flowing behind him. He bustled about the office corridor in a vague and forgetful manner. He paid young men with working-class accents to fellate him in dingy hotel rooms.

'How are things developing with Jackson?'

'Every time I see him I think he's about to put a bullet in me.'

'That is a sensation which is shared by quite a few people. Grim really. Nevertheless, Jackson is fighting this war on the only level where it is winnable. He is an important asset. But I think we need to do more in terms of creating a legend, leaks to the papers, that sort of thing. Generate a little more fear and trepidation in the local population. Mr Jackson is not getting his due.'

'I thought you'd want to keep him out of the papers.'

'On the contrary. Not under his own name, of course. Does he have a nickname?'

'They call him Jacko sometimes.'

'Jacko? Not good. A little clownish.'

'What about Jackal?'

Knox straightened up. His eyes were glittering.

'Well done, Agnew. Jackal is good. What about the Jackal? After the book. That's what I like about you, Agnew. You have a lurid imagination. You should work for the newspapers. Perhaps I could arrange an opening.'

'No thanks.'

Agnew had always tried to steer clear of reporters at preserved scenes. The way they thought they were part of it.

'Perhaps not. You are fairly useful as things stand. The Jackal it is, then. Would you like tea?'

'I could do with a drink.'

'Afraid there's nothing I can do for you there. You've had one or two already today, I see. I suppose I should disapprove, but in a way it's all for the best. It gives you a certain credibility among the assets. That sullen face of yours. The atmosphere of ill-discipline that surrounds you. In fact I would go so far as to say that it has saved your life on occasion.'

'Jackson has something going on with the British captain.'

'How do you know?'

'Hoppy's got a big mouth.'

'Any idea of the target?'

'Cross-border is the word.'

'Excellent. And the target?'

'PIRA, far as I can tell.'

'Is Nairac going to undertake the op himself?'

'Hoppy thinks he is. Jackson says Nairac can't wait. It looks like Jackson, Somerville and Boyle are going along. So I hear anyway.'

'Good, good.'

'There's more to it as well. Somerville says he wants a bigger op. He's itchy as fuck to do a big headliner. Hoppy has this idea, he won't say what it is.'

'I thought this man Hoppy was a little bit slow in his thinking.'

'He's a fucking dimwit, but Jackson listens to him. He's about the only one that Jackson listens to.'

'Keep me posted, Agnew. Don't stray too far.'

'I got a disciplinary hearing coming up.'

'I'll see if I can have it postponed.'

Agnew found that old colleagues were starting to hold him at checkpoints, turn their backs on him in the canteen. He wondered if word about the murder of Sergeant Campbell had leaked out. He knew that none of Jackson's crew would give evidence that he had been there. But there were always the nightmare charges. The doctrine of common purpose. Conspiracy with people unknown on dates unknown to murder people unknown. Conspiracy to conspire. When he got back to the house that evening, he found that Janet had packed her bags and was waiting in the hallway. She could have slipped away during the day, before he came home, he thought, but it would have dissipated the drama, the yearning for blame. Her mascara was smudged.

'I'm leaving.'

'So I see.'

'I can't keep on like this, Blair. There's nothing here for me.'

There was a smell of gin from her breath. She sounded as if she was talking from a long way away, her voice coming through the Valium haze.

'I don't have any life with you.'

He knew that this was an important part of the drama. That the phrases would be tired and derivative.

He remembered that she liked him to talk to her during sex, invent stories. He would find a rhythm, a chant of monotone obscenity. She urged him on to descriptions of female helplessness, submission, men with cruel mouths performing acts of desolate intimacy. Sometimes she would sit up in bed afterwards weeping quietly and he would lie on the other side of the bed without going to her, knowing that she could not bear to be comforted.

He felt that he would be undermining her conviction that she was a failure if he begged her to stay. He knew that it was the only conviction she truly held and that it would be irresponsible to subvert it. When the taxi came he did not help her to carry her bags to the car.

But when she had gone he realized that he had underestimated her. He noticed a letter in the fireplace which had been torn in half. He put the two pieces together on the kitchen table. The envelope was postmarked in Portadown. The letter was made up of cut-out words pasted down. There were frequent misspellings, errors of punctuation which added a whole frightening dimension, an essential part of the grammar of the threatening letter. You were meant to imagine a man from a lower socio-economic group, consumed by hatreds that he only half understood. The cutting out of the letters was not so much to disguise the handwriting as to indicate someone who was painstaking, mildly retarded, relentless. Get out or your dead you hore.

Agnew thought there were two possibilities. The letter had been posted either by Boyle through malice or by Knox. He knew that Knox favoured isolating his assets from friends and family. He thought that men were better operating on their own. It increased their sense of being set aside from society. You could see them acquire a honed look, pinched and ascetic. There were undertones of unbearable stress. Agnew thought about developing nervous mannerisms. In the hospital he had worked on a repertoire of tics, twitches, startled blinking. If required he could resort to repetitive hand-washing or incessant rocking.

Two weeks later Boyle called him and told him to drive to Portadown that afternoon.

'And bring your nightie, Agnew, you're going to be staying over.'

Boyle told him to drive to a light-engineering works on the outskirts of the town. Jackson was there with Boyle and

Somerville. They were wearing blue boiler suits. Jackson told Agnew to park his car around the back of the corrugated-iron shed. When Agnew went back into the shed he saw that Somerville had cleared a workbench and was stripping down a Galliel assault rifle, cleaning grease from the barrel with gun oil and a rag, which meant that it was new. Knox had shown him a photograph of the Israeli weapon and told him to look out for it.

'It's some fucking gun, so it is,' Somerville said.

'You'll never get to use it,' Jackson said. 'It's a liability taking it along at all. I keep saying, you got to get up close to the subject, use small arms.'

'We might have to fight our way out,' Somerville said.

'It's sanitized, so it is. There'll be nobody there to fight, no checkpoints neither,' Boyle said. 'Which is just as well with you along, you fucking retard.'

'What am I doing here?' Agnew said.

'You're the driver. Somerville robbed you a motor,' Jackson said.

'Nice job too,' Somerville said. 'Triumph. Got overdrive and all.'

Agnew watched the way Somerville worked at the rifle, disassembling it rapidly, only barely referring to the manual, which was open beside him. He knew that Somerville was not bright, but there seemed to be an aptitude towards mechanical things, with springs, coils, slides. Agnew was useless with mechanical work. He could not abide things that were threaded, dovetailed, snapped.

The workbenches held steel presses, bench lathes, metal-cutting equipment. There were oil cans under the benches, enamel signs for Mobil, Castrol. He had driven past the place many times, noted the presence of stocky men of unknown capabilities.

'Who owns this place anyhow?'

'A supporter. A man who knows when to keep the beak shut. Are you right?'

'Where are we headed for?'

'A cross-border op the night, so it is,' Somerville said. 'We got this PIRA boy cold.'

Somerville finished reassembling the SLR. Boyle put a 9mm with an extended magazine in his pocket. Somerville showed Agnew how to start the Triumph using the exposed ignition wires. Jackson got into the front of the car. Boyle and Somerville got into the back.

They drove for twenty minutes in the direction of Newry, then turned off towards Newtonhamilton. There were few other cars on the road. Nothing on the radio, just the sound of the tyres on the tarmac. They passed through Newtonhamilton. Agnew always found these small border towns atmospheric. The lit windows and the sense of small lives lived in a fulsome way. The streetscape family businesses and sole traders, the continuity. The sense of debilitating nostalgia just held at bay. On the outskirts of the town there were well-kept lawns and municipal flower displays, compact housing estates. Agnew wondered if Jackson had deliberately directed them this way. To reinforce their sense of being outside of things. To make them think in terms of a grizzled outlaw sensibility. Agnew had the feeling that someone watched them until they reached the town boundary. A teacher or a doctor, a level-headed, small-town rationalist who regarded a certain watchfulness within reasonable limits as being within the sphere of his duties.

The town gave way to fields and then to a landscape of fir plantations, isolated filling stations, scrubby fields. They turned on to an unapproved road heading south. Somerville had a compass and an Ordnance Survey map on his knee. The land around them had an uncharted feel. Agnew looked over at the map. The dense contour lines of small hills and drumlins suggested unique geophysical densities. Agnew was not sure if he regarded this landscape as being trustworthy. You expected unreliable compass readings, a wildly swinging needle. The air was damp and mutable. The road surface was rutted with lorry tracks. A place of contraband being moved by night, single trucks lurching along narrow roads on sidelights, the low-geared diesel grind.

'Fucking speed up, Agnew,' Boyle said. 'We got an appointment.'

'Somebody taking you in?' Agnew asked.

'You're wild inquisitive the day,' Jackson said.

'Just like to know what's going on, who I'm getting involved with.'

'You wouldn't want to be falling into bad company,' Boyle said.

Jackson took the map from Somerville.

'There's a forestry entrance up ahead on the right. Pull in there.'

When they reached the entrance Agnew pulled in. He saw an old forestry tractor half sunk in a ditch. A sign warning of the danger of forest fires was pockmarked with shotgun pellets. He felt Boyle lean in close to his left ear.

'Did you ever think that you might be the job, Agnew?' Boyle said in a whisper. 'It's a good place to dump a stiff.'

'Cut it out, to fuck, Boyle, and keep your eyes open.'

On the map Agnew could see the red line of the border cutting through the area in front of them. He knew that there was nothing to see. There were no markers or watchtowers. The border was notional. It was the distillation of the idea of boundary. It ran across damp boggy fields and low hills, rainy and remote pastures. It disappeared into rain-washed haze. In front of the car a narrow shale track led up into the plantation. Agnew knew that he didn't want to go up it. He was troubled by the idea of crossings. He was troubled by concepts of the forbidden. As he stared up the track he saw two figures emerge from the trees. Both appeared to be carrying weapons, but they were too far away and it was too dark for him to make them out clearly. The foremost figure raised a hand towards them. It had to be Nairac, Agnew thought, although the figure was indistinct. It was the way he waved.

It was not the cautious movement of the hand you would expect here, the gesture half revoked before it was finished. It was a confident motion, slow and assured.

'Flash your headlights,' Jackson said.

Agnew flashed the lights. The other men got out of the car. Agnew could hear weapons being cocked. Jackson leaned in through the driver's window.

'We've got a brave long walk in front of us. Chances are we'll not be back much before dawn. Make sure you're still here. I'd be wild disappointed if you weren't here.'

Agnew nodded.

They walked up the path towards the two other men. Agnew could hear their boots crunching in the shale. Jackson went straight up to them, Somerville and Boyle hanging back. In the dark and the mist, the two men seemed to tower over Jackson. They were looming and mythic and there seemed to be some kind of optical illusion whereby you could see their shadows against the whitish mist that surrounded them, the shadows bigger than them, huge and outlandish. Jackson gestured towards the car and the taller of the two men looked towards Agnew. He kept his head turned towards Agnew for what seemed like a long time. Agnew could feel the force of the man's regard. It felt weighty, as if it conferred responsibilities upon him. Agnew thought that the man might start down the track towards him. Agnew thought that the man was a little bent at the shoulders, although this might have been an effect of the night and the mist. Agnew pushed himself into his seat. He did not want the man to approach him, wreathed in mist, a legendary figure, stooped with the weight of the night and its secrets. But as he looked again the man slipped off into the trees and the others followed.

Agnew produced a bottle of Powers from his pocket and took a long drink. He was sure that the tall figure was Nairac. The other man could have been Lieutenant Tony Ball, who was operating in this area, detached from his unit to the SAS. He wondered how far they were from the target. From what

Knox had said, Nairac was given to long, punishing treks in wild country. The world of improvised bivouacs, C-rations eaten cold, extreme discomfort in the field. He knew that it would not make any difference to Jackson, but he could not see Somerville and Boyle being able to walk too far. He turned on the radio, then turned it off again and opened the window slightly so that he would be able to see anyone approaching the car. The mist had closed in, swirling about the car then parting to reveal strange scenes of dripping rowans and bare wet rock before closing in again. The interior of the car felt clammy and he was afraid to start the engine for heat. The mist smelt metallic, like an industrial by-process, but you found yourself trying to smell musks, feral stink. Agnew needed to piss but he didn't want to open the door. Something barked in the trees, a fox, the sound muted but still replete with snarl and lonesomeness. Agnew found himself thinking about something creeping towards the car, a stealthy carnivore moving on its belly and consumed with blood yearning, the ignominy of its race.

Later he would know that a PIRA operative called John Francis Green was killed that night in a house located across six miles of rough terrain. Green was also known as Benny Green. He had been in the house belonging to his friend, Gerry Carville. Carville describes leaving the house for a few hours, then coming back to find Green dead on the kitchen floor. The ballistic report identified the wounds as being caused by bullets fired from a Star pistol. There were no indications of a struggle. No forensic evidence of any significance was recovered from the scene. There were no witnesses. The farmhouse where the assassination took place was situated at the end of a lane which was over a mile long. There were no other houses on the lane. There are no accounts of the killing apart from the one allegedly given by Robert.

* * *

This was the incident that generated the Polaroid photograph shown by Robert to a range of people. Different accounts are given as to how the Polaroid came into circulation. It has been asserted that it was taken by local police attending the scene, but it has also been asserted that the local police force did not possess a Polaroid camera. The alternative is that the photograph was taken by one of the killers, either as evidence to show that the killing had in fact been carried out or as a gruesome memento.

18

Lorna thought that Agnew was getting smaller. He wore big square glasses that didn't fit his face any more and he peered at things as if he'd never seen them before. She thought that was getting old when things don't fit and things don't look like themselves they could both get smaller and smaller together and thinner and thinner so that nobody could find them. She looks she sees a fat girl in the mirror why can't they see it. She didn't know if the boys on the wall could see her any more sometimes they just looked out to sea but that was all right sometimes they looked so cold the wind was freezing. The way that people looked at her in school is that pity is it all about looking. Mrs Manning her form teacher called her mother in to say that her concentration is not what it should be in fact she doesn't concentrate at all what do they know do they ever think that she is concentrating very hard on things they can't see with their big eyes Mrs Manning form teacher should do something about her own form. She's like a whale and her make-up goes into the edges of her hair. What do you do with a very small father put him on the mantelpiece.

She once asked him if he ever had nightmares about things that he did and he said not so why does he cry out at night. She didn't like Mrs Manning she is a loathsome. She didn't like her mother's what is it partner is the word he is a loathsome also. I read about situations of a daughter who hates mother's new partner in girl magazines but they only give it the importance of acne periods etc and say that you are not unique that you are not alone when she knows well that she is alone.

Agnew thought that the photograph of the dead John Francis Green belonged with the material that he had compiled in the caravan. He had thought that he was the only person to have seen the photograph, but Knox had told him how Robert had gone around the base at Lisburn showing it to people. He imagined the Polaroid colours bleached out now, light draining from it over the years, the greenish tinge that would give the kitchen the look of a flooded interior, a sunken hulk, the colours eerie and muted. He owned a copy of the ballistics report on the bullets taken from Green's body. Three of them had fragmented and were unidentifiable. Five others were grouped as 9mm ordnance with clockwise grooving. The fragmentation of the three bullets on impact, taken along with the characteristics displayed by the wounds associated with those bullets, suggested that at least some of the ammunition used had been altered by means of a cross cut into the tip of the bullet which caused the lead to flatten and expand. External characteristics of ordnance were consistent with the use of a Spanish-manufactured Star pistol.

'Dum-dum bullets,' Mallon said. 'They were used a brave bit at the time. The worst was they used to hollow them out and fill them with mercury. Blow a hole the size of a dinner plate in you.'

'What about this photograph? You know they say it couldn't have been took by the killers, that it was took by the police later on.'

'Possible, I suppose.'

'Then Nairac wasn't there.'

'He told David Erskine that he was there. He showed him the photograph. That's if you can believe Erskine. Besides, he could still have been there if the photograph was taken by a police photographer. He could have obtained the photograph afterwards and still have been there.'

'If he wasn't there?'

'If he wasn't there, he showed the photograph to Erskine in order to pretend that he was there. How come he done that?'

'Because it's the sort of thing that Nairac would have done.'

There was the attraction of the lie, of transgression. Agnew knew that Robert had been in the habit of telling friends and colleagues in England that he had penetrated the PIRA brigade structure. That he was in fact a brigade commander, an assertion which would have been denied by all intelligence agencies on the ground. There was the uncertainty introduced into the situation. Who killed Green? Was Robert there? Agnew recognized it as being within Robert's field. The uncertainty caused by the unclaimed assassination. The fear it engendered.

'Did none of them say anything when they got back to the car?'

'There wasn't that much talk. A bit. They were all tired, far as I could see, except Jackson.'

'They came back on their own?'

He remembered that they had come back on their own. He had finished the whiskey and had half dozed through the night, waking when Somerville rapped the driver's window with the butt of the 9mm. Agnew saw the other two men step forward out of the mist, something rank-seeming in the air now, something of fenland vapours, foul and gaseous. The air inside the car was stale and cold. The three men were wet and covered in mud. They brought a smell of ditchwater into the car and a smell of cordite, the small-arms reek.

'I'm fucking destroyed,' Boyle said. 'I never seen any cunt move as fast as that English bastard going through a fucking bog. He never let fucking up.'

Agnew was going to ask Jackson if the operation had been successful. Then Jackson turned to him and Agnew saw that his face was spattered with blood.

'Drive on, to fuck.'

'Did youse get the job done?' Agnew asked as they drove into Portadown. He didn't look at anyone.

When they got back to the engineering works Somerville insisted on cleaning the Galliel before it was put away.

'You never fired the fucker,' Boyle said.

Somerville ignored him and went on cleaning the SLR.

'You never fired it. He never fired the fucking thing. What's he cleaning it for?'

Agnew thought that Boyle looked terrible suddenly. There were dark shadows under his eyes. His skin was blotched. Agnew saw that Jackson was looking at Boyle as well.

'What the fuck's wrong with you?' Jackson said.

'Didn't like it out under them trees. You couldn't see a stime.'

'Some operative you are,' Somerville said. 'Staff-Captain Boyle, Mid-Ulster Brigade.'

'I can't help it if I got an imagination,' Boyle said.

Jackson walked right up to him, put himself in Boyle's eye-line. He studied him with his head on one side. He put his hand out and placed it against Boyle's face, pinching the skin of his cheek gently as if to test the texture and elasticity of the other man's flesh. As if he suspected that Boyle had shed some of his animate force during their journey on foot. Or that in the midst of troublesome night he had given way to reflections of mortality.

'Take her handy,' Jackson said. 'We'll look after you.'

'I don't know about thon English boy,' Boyle said. 'I don't know about thon English boy at all.'

Somerville started to put the weapons away. Agnew couldn't see the Star pistol, but it was possible that Jackson had kept it in the car.

'So you're saying that Nairac might have had the pistol after all and that he might have fired the shots?' Mallon said.

'I just don't know. I can't remember.'

He could not remember the disposition of firearms, but he could remember vividly the look on Boyle's face, the sweat on his upper lip and the sudden onset of consternation. He thought that Boyle had been subject to sudden terrible insight as he walked through the trees that night, a crippling intuition that his own fate was at hand and that it was connected to the British captain.

Looking back, the scene in the engineering works in Portadown thirty years before seemed to have been devised in order to illustrate lost values, a paradigm of interiors carefully lit to suggest honest toil, of lathes and warm-oil smells, of crafted objects, mechanical tolerances. He remembered Somerville wiping the SLR carefully with a rag, Jackson with a bullet clamped in a bench vice cutting a cross into the tip with a file, a range of artisanal values on display. Even Boyle, slumped between two benches, his face awash with complex woe, seemed to have a place in the composition, the glum visionary, the man who sees it all come to nothing.

'If you don't remember,' Mallon said quietly, 'then who the fuck will?'

That evening Agnew drove to Newry to pick up Lorna. She was waiting in the porch when he pulled into the driveway. She walked towards the car carrying her bag. She looked frail and her face was drawn and ascetic, as though she spent wakeful nights testing herself against the darkness in lonely feats of endurance. As she approached the car, he saw Angela at the porch. She was watching her daughter with a frown, her gaze travelling down the girl's body, a stern assay, as though she were tasked with giving an account of her to some other authority exceeding that of mother. As Lorna was climbing painfully into the car, Angela caught Agnew's eye and pointed at the girl's shoulder bag, mouthing words as she did so. Agnew knew that she was telling him that the diary was in the bag. That he should take it from the bag when the girl wasn't looking. Agnew nodded as if he understood. As they drove off, Lorna turned to watch her mother. The woman stood still in the porch, her arms folded, and as they turned the corner Agnew glanced in the mirror and saw her standing there and had the impression that she intended to remain there all night, that there was something in the suburbs that must be warded against, that vigil must be maintained.

'You look fucking terrible,' Agnew said.

'Pot kettle,' Lorna said. 'I've never seen that shade of yellow before. Not on skin, anyhow.'

'It's called sclerosis. You're a great shade of grey yourself. What's that called?'

'Ash nervosa. Very popular in school.'

'I'd say.'

'Don't tell me to start eating or anything like that. I am eating a bit. Don't tell me how thin I am. I know I'm not. Don't tell me I'm an intelligent girl.'

'You're not an intelligent girl, you're a fucking retard.'

'And you're a spastic alco.'

'Less of the spastic now, take her handy on the spastic front. I'll give you the alco right enough. I might be on my last legs but I'm not a spa. Make sure you put flowers on my grave when I go.'

'What sort of flowers?'

'I don't know. Something sickly, with mad artificial colours that you never get in nature. You know the kind of flower that lasts for six months with no water.'

'Carnations.'

'That's a girl.'

'I suppose I better visit your grave. There's not much chance of anyone else doing it.'

'That's true.'

'Especially not my mother.'

'You said it. Now that I come to think of it, maybe you shouldn't come. It would be sadder that way. An unmarked grave. Weeds growing on it.'

He felt himself swept along with the melancholy of it, the unkempt corner of the graveyard, lonely and unvisited.

'No way.'

'How come?'

'You're not allowed that much of the glooms. There'll be none left for me.'

This was when they were at their best, seeing themselves as beset with comic gloom, driving at sea level towards the campsite, the ebb stench of the shallow bay coming through the darkness to them, its tidal flats, its wracks and salty bents.

That night he left her in the caravan and walked up to the hotel above the campsite. The hotel bar was almost empty, two women sitting over Bacardis in the corner, a livid-faced man almost asleep at the bar. It was the kind of atmosphere for drinking that he liked best. He thought that this was the hotel most appropriate to the campsite, as if the campsite had willed the hotel upon itself, with its worn carpets, unmanned reception desk, stained flock wallpaper, features of provincial despondency. Sand from the beach blew along the driveway and drifted against the seaward wall. The owner was a man in his fifties with papery white skin who wore a black suit. He served Agnew with murmured generalities about the weather and the scarcity of custom. He seemed aware of his own timelessness. He would talk to Agnew for hours in neat crafted sentences, world events encompassed in careful, non-judgemental phrasings. He seemed to have drifted down from some forgotten idea of service. When Agnew was ready to leave, the man steered him to the door, holding him carefully by the sleeve.

He saw Lorna was sleeping when he got back to the caravan. He poured himself a Crested Ten. At this stage of the evening he tended towards drinks which had complex label designs, an element of the baroque. Lorna had left her shoulder bag on the banquette. The bag had Eastern motifs, little mirrored tassels, a hand-dyed look to it. He opened it. He could see the diary, the top edge slightly frayed. He could hear Lorna's soft, even breathing. Lately he had noticed that she slept deeply and was difficult to wake. As he reached for the edge of the diary, his sleeve caught the tumbler of whiskey and spilled it. It was enough to make him drop the diary back into the bag. He felt that he did not have the mental deftness required to open it and start reading. Because you did not know what you would find once you started. He knew that Lorna was aware of the power of the hidden, of that which was removed from the common gaze. He wondered if she concealed the diary to protect her own thoughts as they were written or to protect those who would read it as the hidden words began to clothe themselves in lore, drawing authority to themselves, that a teenage girl's diary had gathered in aloofness and mystery by making itself a sought-after thing. He wondered if the diary would provide an explanation for her illness, or was the book, the text the thing that was driving her, its unseen liturgy, each sentence she added to it picking up on the stealthy cadences, the jurisdiction of the unseen.

He noticed that certain parts of information he had collected in relation to Robert had started to disappear. Pieces of original documentation, newspaper cuttings, photographs. He suspected that Lorna was taking them but he didn't ask her about it. He saw the way that everything she did had begun to take on terrible meaning. He began to drink in the hotel every night. He received the results of a liver biopsy which suggested enlargement, fatty deposits, spontaneous cell death. He received letters with appointments for further tests in distant hospitals which he ignored. They joined the pile of unopened post that he left just inside the front door. The brown envelopes, the envelopes with windows. It was important that unopened letters be out in the open. It was important to be rebuked by them.

'Why aren't you opening the hospital letters?' she asked.

'I don't like their tone,' he said.

'They're trying to save your life.'

'That's not what they're after. They don't give two fucks about my life. They don't even know me. If they knew me they'd just let me die.'

She looked at him without smiling. It was the same look that he used to get from her mother.

'What were you in prison for?'

'Conspiracy to murder.'

'Who did you conspire with?'

'Some men. Men from around Portadown. Others. I don't know.'

'What happened to them?'

'Some were dead by that time, others weren't charged.'

'Why not?'

'Operational reasons, was the phrase that was used in court.'

'What did that mean?'

'I think it meant that they were being protected by somebody in the establishment. That they had connections. That they were useful to somebody.'

'Was Robert Nairac involved?'

'Yes, I think so. Yes.'

'I think so too. How did they catch you?'

'They always knew what I was doing, I think.'

'They had evidence?'

'They didn't need that much. I confessed.'

They had held him for a week at Castlereagh. They sent teams of interrogators in to him. They sat at a metal table. There was something half-hearted about it. It was not what he had expected. He had waited for men in shirtsleeves standing over him. The application of a weary expertise, the bonding of accused and accuser. He waited for them to try to break him, the questioning going on past midnight, explosive outbursts followed by the quiet build-up, episodes of terrible durance. He began to suspect that they did not want him to confess.

It was on the last day. Mallon came in on his own. He placed Agnew's file on the desk in front of him and straightened it.

'Who are you?'

'Detective Sergeant Mallon. You're getting out today. Can't hold you any further.'

'Glad to hear it.'

'I'd say Jackson will put a bullet in you, though. Him or Knox. You'd be better off in gaol, son.'

'You reckon?'

'What do you think yourself?'

'You're probably right.'

He gave a full statement to Mallon over five days. A stenographer worked in the background. He had the impression that Mallon was relating everything he said to other events, creating patterns. There was a sense of motifs being identified. He realized that there were areas Mallon did not want him to explore and he began to alter his narrative to avoid them. He noticed that references to Knox were not followed up. When he mentioned Robert, Mallon said to omit him from the statement, that the narrative thrust was being obscured and that the matter of Robert Nairac raised too many unanswered questions. Mallon said that the presence of shadowy figures at the margin of the narrative served only to confuse. In later days it was Agnew's opinion that Mallon had realized that he had been mistaken. That Robert was not at the periphery. That Robert was at the very centre of things.

Sometimes Mallon would stop him, take a sheet of paper from the stenographer and leave the room for an hour or more. Sometimes a man would come to the door and stand there, gazing at Agnew. He would not cross the threshold into the room.

Agnew began to find that the bare outline of the story was no longer enough. He wanted to convey atmospheres, the impressions that lingered. The way that cordite smells clung to your clothing. What murderous camaraderie overtook them as he drove them away from an attack. The fact that it had been raining or foggy, or that the sun had been shining on a particular day, the way that a man who was to be assassinated held his hand over his eyes to shade them as you called to him, and the way you recalled the look, fixed and quizzical.

Agnew wondered what had happened to his statement. It seemed important that it should still exist. When Mallon came to the caravan he asked him about it. Mallon said he didn't know but that it was probably in a basement storage facility, a vast fluorescent-lit archive with metal-frame shelving, poorly indexed. Agnew felt that such documents demanded a more dramatic context, something old and cavernous where fragile ancient scripts were kept, scholarly, pored over. A place of hushed voices with humidity meters and temperature-controlled vaults.

'You're not that fucking important,' Mallon said. 'There's plenty more like you.'

But he could not escape the image of acres of print, carbon-smudged typescript, individual sheets of paper in blue pen, in black pen, signed and witnessed and sweat-stained, the paper becoming yellowed and brittle at the edges, the eyewitness statements, the police statements, the confessions, the court judgements, the coroner's reports, the commissions of inquiry, the medical reports, the forensics, the ballistics, the labs, the autopsies.

'Look at all the paper I got on Nairac,' he said.

'What about it?'

'Can you not see? All that paper and he is just one man. Just one. There's thousands more.'

Agnew paused, lost in awe at the notion of so much paper, the vast and rustling mass of it. The reams and folios. The quartos.

'You gave the statement. You done the confession and then you done the time,' Mallon said. 'Why don't you let it alone?'

Agnew did not want to leave it alone. He felt that there might be correspondence between the confession that he had given and the documentation that he had collected relating to Robert.

19

Robert began college in September 1968. He revived the boxing club and started a falconry newsletter. He attended the
Cadet Corps. He had several letters from Walmsley in his first
term. It was a mild autumn. The college had a staged feel.
Sunlight filtering through mullioned windows. Students
walking in groups in the squares and quadrangles. Robert
undertook manoeuvres on Salisbury Plain with other cadets.
The plain had been used for training for decades. There were
banks where if you just put your hand in you could take out
a handful of spent bullets. There were burnt areas of vegeta-
tion where nothing grew. There were shell holes filled with
rank oily water. There was a feeling of warfare about the
place, the battlefield, the enfilade. The cadets crawled along
the ground, machine guns being fired just above their heads.
There were complex and testing obstacle courses. There were
long and demanding route marches.

In January of his first year Robert was told that he had a
visitor. He went to his rooms and found Walmsley sitting in
the armchair beside the fire. He thought that Walmsley looked
older.

'This room is no place to keep a bird of prey, Nairac,'
Walmsley said, inclining his head towards the kite which
stood on a perch near the window.

'He's happy enough, sir. He likes to watch people come
and go. Gets sort of chummy with the staff.'

'I wonder. The kite is not a bird of prey, you know. It is par-
tial to dead things, rotting flesh.'

'I get meat from the butcher for her,' Robert said. 'Something a bit ripe. Pong drives the bursar wild.'

The kite watched Walmsley unblinkingly from its perch, as

though it regarded him as pertaining to a species of carrion. Walmsley ignored the bird.

'It does not befit a bird of its nature to be housed in a dingy sitting room along with an assortment of fishing rods and armaments. However, be that as it may, that is not the purpose of my visit.'

Robert vaulted the back of the sofa and dropped into a sitting position facing Walmsley. He was prone to acts of boyish exuberance. However, Walmsley noted that Robert's head was now level with that of the bird and that Robert was looking at him with the same level, unblinking stare as the kite. He felt that he had come under scrutiny by members of the same stern caste.

'Colleagues of mine at Five have indicated that I should approach you. Normally the approach is undertaken by someone on the college staff, but they were aware that I knew you.'

'Five?'

'MI5 is known as Five, Nairac.'

'Why are you asking me?'

'One likes to achieve a spread of resources. I believe you have applied for the army.'

'Sandhurst.'

'Internal security is important in all branches of the services.'

'I didn't know that you were involved in this sort of thing. It's a bit rummy, if you ask me. A bit odd.'

'Nothing odd about it.'

'I don't know about this, sir. I don't know if I'm cut out for all this spy business.'

'Cut out for it,' Walmsley said slowly. 'I think you're cut out for it very well, Nairac. I think that Five would be very glad to see you in their ranks.'

'I'm not good at keeping secrets. Talk too bloody much.'

Walmsley knew that Robert had in fact a talent for keeping secrets. Shortly before Robert had left Ampleforth he had been seen going into a house in the town with one of the girls who worked in the kitchen. Walmsley called her into his study. He recognized her as one of the girls from the laundry. Her face and the backs of her hands were covered in dermatitis. She had been reluctant to talk about Robert but Walmsley made her. She said that Robert had borrowed the house from one of the boxers who used the gymnasium. He had taken her into an upstairs bedroom and drawn the curtains. She said that he had told her to undress and that she would have done anything he told her to do because she was frightened, although she could not say why she had been frightened. He had watched her in the half-light. She said he watched at all times and did not touch. When she had taken off her dress she thought about asking him if it was all right to stop but did not. He watched her as if he meant to describe in detail her body at a later time. He told her that his father was a doctor of the eye. When she had undressed completely, she stood without moving. She told Walmsley that the dermatitis did not extend beyond her hands and face. She stood there with her kitchen pinafore on the back of a chair and her cotton utility underwear on the ground at her feet while Robert walked around her. She felt his breath on the back of her neck where the damaged skin ended. Derma meaning of the skin. She thought that she was a thing to be pitied. She had come to the room prepared for shy and clumsy sexual advances. A patient guiding of hands. She felt that her naked body was something he had read about in a science book or an anatomy book and was now seeing for the first time, or as if he did not know that there was more to a woman than anatomy. She felt like telling him that she knew what boys did – she washed the sheets and sometimes the older boys took to a younger boy and she knew what happened then as well. Robert had stood in front of her and for a moment he met her eyes and then she felt his gaze travelling down her front and she looked straight ahead. Femme meaning of a

147

woman. Don't hurt me please, she thought. Mons meaning mound.

'It's all a bit cloak and dagger. I can do accents though. Could pretend to be a German or something. A bloody Kraut. Gott in Himmel, Tommy.'

Walmsley had heard him say before that he could imitate any accent he chose. He would stand in front of the other students at Ampleforth and pretend to be from France, to be from America. Self-absorbed little performances. The accents were not good but he could hold an audience by the way he immersed himself totally in what he was doing. They held their breath. Willing him on.

'Blitzkreig,' Robert said. 'Surrender or ve vill shoot you all.'

'You haven't answered my question yet,' Walmsley said.

'I don't know. I'll have to think about it,' Robert said.

Robert told Walmsley that one of the kestrels he had reared was to be used in a film. He said that the film would be about a boy who lived in poverty but took a kestrel out on to the moors and that the kestrel soaring through the air was a symbol of the boy rising above his drab surroundings. Walmsley did not believe him.

Robert boxed for the college and gained four blues. He played open-side wing forward for the Greyhounds. In 1969 he fought his college friend Julian Malins in a bare-knuckle fight at a summer party on the college barge. Malins said that he 'took some terrible punishment'. Malins's father later sponsored Robert's application to join the Grenadier Guards. In 1971 Robert's car was stolen. When it was found by the police his third-year history notes were apparently missing. He was allowed to continue without taking the exam. It was later confirmed that the history notes did not exist. That in fact Robert had left old notes from Ample-forth in the car.

In the college years Robert is described as popular, charismatic. But the impression persists that he is already beginning to evade scrutiny, that he is beginning to drop out of sight. There are contradictions with later accounts, anomalies. He is described as without guile and incapable of a 'biting or satirical jest'. But his capacity for cruel practical jokes is recorded by witnesses later on. Contemporaries talk about his charm and wit. Later on his capacity for foul language, for gratuitous obscenity is noted. You have a sense of a violent and equivocal undertow.

Nothing is said of the fact that he studied military history and continued to do so at Sandhurst. The amassed knowledge of violent death inflicted. A time of change. A new vocabulary of war starting to drift in, the old language drifting away. Low-intensity ops. Delivery systems. The learning of tactics, of strategy. Techniques of camouflage, of concealment. Arts of subterfuge. This is the era of tactical nuclear weapons. You learn to move softly. You learn to move in the shadow of things. There are nuclear submarines gliding beneath the ice pack. There are new ways to be deadly, new ways of thinking, barely taught yet. Robert went to see Frank Kitson lecture at Oxford. Kitson telling how he used low-intensity warfare in Kenya against the Mau Mau. The recruitment of pseudo-gangs among local militias to carry out your aims. The use of the six techniques in interrogation. The hiss of white noise. The missiles are targeting your capital cities, your command centres thirty metres down under reinforced concrete. It is necessary to mask your footfall. There are mock-ups of entire jet squadrons in Siberia. There are flimsy aircraft bearing sophisticated instruments in the high atmosphere. There would be no such thing as a front in the new warfare, Kitson said. You looked for small groups of men lightly armed and moving silently. You gather detail. You subvert. You infiltrate. War as subtext.

Robert sat at the back, taking notes. There was a sophisti-cation to Kitson's ideas that appealed to him, but he was drawn more to the dark undertow that underpinned Kitson's thinking, the sense of moral void.

Pseudo meaning sham, false, spurious.

20

There were themes of the occult running through the post-war history of the intelligence services. Occult fiction was written by operatives under pseudonyms. The Devil Rides Out. David found the paperbacks at a stall at Nutts Corner. Fiction with psycho-sexual overtones. There were themes of mild fetish. Nude virgins straining against ropes. Overall, David thought that there was a Home Counties feel to the writing. An atmosphere of mild baroque. Black masses taking place against a backdrop of oak panelling, red velvet drapery. You thought of priapic middle-aged men wearing goats' heads and robes. David thought that he could exploit these ideas. He planted stories of satanic ritual in the local press. Gravestones were desecrated with obscene slogans. A dead cat was eviscerated and thrown over the wall of a presbytery. Knox thought that there was evidence of an unease in the population following the operation.

'You have to remember you're dealing with the Roman Catholic mentality,' he said. 'There is a culture of miracles, rosaries, virgin birth.'

He said that it was worth remembering there was a belief in transubstantiation out there and that historically occult events were associated with civil unrest. He suggested crude daubings of pentangles and other satanic symbols in bus depots and other public spaces. He talked about making ouija boards available in shabby second-hand outlets in the city centre. Anything that made mothers hold their offspring closer. You wanted to see teenagers whispering fearfully at bus stops.

David had spent a month in Norway. He was dropped in the mountains by a Lynx helicopter and skied out. He camped at remote fiords. He learned the use of snares and trapped an Arctic hare. He did weapons drill at below-zero temperatures. When he returned to the corridor he gradually got a sense that things were different. Nothing had changed outwardly but there were nuances. The slight hesitation in the face of a supply clerk when he asked to requisition supplies for Gemini. He thought that Knox seemed remote at briefings. He began to wonder if he had been sent to Norway to keep him out of the way while certain changes were being effected. Joyce told him that he was being silly. He saw how she behaved around the camera tech. He thought there was a flirtatiousness there, the slow-eyed way she watched him, a sense of slovenly allurements being proffered. He became alert for signs of illicit sexual activity.

He met Knox in the mess one evening. Knox patted the bar stool beside him.

'I was just reflecting on a colleague of mine. Fine soldier. Got shell shock in Dhofar. Sat in a trench for thirty-six hours with shells landing all round him. Man beside him was killed first hour. Never recovered from it. Had to be invalided out, of course. Pension and all that. Lives in Hastings now.'

'Very sad, sir.'

'I suppose nowadays you'd say the poor chap was suffering from stress.'

'Different kind of war, sir.'

'Do you think so?' Knox said, turning to look at him. 'Do you really think so?'

The next day David wondered if Knox had been talking about him. He asked Joyce if he looked tired. He noticed white flecks in the pupil of his eye. Joyce told him to go to the MO. Knox asked him if he had considered cutting a cockerel's throat, leaving it in a school playground.

'Children are often the most effective medium for conveying information,' Knox said. 'They have such lurid imaginations.'

David started spending less time on the corridor. He would drive to Gemini, using a different route every time. He would park several streets away and walk up the Antrim road. He felt that it offered certainties. The certitudes of guilty desire. The place had a constancy derived from the atmosphere of mild depravity. He remembered the way that Joyce would say the word 'men', then throw her eyes up to heaven. She relied upon them to be unfaithful, subordinate to the moment. Their infidelities and shifting appetites provided a fixed point to her, something you could align yourself to.

David took to sitting in the back room, watching the tech wordlessly as he loaded film spools into the cameras. He had noticed that he rarely got to screen the films on his own at Theipval. He was normally joined by Knox, and sometimes by a man in civilian clothes whom Knox did not introduce. Sometimes Knox would remove the film from the camera and hand it to the man, who would put it in his briefcase. The film was not returned. David got the tech to rig a proper screen and a 16mm camera in the back kitchen with a sound feed. He took P-cards from the corridor and tried to match faces, but he was in fact drawn to the atmosphere of contrived intimacy that existed in the girls' rooms, the unmade beds, unwashed towels.

He matched several P-cards each week. After a few weeks he knew the location of the P-card in the index on recognizing a face. On 16 June he P-carded Harris Boyle, twenty-four. Boyle P-carded as a telephone wireman and major in the UDA. He had been acquitted on charges of possessing a firearm and automobile theft in 1971. Boyle asked for the Polish girl. She sat on the bed and watched as Boyle examined the room, looking under the bed and trying the door to ensure it was locked.

'You want ride?' the Polish girl said.

'Shut up to fuck,' Boyle said.

'I do fuck, oral. No problem.'

David wondered if Boyle had seen the camera lens. At one point he seemed to be looking straight at it. The tech came into the room.

'He's jumpy,' he said. 'Got some guilty secret, if you ask me.'

'Come sit,' the Polish girl said. 'Sit. I tell you things. I talk you dirty.'

Boyle sat down on the bed beside her. She put her hand on his crotch.

'What I feel here?' she said.

She knelt in front of him and started to unfasten his trousers. She stopped. David could see the handgrip of an automatic tucked into Boyle's belt.

'You got gun? What need gun here?'

'It's all right,' Boyle said. 'It's only for protection.'

'You need protection?'

'I need protection in case somebody tries to kill me.'

'You not need gun here. I not going to kill you.'

'There's plenty out there ready to put a bullet in me. You fight for your country, a man has enemies. You see them people in the street out there, any of them knew who I was, I'd be stiffed where I stood.'

Boyle took the gun out of his belt and put it on the shelf above the sink. He sat down on the bed again and the girl resumed opening his belt. She took off her dressing gown. Boyle lay back on the bed.

'No?' the girl said. 'You want me to be something for you? You want I be little girl?'

'Do what you want,' Boyle said.

She went to the mirror and put her hair up quickly in pigtails. She stood in front of him with her head on one side, a dismal coquette. Boyle reached up for her and pulled her on to the bed.

David thought that there was a chemistry between Boyle and the girl. There was an air of sullen erotics.

Afterwards Boyle asked her if she liked music. He said he was going to see a band that night.

'I like music. I like dancing.'

'Well, you'll be doing fuck all dancing coming with us the night. This is a recce for an op.'

154

David sat up.

'Op? What is op?' the girl said.

'An operation, for fuck's sakes. You think I'm carrying thon gun for the good of my health?'

'I like dance,' the girl said.

'This crew won't be doing any dancing by the time we get done with them,' Boyle said.

'I tell you. I phone.'

When Boyle was gone David brought the Polish girl into the back room. She said that she didn't want to go anywhere with Boyle.

'You have to,' David said. 'We need to find out what he's up to.'

'I don't like,' she said.

'If you don't go I can get you sent home to Poland,' Joyce said.

'I come for fuck, not for dance.'

'You have to go,' David said. 'Just find out what he is up to.'

'I don't want.'

'Why?'

'I don't want. He smell like dead.'

That evening David rang Knox. He knew that Knox had a house somewhere outside Bangor. You thought gravel driveways. You thought understated opulence. He told Knox that he had something important to show him. He did not say what it was. He wanted to retain control of the op, which meant keeping the film of Boyle in Gemini.

It was after eleven before Knox arrived. The street outside was empty. David could see a military checkpoint further down the street at Carlisle Circus. You could hear radio traffic drifting up towards Gemini. Oscar Tango Foxtrot. He saw Knox's Rover coming through the checkpoint. He waited until Knox had parked and held the door open for him. Knox was wearing an Aquascutum coat and red flannel scarf.

When they sat down at the table in the back room he took out a hip flask. You felt that the formalities were being observed. The hip flask contained Islay. You felt the deep functioning of class structure.

David played the film for Knox.

'Do you know this chap Boyle?' David asked.

Knox didn't answer. He walked up to the screen as the film was playing, stood close to it, as if there was something more to be learned from the texture of the act being performed onscreen that would prove instructive, the graining of the film stock, the sexual weft of it.

'I take it you got the girl to agree to report on the activities of Boyle?' Knox said.

'She's gone out with him tonight, something to do with some band or other.'

'Did he happen to mention any of his associates?'

'Not so far.'

'Let me know if he does so.'

'I will.'

'And he hasn't let slip anything about the nature of the op?'

'Negative again. Oddly enough, it seems to have something to do with this band.'

'If you ask me, the whole thing has a slightly improbable feel to it.'

Knox looked amused. Months afterwards David realized the significance of this remark. Knox was an advocate of the power of the unlikely. The distribution of the morgue photographs. The spread of rumours about the occult. It was improbable events which set society on edge, sowed disquiet, created the uneasy spaces on the margin.

'This Polish girl, is she discreet?'

'As far as I can tell.'

Joyce said that the girl did not seem to have any friends and spent her free time in her room, playing records. She had no interest in gossip and was inattentive to the needs of the other girls. The film played on and the two men turned to the screen again. As they did, the girl raised her head and looked directly at the camera. You could hear the sound of Boyle's labouring, but it was the girl's face that held you, the full lips half parted and the half-closed eyes and the direct look at the camera, knowing they would watch the film long after she was gone and drawing them into the atmosphere of feigned erotics.

'She is good, this girl,' Knox said. 'She knows her work.'

And as they watched, the girl's eyes returned again and again to the camera, a lingering glance of dark connivance.

David locked Gemini and drove back to Theipval. He went to the mess. They told him that Joyce had left ten minutes before. It occurred to him that every question asked by Knox had been directed at ascertaining how much information Gemini had acquired about the Op Boyle had talked about. He had asked to be kept informed if David found out about whom Boyle was working with but had not asked to be told if he found out about the nature of the Op.

He drank in the mess until 3.30, then he started to walk back towards the married quarters. He knew that he would not find Joyce in bed. He met her on the narrow walkway between the officers' chalets.

'Where were fucking you?'

'I don't have to answer that. You don't own me.'

They both knew the commonplaces of it. You heard it every weekend night outside the married quarters. The brief exchange of accusation. The defiant retort. That he should feel complex and wounded. He swung his fist at her but overbalanced and missed, falling against the wooden wall of the chalet. The clumsiness of the violence was part of the formal structure of the encounter. Joyce's laughter, standing with her arms folded, looking down at him with feigned amusement as he got to his feet, both of them knowing that he would have to hit her properly this time. He caught her on the side of the face and she fell and he stood over her, breathing hard, knowing what the scene looked like at that precise moment, the woman raising herself on one elbow, feeling the side of her face, the man staring down at her and at the thing he had done, the stance of rage and dismay. The first of the two MPs that approached them pushed him backwards. The second went to Joyce.

'You all right, love?'

The man with corporal's stripes glared at David, everyone aware of the choreography of the event.

'Fucking despicable is what I call it,' the second man said. 'You want the MO, love?'

'I think I'm all right, thank you,' Joyce said, her voice polite, modulated.

There were usages to be observed here. It was important that the two MPs were allowed to see her as shocked but calm, as holding up well despite what had happened, as upholding certain proprieties despite everything. She was the only one who could restore the order that they needed. She straightened her skirt, brushed off pieces of gravel.

'Really, officers, it's nothing. I'm dreadfully sorry to have alarmed you.'

The voice was Celia Johnston in Brief Encounter, David realized, the glassy repressed tones, the bitten-off syllables.

'Nothing I hate more,' the corporal said, ramming his baton into David's stomach and pushing him back against the wall of the married quarters.

'Got too much to drink, did we, sir?' the sergeant said.

'Decided we'd come down the married quarters, give the girlfriend a bit of a hiding?' the corporal said.

They all knew that the convention in such circumstances was to refer to David in a collective sense. 'Going to be any trouble, are we, sir?' 'Not thinking about doing it again, are we, sir?' 'Just take off the tie and shoelaces, sir. That's lovely.'

21

Agnew knew that Jackson was putting an op together but he couldn't work out what it was. He knew that the core people were Jackson, Somerville and Boyle. Jackson had brought in other peripheral figures, men with access to UDR uniforms. Agnew asked Hoppy to meet him in the car park of a bird sanctuary on the outskirts of Lurgan. It was raining. A hoarding giving descriptions of wading birds was peppered with shotgun pellets. Agnew arrived first, then Hoppy pulled up in his van with his disco gear in a small trailer towed behind. He explained that he was doing a disco that night in Larne. They sat in Agnew's car, looking out over the reed beds, the manmade lagoon.

'Come on, Hoppy. What the fuck is this op about? Give us a clue or something.'

'Routine, says Jackson.'

'There's a lot of personnel for a routine job.'

'I can't believe they put fucking Specs on an op. Thon blind cunt's as likely to shoot his own fucking foot off as hit a target.'

'Give us a clue, Hoppy.'

'What are you so fucking curious for all of a sudden?'

'I want to go along. Get the hands dirty. You know the way Jackson's always getting on my wick about it.'

'Says you're scared clean out of the mind.'

'Go on, tell us.'

'Says you're a big fucking woman, jumping at your own shadow.'

'Come on, Hoppy.'

Hoppy smiled. He pointed out of the window of the car towards the trailer behind the van.

'My discotheque,' he said.

Hoppy always referred to it as a discotheque. He thought it sounded sophisticated. He handed out flyers in the street with the word 'discotheque' printed in bold. He smoked Peter Stuyvesant cigarettes and spoke to women in a jaded, suggestive whine intended to suggest time spent in the company of world-weary continental elites.

'Jesus, what about the disco, Hoppy?' Agnew said. 'Come on, the fuck. What's the disco got to do with anything?'

'Everything,' Hoppy said. 'You know what the major threat to the discotheque is, Agnew? Live music. That's a fact. Live music.'

Hoppy started to laugh. Agnew wound down his window and threw his cigarette out. He could hear the sounds of birds concealed in the reeds, the waders. There were cigarette packets floating in the water, beer cans. Hoppy got out of the car. Agnew watched him drive off, then sat in the car park until the light began to fade, finding that the migratory wildfowl, their muddy alien cries and glum wetland habitats, fell within the limited range of empathies left open to him.

Knox told him to establish contact with the other members of the unit being assembled by Jackson. A group of them drank in the pool room of the Blues Bar. James Somerville, Wesley's younger brother, Specs, and Thomas Crozier. Specs was a tall youth who wore glasses so thick that his eyes were barely visible. You tried to make eye contact with him but all you could see was a blurred mass, shifting colour spectrums. The glasses seemed to give him an authority among the younger men. They deferred to him. Their attitude suggested that here was something outside the normal range. Specs, Somerville and McDowell were older than everyone else in the bar and Agnew realized there was a gang ethos here. You expected gestures of defiance towards authority figures, a transfer of sibling loyalty, acts of violent surrogacy. Agnew went to the bar. There was a pool game in the middle of the bar, a game of darts at the far end. Specs stood with his back against the bar with McDowell and Crozier.

'You looking something mister?' Crozier said.

'Got to talk to you boys. Jackson wants to know if you're ready for the job.'

Agnew found himself wishing that he had taken the route of sly dissimulation rather than the outright lie.

'Course we're ready,' McDowell said.

'Thing is, boys, Jackson doesn't mind, but the British captain doesn't know if you're up to it. Haven't got the military training.'

'We're military all right. A regiment of the army,' Crozier said. 'I done two months' basic at Catterick.'

'You never said who you were,' Specs said. 'He never said who he was.'

'Agnew.'

'You're the peeler,' Specs said.

'Take her handy, boys,' Agnew said. 'We're all in this together.'

Agnew could feel the youths coming up behind them. He didn't need to turn to know he was in trouble. You thought parallels and check shirts. You thought Crombie coats and bicycle chains. This town lent itself to the worst of post-industrial imaginings. Skinheads. Suedeheads. Tartan gangs. Formal narrative acts carried out in the context of post-industrial underclass.

'What do you reckon, Specs?'

'Looks like trouble to me. Looks like a bad egg,' Specs said.

'He looks like fuck all to you, Specs, because that's all you can see.'

Agnew turned and saw that Jackson had come through the connecting door from the bar. He wasn't sure if he was relieved or not. Jackson crooked his finger at Agnew.

'A source tells me that there is agent penetration of this unit. You know anything about that, Agnew?'

They were sitting at the main bar. Jackson was drinking Smirnoff and White. Agnew was drinking brandy and port. It was his fifth. He found himself raising the glass in valedictory gestures. Agent penetration. He wondered if Jackson was referring to him. He didn't think of himself as an agent. He wanted to explain that his life was errant, subject to lethal drift, dictated by bluster and spurious attempts at self-justification. He had been under the impression that Jackson understood some elements of this. Agnew lifted his hands to demonstrate bewilderment, injured innocence.

'I come with you on them jobs, didn't I? Nothing went wrong, nobody got lifted.'

'Agents isn't for getting people lifted. Agents is for finding out things. You were asking some questions in the bar there.'

'Curious is all.'

'You were at Hoppy with them same questions as well.'

'Mr Personality. Discotheque.'

'Discotheque. Sometimes I wonder how come you're still alive, Agnew,' Jackson said. Agnew smiled at him and raised his glass. He thought he detected a mood of cadaverous bonhomie in Jackson and he was keen to encourage it.

'All I know is there's a big job going on.'

'You want to come along, is that it?'

'Yes.'

'Fair enough, you come along, but you don't find out what's going on until the day and hour it happens and you stop asking fucking questions. Am I clear about that, Agnew?'

The door into the back bar was open. Agnew looked up and saw Specs still standing at the bar. He was looking directly at Agnew. His glasses shone in the half-light. Agnew had the impression that he was being looked at through a finely tuned instrument, an advanced technology that could break down its subject into particles, see its way into the deep structures.

Robert was operating on the border most of the time. He claimed to belong to a unit called 4 Field Survey Troop. He had moved to the base at Castledillon. The castle was Gothic revival with mock turrets and battlements in limestone. There were weeds on the driveway. In certain places you could see the sky through the roof. There were rots and fungi growing up through the floors. At night foxes barked in the shrubbery. Robert moved his gear into the master bedroom. Tony Ball took the mistress's bedroom. Foxhunting scenes in oil hung in the hallway. There were representations of Graeco-Roman wrestling in the billiard room. There were themes of corrosion. There were themes of big-house decay. Robert found a Vincent Black Shadow in an outhouse at the back of the house and worked on it at night. He saw himself riding the motorcycle through deserted villages at night, crouched over the handlebars, angular and gauntleted.

The base was lightly guarded when Robert and Tony Ball moved in. Command structures were run from Lisburn, which meant that they were in control of their own movements. The emphasis was on initiative. In the following year things would change, but in the first days they regarded themselves as free-spirited. They drove around in open-top Land Rovers with the windshield folded down to enhance field of fire. This was the way Robert saw the conflict developing. Small lightly armed tactical units operating at will. He did not envisage the 160-foot-high communication structures, the vehicle armouring, the body-heat detectors. He did not think of the war as being fought from behind one-inch non-penetrative Armorall. Robert and Tony Ball thought handpicked. They thought seasoned veteran. They drove Q-cars into small towns on the outskirts of conurbations, looking for the new housing estates, tight-packed and rancorous, hoping to expand on what had been achieved with Jackson. They wanted to make contact with men who had army backgrounds. They were looking for men who felt that society had let them down. The men they were looking for were members of a range of organizations. Gun clubs, the British Legion. They wore military-style moustaches and were given to resentful outbursts. They had small-arms expertise and were collectors of regimental memorabilia from narrowly defined periods of conflict.

In the evening Robert stalked small birds in the shrubbery with an air rifle. He found that there was less and less time for hunting pursuits. Robert and Tony Ball drove the Land Rover into the Kilwilkee Estate outside Lurgan three days in succession, hoping to draw fire from PIRA elements. They would pull up beside groups of youths and attempt to engage them in conversation. Robert regarded himself as having an affinity with young men from working-class backgrounds. He explained to Ball that he was familiar with disaffected youth through the boxing gym he had attended. Robert tried out accents on them. The youths wore pained expressions. Robert listened to the way they talked. The complex and volatile sentence construction. Arcane word patterns with overtones of communal violence that seemed to Ball to be the rudiments of language, someone trying to put sounds to the unearthed fragments. Robert memorized whole phrases and tried them out when he got back to Castledillon, working on the gutturals, the glottal stops. Fuck you looking at. Dug out of you. Robert's voice would find its way through the building, its vents and gapped skirting and collapsed ducting, becoming a nasal chant, a monkish and high-sounding thing, by the time it found its way to the drawing room, the entrance hall with its oak panelling and Masonic insignia.

They spent the winter there. It snowed for two weeks in February. Robert and Tony Ball lit huge fires in the ornate fireplace in the drawing room. Robert said that they should be partisans. Like Tito's men with sheepskins around their shoulders, ammunition belts. They dragged logs from the woods and dumped them on the Persian rugs. They lounged about on antique French furniture and drank vintage wine from the cellar. They developed habits belonging to rude peasants. Tony Ball stood at the French doors and urinated into the garden. They went unshaven for days. They made lewd comments concerning the portraits of women in the drawing room. They spoke to each other in gruff, heavily accented English.

At night Robert lay awake and thought about the forest crowding around. He remembered the woods in Germany and the story that Fulbright had told about bear-baiting.

He pinned an OS map of the border area to the wall in the drawing room. He stood in front of it for hours. He drew lines on it, put small Xs beside isolated border farmhouses. At first Ball thought that he was targeting known PIRA individuals, but as the snow persisted the markings became less clear. Question marks were added, lines looped around geographical features for no discernible reason. Cryptic acronyms were added in a minute hand. Robert returned to it again and again. Lines were added in different-coloured pen. Many of the lines petered out.

'I can't get bearings on this bloody border,' Robert said.

'It's just a line on a map,' Ball said. 'Talking about maps, that one is fairly shit.'

He watched as Robert moved his finger down the legend. Legend meaning explanatory words. River. Contour line. Antiquity. His lips moved as he read. He had a puzzled expression on his face, as if there were another, more detailed and clandestine legend elsewhere. One that gave reference points to the shifting nature of the place. The zones of infiltration. The cartographies of subterfuge.

At night men came to Castledillon to see Robert. Cars coming up the drive, tyres crunching in the snow. Late-model Cortinas, Capris, Escorts in rally livery. They had the look of paramilitary figures, informants, minor politicians with an opportunistic demeanour. They paused at the top of the limestone steps and cast shrewd looks around. Some of them had that rogue-cop look: hard, liverish, vain. They sat on the edge of the sofa in the drawing room, holding glasses that seemed too small for their hands. Robert lounged across several gilt-framed chairs, wearing combat fatigues. There was a sense of uneasy alliances in the room. The men talked about PIRA activity in the border area. 'It's war,' they said. They kept using the word war. There was a sense of assassination in the air, dumped bodies, proxy killings. They stopped to look at Robert's border map on the way out. It seemed to have a calming effect. They seemed to think that Robert was sensitive to deeper structures, strategic and spiritual dimensions that were not immediately apparent.

When the snow thawed Robert resumed missions on the border. He liked to slip away before first light. It was the pre-dawn thing again. He read that it was the time when people were least alert. When they were sunk in REM sleep, lost in the neural structures, the cell pathology, the deep cortex so that Robert wondered if they could feel him, tugging at the edge of their consciousness as he skirted their farmyards on foot, their back gardens. An uneasy stirring at the level of the cerebrum, a level of apprehension. Sometimes he would dig into a hide close to a house and spend the day focusing his attention on one member of the family, a farmer or an older woman, feeling their discomfort as the day went on, the way they gradually retreated into the house and stood at a window looking out, brow furrowed. He felt that he was doing them a favour. That he was making them aware of their own mortality, that he was letting them know that the bad thing was closer than they thought.

22

Knox met David on the corridor the following morning.

'Woman trouble?' he said.

He put his arm around David's shoulder and led him into his office. The Polish girl was sitting in front of Knox's desk. She was staring at a group of bird skulls on the windowsill. David felt that things were even more out of control than he had expected. He had wanted to be the first to speak to her after she had been out with Boyle.

'Picked them up off the beach in Sullom Voe,' Knox said, lifting one of the skulls and handing it to David.

David turned it over. Almost weightless, chalky, with slant apertures for the nostrils and ears, the eye sockets delineated with etched lines, a precision-tooled feel to it, the sockets, the scribed platelets of bone, the whole thing seeming constructed towards ends that exceeded mere flight.

'Tell Mr Erskine where you went with Boyle,' Knox said.

'We go to watch band. He drink much.'

'Did he tell you anything about what they were planning?'

'He say they kill some people. He not say who.'

'What was the band called?' David said.

'Miami something. I don't know.'

'They're definitely up to something big,' David said.

'I wouldn't be surprised,' Knox said. 'Not a bad thing from an operational point of view, I suppose.'

'What do you mean?'

'I would think there needs to be a major Op. Isolated events no longer suffice at certain points. It's the way the thing works. You need an atrocity to move things along. It's important that a brisk momentum is maintained. People shouldn't be allowed to dwell on things.'

'I don't believe what I'm hearing.'

'Of course we wouldn't allow such a thing to happen,' Knox said, 'if we can find out what they're up to.'

'I'll pull out all the stops,' David said.

'I think that would be a very good idea, David. There are some people on the base who are questioning your ability to work under stress. The incident last night didn't help your case.'

'There won't be any more incidents.'

'That's good to hear. Perhaps you would be kind enough to take this young lady back to Gemini and conduct a thorough debrief. You may pick up something.'

The Polish girl sat in silence until they reached the outskirts of the city, the zone of tyre depots and railway wastelands and failing business enterprises. Then she spoke without looking at him.

'They kill band.'

'Sorry?'

'What they do. They kill Miami band.'

'What are you saying? They're going to shoot the band? All of them?'

'Not shoot. Bomb.'

'Bomb? That lot can't make bombs.'

'Maybe somebody make it for them. I not ask.'

'Why didn't you tell Knox this?'

'I think that man knows already. He knows much things.'

'Why do they need all the uniform soldiers?'

'Not ask.'

'Do you know when they're going to do it?'

'Not ask.'

He knew that she would not tell him any more. He unlocked the door of the Gemini for her and stood back to let her in. He knew that no one was due at the club until late afternoon. He followed her down the corridor to her room. She sat on the bed. He found himself telling her to take her clothes off. He spoke roughly to her. He used uncouth expressions that he had heard on the streets.

There was an understanding between them that the sex would involve degrading acts, that he would wish to humiliate her. There would be elements of coercion. It would be understood that she would remain passive. They both knew it was necessary for him that an atmosphere of duress existed in the room.

Knox rang Agnew at home and said that Nairac was expecting him at Castledillon.

'What am I supposed to be doing there?'

'You're a disgruntled cop. You think the authorities expect you to operate with one hand tied behind your back. You think there is excessive emphasis on civil liberties. You want to take the gloves off.'

'What about Jackson?'

'I'll look after Jackson. There's no reason he should know.'

'Jackson thinks I'm an agent.'

'That's not a bad thing. It gives you some protection. If you were just an ordinary honest to goodness suspended police officer you'd be no use to him.'

'What am I supposed to ask Nairac?'

'Try to work your way into his confidence. Try to establish how deeply he is in. Goad him a little. Make him brag about what he is up to. He has a habit of taking photographs apparently. Kind of a trophy thing. See what he knows about the big Op.'

When he put down the phone Agnew knew that he should have refused. He knew that there was nothing straightforward about Knox's request. But part of him wanted to get close to Robert. He knew that the whole thing was slipping away, but there were areas of his life that he thought might be improved by meeting Robert. He thought that some of the shadowy areas might be dealt with, the problems he had with motivation, with belief in what he was doing.

The meeting had been arranged for the following evening. Agnew drove to Castledillon from Portadown. The sand-bagged hut at the entrance had a deserted look to it. The drive-way was partly blocked by rhododendrons that had grown across it, the flowers overblown and pink and looking artificial, a sickly futurist hue to them. Agnew parked at the front of the castle. He walked around the side. There were two Saracens parked at the rear, their engine bays open. There were piles of torn khaki webbing, a broken gun carriage, several dented helmets. Rain from a broken gutter spilled on to burst sand-bags. There was a sense of armies in retreat, roads covered in discarded militaria. He realized now why the soldiers who lived on police bases spent so much time repairing gear, paint-ing vehicles. It was important to keep this kind of melancholia at bay, the historic sense of lost causes. He stopped at the French doors leading on to the lawn. He saw Robert standing in the room. He was looking at a map he had pinned to the wall. Agnew recognized the Guardsman's stance. He coughed softly to let Robert know that he was there. Robert turned around.

'Blair Agnew,' he said. 'I P-carded you. Got your photo-graph. You look younger in it.'

'I been under a bit of stress.'

'Did you ever box? You have a boxer's shoulders.'

Robert dropped his shoulder. He feinted and aimed a jab at Agnew's stomach.

'I never had the chance,' Agnew said.

'I boxed Martin Meehan once. The PIRA activist. Had a fucking good hook too. The bastard. I learned the Belfast accent listening to him.'

'Should have shot the fucker,' Agnew said.

'I understand your impatience. But we have to go at the thing properly. Remove people from the picture in a con-trolled way.'

'If more people was took out we wouldn't have half the problems. Only language they understand.'

Agnew was starting to enjoy the persona of disgruntled middle-ranking policeman. He tried to project the fact that his bitterness was more than just political. That it was related to lack of promotional prospects, domestic problems. He wanted his speech to be subtly inflected.

'Rest assured, Sergeant Agnew, we're doing what we can. We don't have to operate within conventional frameworks. We're playing a long game here and local men like yourself are vital.'

'I want to do something. The province is on its knees. They're coming out of housing estates with rifles. The judges are letting them off with warnings.'

'Let me show you something, Sergeant. Just come with fucking me.'

Robert walked off down the corridor. Agnew followed. Robert brought him to his room. Agnew noted the carefully made bed. The polished boots. Hairbrush and razor in line on the wash hand basin. The Grenadier Guardsman, Agnew thought. He followed Robert through into the dressing room.

'This is the armaments room,' Robert said.

Agnew recognized mercury tilt switches, power timing units. There were two Armalites, a general-purpose machine gun and an M16 with tripod. There were sidearms and automatic weapons that he did not recognize. Cases of ammunition with black poker marks where military decals had been erased were stacked neatly at the back of the room.

'You can see that we're prepared to take the war to PIRA,' Robert said.

He showed him a box of gun parts – barrels, extractors, firing pins.

'They're cast,' Robert said. 'It means cast aside. Supposed to be worn out and destroyed. Means you can fit them and use them and no one can trace them. The parts are destroyed and the records are destroyed. The gun doesn't exist.'

Agnew remembered that he had seen gun parts at the farmhouse.

171

'Just because you got them doesn't mean you're using them,' he said.

He wanted a sour tone. He wanted Robert to feel how much he resented his gleaming armaments, his intimations of complex political analysis. He wanted Robert to feel his desire to go out and direct extreme violence at unsuspecting targets.

Robert showed him a case of Powergel.

'Unnumbered consignment taken from a quarry. Can't be traced.'

He showed Agnew a Star pistol. Agnew remembered seeing the pistol before.

'Taken from a PIRA dump. There's no path back to the security forces.'

He showed him Eastern European automatics with the serial numbers etched off with acid. He showed him generic hand grenades manufactured in South Africa without identifying marks. The emphasis was on the unattributable, the deniable. Robert seemed to be saying that it was necessary to move quickly on from the act of violence itself, the riddled car, the dumped body, the processes and bodily by-products, the corpse murk of political murder. You had to get to the meaning of the thing. There was a shadowy grandeur implicit in each operation. There were contexts to be respected. Agnew encouraged Robert. They moved to the drawing room. The outlines of a new operation began to emerge. Robert said that the targets would be miles away when the final part of the operation took place. That was part of the beauty of it. The other part was that the targets would have crossed the border from one side to the other. It was important that the border itself be brought into play. There were powerful ambiguities associated with the idea of frontier that could be drawn on. The targets themselves were unimpeachable. Their very innocence made them vulnerable and Robert seemed to imply that it was only a matter of time before they were drawn into events against their will.

'It's five o'clock, fuck me,' Robert said. 'Reckon the sun is well over the yardarm. Feel like a drink?'

Agnew noticed that Robert swore continuously but that there was something awkward in the way he swore, stilted, as if he had learned the words late in life. That he would sometimes insert the swearwords into the wrong part of the sentence. You had the feeling that he was working too hard at the sentence. The constructions seemed laboured over and unwieldy.

Robert opened a bottle of gin and poured two glasses, over-filling them and leaving little room for tonic. Agnew regarded himself as an expert on the subject of drinkers. He drank in a self-aware way, controlled and durable. There was a grim determination to the way he drank. There was a lifetime project involved. There were skills to be honed, wisdoms in the field of self-delusion to be acquired. There had to be a husbanding of resources. He saw himself as a lean and focused careerist in the matter of drink.

Robert was a different matter. He seemed genuinely indifferent to the amount that he poured as long as the drinks were substantial. He drank fast. Agnew could see that there could be a tendency towards undergraduate drinking games. He became louder. He insisted on showing Agnew defensive boxing stances. He insisted on trying out accents on Agnew. He told Agnew that once he had the accent of a town he then studied the OS map of the town. If he was questioned by a native he would then be able to display his knowledge. You go along Buttercrane Quay all the way until you turn right into island. You come down Cathedral Hill until you're in the Shambles.

It was dark. The drinking was heavy. Agnew thought that Robert had drunk almost two bottles of gin. He was sweating profusely, but otherwise the drink did not seem to have affected him. He had produced an old cavalry sword and was demonstrating fencing techniques. This was the hour when introspection normally took hold of you, Agnew thought.

173

This was the hour for episodes of painful and halting reminiscence. This was the hour when you began to blank things out. When you began to accumulate the self-reproach you would need for the following day. Robert didn't do any of these things.

'I want to show you something,' Robert said.

He went out of the room and came back a minute later. He handed Agnew a Polaroid photograph.

'You wanted to see what we were doing to the bastards. Here's your proof, fuck it. We're out there working on this kind of thing every day.'

There was an unmistakable aura of political assassination about the photograph: shot men in shirtsleeves lying in gutters, a prominent public figure minutes before in the middle of a crowd, a man with a hint of scandal about him but doing now what he does best, grinning and waving, loving the crowd and being loved back. A moment that will be stilled for future consumption. A man on his own, smiling and tainted. The moment already drifting into melancholy as a highlight picks out a man at the edge of the frame, an object in his hand and then the shots, the disbelief. You are intended to notice the vulnerable elements. The poignancy is in the details. The fact that the dead man's shoe has come off. The fact that several buttons on his shirt are undone.

'Who is he?' Agnew said.

'Name of John Francis Green, PIRA operative. Lived the other side of the border. We crossed one bastard of a wet night and took him out of the picture.'

Agnew remembered the night. The fog. The dripping plantations. He remembered the men he had seen standing under the trees.

'See what you can achieve when you work with local men? Pseudo-gangs, Kitson calls them. Fight your enemy on their own terms and send the bastards all to buggery.'

Agnew could feel Robert watching him, willing him to look at the photograph again, to subject it to intense scrutiny.

174

The man was lying on a tiled floor. The base of an electric cooker was visible beside his out-flung right hand. There was a scuffed metal chair leg close to his hand. His hair was matted with blood on the side which was in contact with the floor. There were no wounds visible on the back of his white shirt. He would have been shot first in the chest and the blood and brain matter would have come from the bullet wound behind his right ear. Agnew thought that he could feel the atmosphere of the room where the shooting had taken place. The slowly dissipating sense of affray. Later in his life he would say that something in him anticipated the shadowy trajectory that the photograph would take, its provenance becoming uncertain, its very existence being questioned, its meaning transmuting. It gathered authority to itself. Its jurisdiction was unwavering.

Agnew felt somehow that events had reached a narrative point. The place where things hinge and turn.

He looked up. Robert was standing in the shadows at the corner of the fireplace, smiling at him as if the photograph was the reason he had been brought here. In the flickering light you could relate Robert's faces to the portraits that hung on the walls around the fireplace, the faces looking across the centuries, thin-lipped with dark knowing eyes, a feeling of tainted bloodlines about them.

23

Agnew had not seen Mallon for several weeks. There had been a succession of storms, easterlies blowing down along the coast. The tidal race seethed and he walked the beach in the mornings to see what had been washed up. Torn fishing gear, plastic bottles, rafts of weed going black in the wind, swathes of it giving the beach the look of catastrophe. It was the kind of day that Mallon chose to show up on. The kind of day you picked over things, examined the debris. As he approached the caravan he saw Mallon's car. He walked past the caravan and went down to the dock. As he did so he thought he saw Lorna walking in the sand dunes, dressed in black with a bag over her shoulder, as if she were carrying off some sad plunder. Mallon was sitting on a balk of timber.

'About you.'

'What's the score?'

'No score. Just sitting around on this here timber.'

'You'll get piles.'

'I got piles.'

'What are you here for?'

'Been thinking.'

'About what?'

'About the Miami job.'

'And?'

'There's something that I don't get about it. It's the fucking logic of it. There's something wrong about it.'

'How's that?'

'The big idea was they would put the bomb in the van without the band knowing. The band would drive on their merry way. When they crossed the border the bomb would explode.'

'The band would be portrayed as being sympathizers carrying a bomb.'

'Can you trust nobody?'

'It would have the cross-border dimension.'

'War doesn't respect borders. It internationalizes the incident.'

'It doesn't add up. The whole thing is too complicated. The aims are vague and ill-defined. The thinking isn't right. They had to draw in a dozen men. Jackson and them boys didn't do complicated. They like to get in, hit a target, maximum eye-contact, maximum hate.'

'So what sort of thinking was going on?'

'You got a man, he's already out there too long. He's working between agencies. Nobody really knows who's running him or what is going on.'

'Nairac?'

'It's all there. The use of pseudo-gangs. The over-elaborate planning. The ruthless disregard for human life. There's a tiredness to the plan. It's what, it's morally jaded.'

'Did you ever hear of a man by the name of Reeks?'

'Rings a bell.'

'He was PIRA. He went about telling people that Nairac was supplying explosives to PIRA. They thought he was a sympathizer.'

'What the fuck was he doing that for?'

'To gain their trust. To work his way into their confidence.'

'You see what I mean about the thinking?'

'He says that Robert McConnell found out what Nairac was doing.'

'Lance-Corporal McConnell got a PIRA nut job shortly afterwards.'

'The implication being that Nairac set him up. You're looking at the same precise mentality, so you are.'

Agnew leaned his elbows and spat in the sand. For a few weeks now he hadn't been able to stop spitting. At the same time he had a long hacking cough. He felt that the cough brought dignity to the spitting. It was gravelled, authoritative.

'You want to get that looked at,' Mallon said.

'Away and fuck yourself, Mallon.'

'You know what your problem is, Agnew? You don't know anything really. You never really learned anything that was worth knowing. Else you'd be dead. Be grateful.'

'I always wanted to know enough to be resettled. That was a kind of ambition for a while.'

Mallon laughed. But Agnew saw himself giving evidence in open court on former accomplices, pale, dressed in a suit, avoiding their eyes. He saw himself in protective custody, spending time in furnished rooms with handlers in shirt-sleeves. But it was the resettlement part that appealed to him. The new name. The new life in a windswept north of England town. He saw it as being close to the sea, with a shingle beach, a depressed industrial base, a promenade lined with dingy amusements. A place where everyone knew that the best times were gone. A place where he could meet some warm-hearted and mildly regretful divorcee with a nest egg and a rueful fondness for damaged men.

Lorna liked to lie in the sand dunes to write her diary. The way the sand dunes went up and down no one could see you but you could look out through the spiky grass and see them. Sometimes she came across lovers particularly married ones you thought adultery in the daytime she thought perhaps they could not afford the shady hotel room. Sometimes she almost stood on them in their what was the word their throes. She wondered did they ever suspect a secret watcher. Sometimes she didn't even see them she heard them a woman's voice using small worn-out words. She came across the places where the boys sat at night around a campfire to drink beer smoke lonesome cigs hash etc. The boys came and went like in a migration in the week they lived in the city and at the weekend they came here. She could see Agnew and Mallon sitting on their lonely plank and talking things that happened years ago and kept on happening. She thought that Agnew looked like a man carrying secret contraband of years something he'd smuggled into today from all those years ago. Her mother said don't you dare talk to me like that I'm suffering from depression and disorders of the personality. She would cry at night then and sit on Lorna's bed and talk about her golden youth. Your father could join his hands around my waist I could sit on my hair my teeth were so white my bust etc. Problem. These were not things that had happened to her mother but things that had happened to her grandmother who had the waist and the hair and the golden youth. Her mother's past was Agnew maybe that was what she was trying to hide from in some other person's memories they're all trying to hide from something. Between the pages of her diary Lorna kept the photograph of Robert she had taken from Agnew's things it was the one where he is sitting with other soldiers his uniform so neat his peak hat down over his eyes in that way that you could hardly see them so he is a hider too and near to her heart in that way though he is all the things that she isn't girl fat afraid. She took some of the old paper that had gone yellow and crackled but not much because she knew that these were the things that Agnew liked the most. But she liked to hold them the ones that said statement of Thomas William Crozier or statement of James Kyle McDowell with the signature at the end and she tried to think of being there when the pen was put to the paper and there it was twenty-five years later still saying yes I did such butchery what more is there to say.

Agnew read late into the night. It seemed that he needed less sleep. Intelligence Digest reported that Colonel Clive Fairweather, former head of the SAS, known as GSO2, had been reprimanded in writing by the Special Forces Disclosure Committee for giving a taped interview to journalist John Parker. The SFDC reprimand seemed to refer to the fact that the GSO2 had been interviewed with specific reference to Robert's links with loyalist paramilitary groupings. The digest had been published in October 1999 and had been posted to Agnew anonymously. Agnew suspected that Mallon had sent it to him. He was already familiar with the story about Fairweather, but Mallon would have known that he would be impressed with the acronyms employed, the existence of faceless committees with narrowly defined functions. The digest said that SFDC met in the Duke of York Barracks in Chelsea. It said that Fairweather was Chief Inspector of HM Prisons in Scotland. Agnew was deeply grateful for these details. He knew that the existence of such detail implied other truths, opened out into other less concrete contexts.

He had taken to watching his daughter while she slept. Lorna gave no indication that she knew he was there. He could see the shape of the diary under the bedclothes. Her mother sent clean white bedsheets with her on her weekend nights in the caravan. Starched linen sheets with a clean, medicinal smell. Agnew thought that they brought an air of the sanatorium to the caravan. He had started to promise her presents, to take her hand when he talked to her, address her by pet names which had never existed when she was a baby, although he pretended that they did. He seemed eager to commit himself to gestures of inappropriate tenderness in the context of years of parental neglect. She seemed to understand this. The meagreness of her flesh seemed to give her an authority among the wretched that ran beyond her years. She seemed informed in the matter of amnesties, of pardon granted. She seemed to understand that his only real expertise lay in the field of weak promises and shallow commitments and she was willing to accept as much as possible of the heartfelt.

On Sunday afternoon Agnew was dozing on the banquette when he heard a car pull up. He looked out and saw Angela getting out of her car. He saw the way she looked around before she walked towards the caravan. He realized that the area around the caravan was open to interpretations of squalor. He opened the door and waited for her. She was wearing a hat and suit. She had been to church that morning. There were times when she liked to see herself as respectful, amenable to concepts of fidelity. She would come home from church and recite the names of hypocrites in the congregation and the precise nature of their hypocrisy. The secret drinkers. The adulterers. They would spend Sunday afternoons in bed. Her lovemaking was precise and dutiful. There were themes of obedience. There were overtones of endurance. She was tolerant of certain salacious practices he had acquired.

She opened the door of the caravan and walked in. She didn't look around or comment on the contents of the room. He realized that she must have decided this on her way there. That she would not comment on any aspect of his life. That there were too many hazardous aspects of life represented in the piles of paper. She had always held the conviction that the present was rife enough with lurid peril without importing more from the past and she had trouble understanding his obsessions. She took the view that he was fortunate to have survived intact from the evils he had surrounded himself with without submitting to the steely dreads of self-examination. She stood in the doorway in her Sunday clothes and gave him a look of stern affront, as if he had already turned down a bounty of righteousness that had been offered. One of Lorna's T-shirts lay over the back of a chair. She picked it up unconsciously and began to fold it.

'Where is she?'

'Probably out for a walk. She goes walking in the dunes.'

'You don't care, do you?'

The words had a bitter outline, but there was an absence in the way she spoke them that robbed them of malice. She ran her fingers over the seam of the T-shirt and turned it over again as if she could enfold apprehension within it. There were small fluting tones of valediction and regret in her voice which he didn't understand, but he realized that they were lucky to have Lorna to talk about since she enabled them to range over themes of blame and responsibility in an extravagant and ultimately pointless way without invoking their own failures.

'I think she likes it here,' Agnew said.

'I don't know what she likes. I know what she doesn't like. And that includes me.'

Certain phrases involving the concept of teenagers and phases that they might be going through came into Agnew's mind but he didn't say anything. If his daughter was going through a phase, then it was one where the outcomes were necessarily haunted.

That night he read that the favoured weaponry available to Special Forces in 1974 was US MACII silenced sub-machine guns. Remington folded butt lightweight pump-action shotguns. Sterling MK5 silenced machine guns. He noted the emphasis on lightweight. He noted the emphasis on silence.

24

The functions of the corridor were expanding to accommo-
date new levels of activity. As well as monitoring subver-
sive activity, Knox knew that it was even more important
that other agencies be kept under surveillance. Jackson's
Portadown unit possessed unique qualities. Jackson had
been dealing with 14th Int and Box. He believed that the
unit had been infiltrated by Special Branch and Five. It
incorporated disgruntled policemen and soldiers. There
were undertones of murderous bigotry. In some cases there
were suggestions of borderline schizophrenia, inherited
mental instability. It was vital that Jackson's unit be
allowed to operate freely. There were classic scenarios of
perfidy that Knox thought must be allowed to develop.
Knox was confident. He knew that Jackson would be
impossible to stop. Everyone was in too deep. They were all
professional operatives. Knox could sense their excitement.
They knew that they were involved in something special,
unforeseen levels of intrigue.

He thought that David was holding back information. He
thought that the Polish asset was passing intelligence to
him. In one way he didn't mind. David had a tendency
towards rigidity in the ethics department. It was good for
him to find himself in the position of lying to his superiors.
It was important that a man like David should find himself
racked by self-doubt, tormented by images of betrayal. You
could see the strain on his face. You wanted him to get past
the moral dimension of things. You wanted him to see the
purity of the conspiracy, to identify it in its abstract and
high-minded qualities. But there was a danger he might do
something to disrupt the Op. Knox knew that that could not

be allowed to happen. There was too much riding on it. They all had an interest in a successful outcome.

Knox didn't know the exact nature of the Op but that wasn't important. What he had learned convinced him that it would possess all the necessary attributes. Everyone would have principals and agents involved. There would be no statement of involvement by any paramilitary grouping. There would be a suggestion of rogue elements. Certain indicators would point to the involvement of men with links to extreme evangelical organizations. The targets would be seemingly beyond reproach but their blamelessness would be undermined in the eyes of the public. Knox appreciated the way that the parties to the conflict were capable of creating continuous images of innocence defiled, that they did not shy away from generating scenes of terrible intimacy – the father gunned down in front of his children, the pram overturned on the blood-soaked pavement.

Knox had hoped that Agnew could have provided him with more information with regard to Robert's intentions but Agnew's memory of the night wasn't good. He seemed most impressed by the drinking, the quantities consumed, the intensity of it. He said that he woke up in his bed the following morning with no memory of how he had got home. His car was neatly parked in front of the house, which led him to believe that Robert or Tony Ball had driven him home. Knox wondered if Agnew had let anything slip about his involvement with Box. It didn't matter if he had. It merely added another layer.

It was springtime. Knox had seedlings in pots on the windowsill of his office. He liked to encourage the view of himself as a keen amateur gardener. A potterer about in gardens in a shapeless hat. A man given to certain homespun wisdoms. However, in private moments he admitted to himself that his position had lineage. There was a constitutional tradition of conspirators. Men who found themselves at the centre of swirling heresies and felt obliged to act. He felt a sense of historical connection. He could empathize with seventeenth-century figures. He felt a sense of connection with their labyrinthine plots, their Jacobean glooms. He could see himself plotting, forging documents in flickering candlelight, driven by mournful conviction.

He felt that there were analogies with the current political landscape. The communist menace. You were aware of currents in foreign affairs, malign influences. The threat looming in the East.

He heard that Robert was increasingly active along the mid-border area and in Portadown. He found that people believed anything they heard about Robert. They yearned after him. They sought the lonely perfection of the conspirator.

David had started to suffer from dizzy spells. He also experienced occasional numbness in the extremities. The MO prescribed Valium. David told Knox that mental stability was not an issue. He continued to operate out of Gemini. Joyce stayed in the front room with the girls and the tech stayed out of his way. The Polish girl was the only person he had contact with. She recognized the tension in him. She said, I give you relief. She said, I do manual stimulation very quick, you like? He said, I can't. He wondered if they were putting something in his tea. Nevertheless, he said, I will continue to function at the highest level. He thought that his blood pressure was elevated.

The Polish girl continued to go out with Boyle. It seemed that his remarks were sparse and cryptic. In fact she said that Boyle sometimes did not speak at all. It was hard to ascertain any further details. David wanted to put operatives in place to watch Jackson, but Knox countermanded the plan with a line of reasoning involving resources that was probably intended to sound limp and spurious. David thought that there had been stealthy incursions into his office. He talked in terms of counter-espionage. He was willing to approach total strangers in the mess and engage them in embittered polemics. Joyce was sharing a small flat on the other side of the base with a Wren. He wrote anonymous letters to the CO, accusing the women of acts of gross indecency. He considered it better than the alternative, in which he saw himself breaking into their flat with a gun in his hand, a mumbler of incoherent threats. He stood at the other side of the parade ground and watched them when they came out of the flat in the morning. They wore headscarves and held their coats tight around them with one hand, scuttling away from him with downcast eyes like the women of a fearful diaspora.

Business at Gemini began to drop off. Since the beginning of the operation there had been an atmosphere of sexual melancholy that felt appropriate to a brothel on the fringes of far-reaching civil unrest. But it seemed that the atmosphere had changed. The girls complained about the tongue-lashings they got from Joyce. They had often complained before about the conditions and the restrictions imposed upon them by reason of being attached to a covert operation, and Joyce had cultivated a puffy-eyed and sulky disposition in them that was appreciated by the clients. But now they seemed to be looking for something with a harder edge. They had tired of the glum coupling on offer. David noticed the degree of rancour that had crept into the house, and the girls seemed unable to maintain the shallow fictions of companionship that made the work tolerable. The atmosphere of counterfeit fondnesses and accepted falsehood had given way to disdain.

David was called to the house late one night. A girl from Swansea had been beaten up in the front bedroom. The girl had worked as a stripper and David knew her by her stage name of Tawnee Ryder. There was blood on the floor of the room and on the sheets and a handprint in blood on the wall. Joyce was trying to staunch the blood coming from the girl's nose and mouth with a tissue. There was a pink nylon negligee on the floor. There were other undergarments draped on the mirror. The dressing table was covered with poppers, condom foils and other carnal debris. The girl was wailing.

'She needs stitches,' Joyce said.

'Who did it?' David said.

'A fucking man done it, what else?' Joyce said. 'Call a taxi and get her took to the hospital and then leave us be.'

David went with the girl to the City Hospital. He gave her name as Tawnee Ryder and her address as c/o Theipval Army Barracks. The receptionist did not comment. There was nothing to be added to the combination of the playful mock-erotic alias and the shifty equivocations of the address. When he got back to Gemini Joyce had gone. He tried to clean up the room. He realized that the attack would have been filmed but he had no appetite for viewing footage of battery with a semi-evidential aspect to it. He wanted to look at the early films that had been shot, the flickering and badly edited 8 mm. More and more he seemed to see themes emerge in them, touching quasi-narratives. There was more than a hint of alle-gory, of difficult inner journeys undertaken. All the girls involved in the early days had left. David thought that the new girls who were being sent over did not show the same talent for spurious approximations of desire. He went into the back room and pulled down the screen. When he went to the steel cabinet where the film was kept he found that it was empty.

The following morning David pulled up in the car park in Theipval. The Four Square Laundry van that had been used for surveillance and acquiring evidence was up against the fence at the far end. Its rear doors lay open and you could see the concealed roof compartment. The back of the van was bloodstained and there were bullet holes in the side. The windscreen was starred. When David entered the corridor he found that no one wanted to talk about what had happened. He went into Knox's office.

'What happened?' he said.

'PIRA ambush,' Knox said.

'Casualties?'

'Of course. But we've slapped a D-notice on it. Vital national interest not served and so forth and all that. PIRA will claim casualties on our side but the papers won't print anything.'

'It's a disaster.'

'You could say that. Or you could say that the incident merely hastened the end of the operation.'

'It's being wound up?'

'It was on its last legs anyway. There was something a little overdone about it, shall we say?'

David could see what he meant. The use of operatives with blacked-out faces. The use of secret compartments.

'I have a new device that might interest you,' Knox said.

He brought David to a table at the back of the office. There was an object covered in a dustsheet. Knox lifted the sheet.

'A gallium-arsenide laser with opto-electrical linkage,' Knox said.

David had never seen anything like it.

'What does it do?'

'Bounces a laser beam off the window of a room containing targets. It picks up the vibrations. You can make out every word that they're saying.'

The laser seemed to fill the room. It projected an aura of stupendous technology. It was in the shape of a gun, with delicate sighting mechanisms on one end constructed from rare and minutely fashioned materials. The other end was dominated by heavy, old-fashioned elements, lead and brass. You could see the need for containment. Unknown forces were being generated. Other men came in from the corridor to look at it. The room grew hushed. The men gave themselves over to tech awe. Gallium arsenide. Knox beamed over the group of men, pipe-smoking, boffinish.

That evening David returned to his car. The Four Square Commer was still parked at the back of the car park. He walked over to it. The rear doors lay open. There was a smell like the taste of blood in your mouth. The van was shadowed, dark with intimations of carnage. David noticed personal effects scattered on the floor of the van. A Dunhill lighter. A penknife. There was a woman's clutch purse lying on a bundle of laundry. David could see tissues with lipstick on them, a powder compact. The MRF used plain-clothes women operatives. They dressed in jeans and T-shirts and kept their hair tied up in ponytails. The clutch bag must have belonged to one of them. There was a tradition of scant make-up in covert units. Wearing small amounts to high-light the fact that you weren't wearing enough. Your hair was badly cut. There was evidence of carelessness in the way you dressed. It was important that your complexion appeared a little pasty, that you had the pallid aura of underground firing ranges. Fingernails bitten to the quick to suggest underlying emotional issues.

He heard his name called and turned to see Robert walking towards him across the tarmac. He was wearing the donkey jacket. He waited for Robert to join him. They stood in silence, staring into the back of the van, the scattered belongings taking on lonely import in the dusk light.

'What happened?' David said.

'PIRA ambush,' Robert said. 'Fired down on them. Through the fucking roof. Fucking SLRs they had.'

'Where?'

'The Ardoyne. Spent some time in the fucker myself. Thought I was a local. Talked like them. Dressed like them. Sixty-two per cent unemployment. You have to look a little stooped. Saw a few of them in the boxing club. Slouching about the place. Hands-in-pockets affair. Life's pulling you down. You got six children, you never had a job. The voice, you know, breaks a little sometimes.'

'You sound like you have some sympathy.'

'Do I now? There would be no sport forby the man pitiest the bear.'

'Sorry?'

'Nothing. I was doing a Lancashire accent. Lancashire is easy.'

Robert unslung his bag from his shoulder. He took out a Polaroid camera, a bulked-out and unwieldy instrument like something from the early days of photography.

'You see that?' Robert said.

He pointed to a clump of scalp with hair attached which adhered to one of the metal stanchions on the side of the van. He unfolded the eyepiece of the camera and photographed the piece of scalp and then the interior of the van and the bullet holes, placing each Polaroid carefully on the bumper so that it could develop. He got David to stand in each photograph to give scale to the image, he said. David could smell the developer and fixative, the mild, barely toxic odours in the evening air, Robert seeming a master of this, barely visible figures resolving themselves from obscurity, tremulous imagery, the half-uncertain smile, and the photograph itself with its box-camera colours already freighted with qualities closely aligned to nostalgia, the longing for a thing which perhaps was never there, the premonitory sadnesses.

They waited for the photographs to dry. David thought that he looked like a photograph of a missing person.

'You were talking to Knox?'

'He shares Daily Int reports with me. Everybody gives me information. Don't even have to ask for it most of the time. Boxes of the stuff. Last time I was in Theipval I went back to the car and there was an envelope on the front seat. New photographs of targets.'

'Most of those things aren't supposed to leave here.'

'I'm kind of a postman to them. They give the stuff to me and I deliver it where it needs to go so things like this don't happen.'

'I'm not sure what you mean.'

'This is a war, fuck it, David. Except that you're not allowed to fight.'

'Proxies?'

'There are plenty of good men out there who want to play their part.'

It seemed to David that the apparatus was resolving itself around Robert, finding focus. He walked with Robert to his car, the Q-car, the Triumph that he would drive to the Three Steps Inn. The rear seat was covered with brown Daily Int Sum files, boxed P-cards. David thought of Robert in Castledillon going through the boxes, intent and bookish, scrutinizing and selecting the subjects, a committed and lethal archivist.

They stopped to watch as the Korean women who had been taking out the laundry for the Four Square op were led towards a minibus. They were carrying sports bags containing their belongings. They came towards David and Robert walking fast, almost striding. They weren't what David expected. You looked for downcast eyes, a shuffling walk, submissive Oriental gestures. When they drew level with the two men, one of the women glanced at Robert. She turned to the other women and said something and the women laughed, their laughter harsh, mocking, charged with sexual innuendo.

When Robert had left, David went to Knox. He told him about the meeting with Robert.

'He's using proxies,' David said. 'He's taking to information you give him and he's putting it in the hands of activists so that they can take people out.'

'I see.'

'You can imagine what could go wrong. The information might be inaccurate. Civilians getting caught in the crossfire. I recommend that the flow of information to Captain Nairac be stopped immediately.'

'Your observations are very astute, David. I will certainly take them on board.'

'I'm very concerned about this.'

'You fear that the ethical remit is being exceeded?'

191

'I'm not sure who is in control.'

David noticed that there were new men in the corridor. They looked like Five to him. They had that look of minor public school. They had that look of homosexual mannerisms suppressed. They talked about collating data. They spoke in terms of systems management. You heard the word focus. The atmosphere was bustling and purposeful. David realized that he hadn't seen the NAAFI ladies for weeks. He missed the way the corridor used to be, the hissing of the tea urn, the smell of wet overcoat, the amateurish and sometimes offhand way of putting an operation together. He thought that there had been deep affinities there, a connection with eventual outcomes, the appearance of armed and masked men on suburban streets intent on heartbreak. There was a recognition that their actions represented a monstrous betrayal of humankind. There was an acknowlegement of interdependency, the need to get past the shattered body on the pavement, a sense that moral issues of great complexity were being generated. All these aspects seemed to have gone missing. The young men wore two-piece suits in recently invented fabrics. They brushed past David in the corridors. They had a hard-eyed modish look to them, a look he suspected they had acquired in foreign fields of operations. Berlin. Vienna. They brought an awareness of a higher order with them, the capacity for greater betrayals, long-running and complex treacheries. He overheard plans being put forward. Strategies with a bare modern feel to them. David remembered the stories he had run about black masses, satanic rituals. He wanted to put in a plea for the virtues of that kind of operation. Operations that were steeped in atmosphere and texture, that functioned on the margins of self-parody.

David wanted to make a plea for the virtues that had made the corridor such a good place to work. Virtues of decency and candour whenever possible.

When David came into work the following day the Four Square van had been towed away. At one stage he looked up and noticed Knox watching him through the glass wall of his office. He didn't think there was anything good in this. Knox didn't speak to him for a week. David tried to concentrate on work. He was looking for themes that would show the value of the old approach.

'Why don't you pop over to Gemini, see how things are going over there? We can't stay cross with our former help-meets for ever, can we?'

'I assume you're referring to Joyce.'

'Exactly.'

Knox seemed to want to be seen as a roguish purveyor of rugged good sense in the matter of splintered relationships, advice tendered with a smirk that was meant to suggest cronyish solidarity.

David was working on a newspaper campaign that involved publishing photographs of cheerful soldiers in conversation with local children at interface areas. He had set strict criteria for himself. It was important that the soldiers were from provincial regiments. The Black Watch. The Welsh Guards. You wanted to suggest characterful regional accents. It was important that the children wore shorts and darned woollen pullovers. There were subliminal criteria relating to working-class lifestyles that had to be fulfilled. The children had to be sufficiently grimy to suggest a struggle against poverty. They had to be freckled, gap-toothed, and possess quantities of urchinish charm. The possibility of malformation due to generations of poverty was alluded to. Polio. Rickets. The possibility of degenerate adulthood was not excluded. There were strong existing models for such children in the context of post-industrialized societies and David was aware that his work would have to survive intense scrutiny.

It was early evening before he went to Gemini. As he turned the corner he saw that there were three Saracens pulled up at the kerb outside, soldiers taking up defensive positions in derelict housing to either side. David approached the soldiers.

'What happened here?'

'Don't know, sir. We come out on relief duty. Whatever happened, it happened earlier on today. Place is right shot up, though. Lot of blood about the place.'

The front door of the club had been knocked off its hinges. David felt that the image contained all that he needed to know about what had taken place, a splintered basement door signalling the violent jurisdiction that had overtaken the Gemini.

'Casualties?'

'Couldn't tell you, sir. All been took away by the time we got here.'

David tried to work out how many people would have been present: two or three girls, possibly punters, the tech, Joyce. David noticed brass .303 shell casings on the floor just inside the door and wondered why they had not been removed by forensics. He stepped over the shell casings. There was blood on the hall lino. Each of the bedroom doors had been kicked open. The beds were covered with lint strips, discarded sterile pads soaked in liquid matter. The dressings were army issue. Then David saw that the ceiling lens and wiring had been ripped out. He wondered if they had been taken afterwards. He wondered if the camera had been rolling through the attack and if there existed a record of what had taken place, scarred and faltering but nevertheless compelling by virtue of the subject matter.

He went through to the kitchen. The table and chairs were smashed but the projector was still in place. The pantry where the tech worked had been destroyed. The chemical baths spilled. The enlarger on its side on the floor. David returned to the kitchen. He saw that the screen had been left intact and in position. He went back to the projector. There was an empty can of film sitting next to it and a reel of film was threaded on to the projector. David turned on the projector and waited for it to warm up. He knew what he would see. The Polish girl's room. The fixed camera position allowing the narrative to spill over the margins, implying another degree of action off-screen, one less stilted than the scene on camera, the gunman seeming conscious of the constricted nature of the setting, the need to stay in frame. He started the film. The Polish girl was sitting with her back against her headboard. There was one gunman in frame carrying an SLR. He seemed to be talking to someone in the corridor. He walked over to the dressing table and pulled out a few drawers, spilling them on to the floor, the action carried out in a self-conscious way, without conviction. There was something wrong with the projector set-up. Every few seconds the action slowed down slightly. In a gesture which seemed predetermined, the Polish girl pulled her dressing gown around her more tightly and fastened the belt. She was not watching the gunman. She was watching something that could not be seen by the camera. David heard what he thought was a door slamming, a woman's voice. You were given the feeling of a production that had gone beyond the obvious drama, the man holding a gun, in favour of glum existential tensions, universal themes of futility heavily underscored. The flickering naturalistic light. The muted nature of the sound recording. The sense that late-twentieth-century concerns were being explored. There were motifs of random senseless activity. The man holding the gun turned suddenly and fired without aiming in the direction of the bed and just as suddenly ran from the room without stopping to examine what he had done. David could not see if the girl had been hit. As soon as the gunman ran from the room, she turned on to her side away from the camera and pulled her knees up to her chin.

David knew that the film had been left there for him. He knew that PIRA would not have left the projector ready to be used. Everything else in the house had been destroyed. When he went upstairs he found that the windows had been broken and the reel-to-reel had been smashed, the tape strewn across the room. He looked for traces of Joyce in all the rooms but only the bathroom gave any indication that she had ever existed. The lipstick-smeared tissues thrown on the floor. The hairbrush with fine blonde hair in it. The rusting mirrored cabinet containing deodorizers, talc, sanitary products, depilatory creams, vitamins. Objects which seemed the property of a low-key and dispirited narcissist. David started to pick things up and put them back into the cabinet. He thought that she would appreciate the prosaic nature of the gesture, the sense of paltry tribute.

When he got back to Theipval he went to the corridor. No one had seen Knox. He telephoned GHQ in the hope of getting information on casualties at Gemini. He rang GCHQ in Cheltenham. He rang Box in London. He spoke to night-switchboard assistants. He engaged in violent arguments with minor operatives. At dawn he drove around the hospitals. He stood in casualty departments.

Porters unloaded elderly people from ambulances, coming in with a sense of visitation. Car accident victims being received like overseas legations. Overworked staff spoke to him tenderly, as though they recognized him as being among the maimed. No one had been brought in that night suffering from gunshot wounds, they said. Morgue attendants, pale and authoritative, were summoned from their melancholy postings to confirm the fact that there were no young women among that night's dead.

David drove back to Theipval through the morning traffic. He got into bed but was awakened at ten o'clock by knocking on the door. He opened it and saw the MO and an assistant. He was aware of how he looked, unshaven and red-eyed and prone to irrational action. He could see they were aware that a sudden, unprovoked outburst of violence was possible.

'Good morning, David,' the MO said. 'Perhaps we could step inside and have a little chat.'

The MO was a large man, balding, tactful. They sat in the front room, David slumped in an armchair, the MO sitting on the edge of the sofa with the assistant standing behind him.

David became aware of the way that Joyce had decorated the room. Of the tasselled furniture, the salmon carpet. He began to think he had missed something about her life, a talent for morose complexity.

'A complaint has been made against you, David, I'm afraid,' the MO said, 'concerning an incident of domestic violence.'

'Joyce?' David said.

'Yes, regrettably,' the MO said.

'An allegation of serious assault,' the assistant said.

'Joyce is dead,' David said. 'She was shot last night. I think so, anyway.'

'You're not sure?' the MO said, sympathy in his voice.

It was important to encourage David's uncertainty. It was important to them all that he find points where he had become disconnected from reality. They were looking for long pauses between sentences, harsh barking laughter at inappropriate conversational points.

'There were no reports of any shootings among security personnel last night,' the assistant said.

His function appeared to be to ensure that the conversation did not stray outside the confines of verifiable fact with due regard to the atmosphere of imploding mental states in the room.

'I'm not sure,' David said.

'Just look at the place,' the MO said.

There was sympathy in his voice. David looked at the table in front of him. He could see an empty Gordon's bottle, an opened Fray Bentos tin with mould growing on the contents. The carpet and wallpaper were stained where things had been thrown against them.

'You must be tired living like this, David,' the MO said. 'You must be very tired.'

The assistant placed a small plastic cup of water on the table and set down two Mogadons beside it. David understood that he was to take them.

25

Jackson told Agnew that the op was on for 31 July. When Agnew told Knox he approved. He said that the weather would be warm and there would be Orange marches and other acts of defiance directed towards the civil authority to provide a context of incipient social collapse.

Jackson said that they were to meet in the engineering works. Agnew drove to the engineering works on 28 July. He wanted to see what preparations were afoot. It was warm. Occluded fronts to the south. Stratocumulus clouds in the high atmosphere. The doors of the corrugated-iron shed were open and there was a smell of warm oil on the evening air. Work had stopped for the day and men's overalls were hung on pegs just inside the door. A scene to encompass values relating to honest toil, to the careful manufacture of metal artefacts with a range of applications, to the summer-evening return of honestly fatigued men to their small houses, their trim gardens, their orderly emotional lives.

'I could have worked here,' Hoppy said. He was standing inside the door. 'My da could have got us a job here the day I left school.'

'You never done a day's work in all your born days,' Agnew said. 'You never lifted the mitt to do a turn since the day and hour you walked out the door of that school.'

'Be that as it may,' Hoppy said, 'be that as it may. The discotheque has brought many hours of quality entertainment to the people who attend in their droves.'

Hoppy brought Agnew to a storeroom at the back of the works. He unlocked it. Agnew saw a row of military uniforms, neatly folded.

'Them's for the boys,' Hoppy said.

'What about arms and all?' Agnew said.

'I don't know nothing about guns and the like, but there's talk that there's a device being made in thon farmhouse.'

It was the first time that Agnew had heard about an explosive device. The presence of the device lifted things on to a different plane. The use of bombs gathering a terminology to itself. The blunt, percussive phrasings of the early designs. Keg bomb. And the visual language. The devastation of whole downtown commercial areas. The gathering of body parts into black plastic bags. Survivors described hearing the sound of the lit fuse, the malevolent hiss of it, sulphurous, reeking of old plots. There was a leisurely aspect to proceedings. There were two-hour warnings. Stripped-down alarm clocks were used as timers. Agnew could see things changing. The technology was being projected in different terms. He heard the disposal men talking in terms of propellants, of power timer units. Highly developed plastic explosives, malleable, odourless, were being manufactured in the closed cities of Eastern Bloc countries and being smuggled in via fraternal trade organizations. Mercury tilt switches were in common use for under-car devices. Agnew had the impression of higher processes being brought into play.

Agnew saw signage normally used at military checkpoints. Signs ordering motorists to halt. Signs warning them to turn off their headlights. He had been on duty at these checkpoints and thought they were an expression of nostalgia for sinister Cold War crossing points, soldiery looming out of the dark, the pale uplifted faces of civilians, the shouts of brusque command.

When they came back into the works, Jackson was there with Somerville and Boyle.

'Good evening, Major Boyle,' Agnew said, clicking his heels and snapping a comic salute, implying the existence of a buffoon officer class that included Boyle in its ranks.

Boyle did not appear to notice. He looked like a man surrounded on all sides by a psychic abyss.

199

'Cut it out to fuck, Agnew,' Jackson said.

'Aye, leave the man be,' Somerville said, 'or you'll get ten different kinds of shite beat out of you.'

There was something about the presence of the two men that produced an inappropriate response in Agnew. A tendency to bad jokes. A need to quote threadbare aphorisms, make inappropriate sexual remarks.

'What are you doing here?' Jackson said.

'I just came to see if everything was ready. Be prepared. That sort of thing.'

'Go home, Agnew.'

'You got the signs in there. A fake checkpoint. Then what? The target pulls up, then you blast them, rifles set on automatic?'

The car rocking on its springs. Headlights popping. The slow-mo aspect of the thing. The victim's body in spasm, the full-body tic, the limb twitch. Then the aftermath, riddled bodies lying out of open car doors, overtones of futility.

'I told you, Agnew, you'll be took along,' Jackson said.

'Fucking leave him there too, with a bullet in him,' Somerville said.

'Dead to the world,' Boyle said.

He was rocking backwards and forwards. Agnew expected a low wailing, the disconsolate expressed on a primal level, the soul chant of nomadic peoples addressing their dead. The others ignored him. Agnew suddenly needed a drink. He turned away from them and walked towards his car. When he got there he looked back. The men stood in the doorway, talking among themselves, half hidden in the warm gloom of the shed, swallows flying under the steel joist at the front, their shirtsleeves rolled up so that you would have thought there was an honesty to the scene, epitomes of warm-hearted masculinity, of lifelong friendships, men with sunburned necks who were well regarded by their neighbours, given to acts of spontaneous generosity or succour. Except for Jackson, standing to one side watching Agnew, a calculating look in his eyes as though he had detected Agnew's treachery and was engaged in making assay of it and calculating what reimbursement was due to him by right.

Robert was working nights. During the day he would sit in the rose garden, drinking with Tony Ball and Sergeant Jim Nightingale. Robert and Ball drank gin slings and Nightingale drank Double Diamond from a crate he left in the fishpond to keep cool. It was important that none of the customary military forms be observed. Nightingale referred to Ball as the gaffer. Otherwise first names were used. Ball and Nightingale were said to have been killed in an accident involving their Land Rover in Oman in 1982. The three men would have understood that Special Forces who were killed in action often had their deaths attributed to a traffic accident in a former colonial possession. They understood the concept of non-attributable death on notional desert highways. It opened up a new aspect to the lexicon of desolate fatality expected from a Special Forces operative and was therefore welcome to them.

When they were in the rose garden they did not talk about their night-time operations. Robert had designated the drawing room as the Ops room and they talked about their work there. They lounged in deckchairs. They climbed trees. They played impromptu games of cricket using twigs as stumps. They were aware that their shouts would carry over the garden wall and be heard and resented by the regular soldiers. One day Nightingale hit the ball through the window of the greenhouse. Robert went to get it. He had to search through the withered remnants of semi-tropical foliage, gnarled, pot-bound, an old vine with desiccated grapes running the length of the roof-span, dusty cacti on the windowsill. There was the sound of running water from somewhere. There was a smell of decay, with mould growing in the underside of the benches, a sluggishness in the air. Robert had to push through the dried-out foliage to reach the cricket ball. Something pricked his skin. Robert didn't like the place, its dank, humid enclosures. He didn't like the gravid, ferny odour of it. He found the ball and went back out into the sunlight.

'It's bloody hot,' Tony Ball said.

'It's fuck me hot,' Robert said. 'Let's go swimming in the lake.'

'Catch something in that bloody lake. It's all bloody weed.'

As Nightingale went to sit down on his deckchair it collapsed. He lay on the ground, holding the base of his spine.

'Look at him,' Robert said. 'Took the fucking bolts out of the chair this morning. Knew he'd fall on his arse. Bloody Nightingale. That got you singing.'

These cruelties were there as token of the craft that the young men practised, as earnest of the cruelties they were tasked with, the lethal nocturnal errantry.

Some nights Robert would drive the Dolomite into Portadown. He would wear the donkey jacket. Tony Ball thought that he was meeting with Jackson. He knew that Robert was running an Op with Jackson. He understood that other members of the forces had problems with the way that Robert did things, but Robert seemed to be able to operate with a freedom that puzzled him. He said afterwards that there seemed to be other contexts where Robert was concerned, authorities other than the purely military.

Two weeks before the op Robert went on leave in London with Tony Ball. Robert wore khaki trousers and a check shirt with oxblood brogues. He wore his hair combed to one side and flattened down with Brylcreem. The collar of the shirt was frayed. The brogues were scuffed. People saw him as tousled, boyish. They went to the Guards Club. They went to the Pall Mall Club. During the day they visited tackle shops and falconry outlets. Robert seemed to like places that were wood-panelled, that had brass fixtures, Portland stone flooring worn smooth by generations of feet. He seemed to be able to find small exclusive outlets with an emphasis on tradition in all quarters of the city. He seemed to be able to have himself

202

tended to by subservient men wearing leather aprons who excelled at a range of bespoke craftwork. Cutlers, tailors, saddlers. He brought Ball to a falconry outlet in an entry off Piccadilly Circus. The shop consisted of a low-ceilinged room which smelt of leather from the jesses and hoods and other bespoke objects. The owner was a small man in his fifties who wore gilt-framed glasses and projected the learned but remote look of a medievalist. The man shook hands with Robert, murmuring a greeting while giving the appearance of a man handing on some powerful lore. He turned the door sign to closed and beckoned them to follow him. He brought them into the back of the shop and then into a shed that stood in a yard to the rear of the shop. The man had bought an African vulture. The bird stood on a perch in the middle of the floor. It was almost five feet tall with a long neck, hairless, so that it could forage in the depths of carcasses without despoiling its feathers. It regarded them with a small, lustreless eye set above the large yellow beak, looking lost to the abstracts of its loathsome thought. Ball was surprised to see that Robert thought the thing beautiful, going so far as to place his hand on its dusty, unkempt plumage, which touch it seemed to tolerate uncomplainingly, its mind bent upon the prospects of gross feasting, upon the procuring of its vile surfeits

Tony Ball thought that it was a strange week. One night in the Reform Club Robert produced a photograph of a girl called Mary Parker.

'That's the girl I'm going to marry,' he said.

Later, when Mary Parker was approached, she expressed surprise. She said that she barely knew Robert and had never gone out with him. It seemed part of Robert's capacity for facile self-dramatizing.

Robert insisted that they go drinking in Camden Town, in Kilburn. He gave them names which he said identified them as natives of Belfast. They entered and drank in pubs which were described as known PIRA haunts.

'We'll get a fight,' Robert said. 'These people love fucking fighting.'

Robert asked people about their accents, where they came from. He told them he was from the Ardoyne. He recited the names of streets in the city. He bought drinks. Speaking in a low voice, he described typical lifestyles to Ball. The prevalence of alcoholism. The ability to work hard at repetitive and dangerous work. The large families. The ability to excel at balladry, to evoke rain-washed rural scenes, to subvert civil society through mayhem.

The night before their leave was due to end Robert brought him to a pub on a side street off Kilburn High Road. It had a low ceiling and a rudimentary wooden bar. The bar was populated by navvies who were in various conditions of drunkenness; the smell was of cheap digs, semi-itinerant lifestyles. Each man sat over his drink alone and did not correspond with others at the bar. Each man seemed sunk in ghost race-memory and would raise the glass to his lips slowly and methodically, as if the act of drinking had been forced upon him, or some impediment attended his drinking. The men wore work boots, a selection of old black suits turned greenish with age and stained white shirts open at the neck, and they ordered more drink by tapping on the side of the glass with a finger, and they smoked cigarettes which they discarded by allowing the unquenched butts to fall to the floor beneath their feet. There was one pay telephone in the bar which was attended by a yellow-faced ganger who sat before a ledger placed on the bar. As each labourer entered he would approach the ganger, who would enter the man's name and the amount of his remuneration before handing over a brown envelope for wage.

Robert ordered drinks, which they took to a table at the back of the room, and they surveyed the men's faces in the tarnished mirror which formed the background of the bar. They drank for several hours, the two Englishmen falling silent as though they had been conscripted into a morose diaspora. A few minutes before eleven o'clock Robert rose to go to the toilet. It was reached by way of a block alley open to the sky and then a small yard. He could barely make out where to step, as the alley had filled with a rank and fetid mist driven inland from the mudflats of the great river so that you thought about the gas-lit Victorian streets, the great fogs that enshrouded the East End, the corpse sprawled on cobblestones.

The toilet was ill-lit and filthy and the odour seemed to pursue Robert as he made his way back towards the bar. Halfway along to the alley he became aware of a man coming the other way and recognized him dimly as one of the drinkers at the bar, a large dark man who had not shaved and who wore a black trench coat, mud-encrusted, with a split down the back. The man turned sideways so that Robert could pass him in the narrow passageway, but as Robert drew level with him the man turned again so that his bulk pinned Robert against the wall, the bare blocks abrading the flesh of his face, the man's damp overcoat enwrapping his arms so that he could not move them. When he tried to punch out he had the impression of layers of clothing, the force of the punch being absorbed by heavy cloth, though he thought that if he had made contact with the actual flesh it would not have made any difference, as the encounter gave all the signs of something that would have come to pass no matter what was ordained by the participants. Robert felt his chin being seized by a large hand and his head being turned outwards until he felt that the sinews of his neck would be torn if he did not yield. His face was turned until he was looking upwards into that of the man, although he could see only its outline in the darkness, his face turned upwards in travesty of a lover offering their mouth or as though he owed the man some deference. The man bent his head down to Robert's and pressed his mouth against Robert's mouth, the lips enveloping Robert's, the tongue working its way into his mouth so that Robert struggled wildly, but the man held him with the strength of whatever mania drove him, the breath rancid, masculine, his lips working against Robert's, the flaccid maw, as though engaged in the slaking of a loathsome thirst, and when he was done he released Robert and thrust him back against the passageway so that his head struck the wall. Robert stumbled and fell to the ground.

'There, there, my dear,' the man said, his voice harsh and resonant in the narrow alley.

He drew his sleeve across his lips and walked off towards the toilets, and Robert could hear him laughing softly and then the sound of his voice speaking in low tones, as though he disputed something with himself, some detail of their encounter that he wished to have made clear.

Robert returned to Castledillon at the end of June. He told Tony Ball that he would be based in Bessbrook Mill from then on, that there were certain operational areas that he wanted to be close to. There were 14th Int and SAS units based in Bessbrook Mill. The SAS had turned the top floor of Bessbrook Mill into a bar that other services were excluded from. Robert was permitted to use the bar. They covered the wall with photographs of Special Forces operatives in zones of conflict.

Robert's room was in a prefab within the compound. A rudimentary heliport had been constructed and traffic was intense, Lynx and Westland choppers coming in low and fast across the perimeter wall, bringing a hysteric edge to things, an edge of embassy evacuation, civilian employees abandoned to advancing armies. Robert liked to stand below the landing pad as they came in, feeling the rotor wash, the hammering downdraught, driven backwards by it, the chopper coming in to land nose high, NCOs barking orders into the noise and dust and swirling debris, night patrols going out, MVCP units, SO units going out in twos and threes, Robert the only man who went out regularly on his own without backup, knowing that this set him apart from others, wanting it to be like that.

He had brought the map of the border region with him and he pinned it to the wall of his room. The original map had been almost obscured by his markings. There seemed to be a reinvention of the idioms of terrain. There were lines that resembled contour lines but were not. The grid disappeared in some places and in others was relocated. Minor routes were altered so that they appeared to skirt centres of habitation. Isolated farmhouses were circled, the names of their male inhabitants written in pencil, escape routes inked in. On clear days Robert would take a chopper up. He would sit in the open doorway with his maps under plastic and refer to the landscape below him. He found that it altered from day to day. He got them to take him up on the June equinox, the sun barely falling below the horizon, the landscape all flat planes and dusty tree masses, the mountains bulked out with spring growth. He flew in the hope of detecting something tremulous and mystic, of being able to develop themes of rebirth.

The Miami Showband played two sets at the Coach Inn in Banbridge on the night of 14 July. They arrived at approximately 8.30 and began to unpack the van. It had been customized with their name on the side and aircraft-style seats had been fitted in the front for the band members, which was thought a stylish thing to do, band members strapped in tightly as though at great altitude, as though the night slipped past a gleaming anodized fuselage, the drama of thousands of miles covered, of altitude, of airports deserted in a pre-dawn light. The band existed to play note-perfect cover versions of chart singles. Consummate musicianship was required. Habits of perfection were developed. They were the premier exponents of this craft. In addition, no other live band was prepared to travel at night to the towns of Portadown, Craigavon, Lisburn, Banbridge in such dark times. No other band would travel and then perform feats of dextrous musicianship. The Miami played to full houses and when they finished the audience considered that they could face the night and cheered them from the depths of their emboldened hearts.

* * *

Six miles away on the A1 Robin Jackson and others were in the process of constructing a fake checkpoint. There were ten men involved, some of whom had made their own way there, others who had been dropped from military vehicles that had then driven off so they would not be associated with the operation. All the men except Agnew were wearing the military uniforms that Jackson had stored in the engineering works. The signage was erected and Harris Boyle was flagging cars down with a torch masked in red and examining their identification. McConnell lay on his stomach with a GPMG pointing down the road in the direction of Banbridge. Agnew stood in the field alongside the road with Specs. Specs had been told to guard the explosive device, which had been placed in a green metal ammunition box.

'I don't know what I'm doing here,' Agnew said.

'Just fucking mind out and don't get in the road,' Specs said.

'If I knew what the plan was,' Agnew said.

He saw Jackson approaching them from the direction of the road.

'You'll find out brave and soon,' Jackson said.

Agnew watched as he crossed the field to the high ground covered with whin that made up the western boundary of the field. He saw Robert coming down the hill on his own. He was wearing fatigues and carried a revolver in his hand. He hoped that Robert was too far away to recognize him. Then he realized that Robert had probably been there for some time, that he had probably constructed a hide among the whin on the high ground and that he would have watched them setting up. Robert knew that Agnew was there.

The Miami left the Coach Inn at 12.40 a.m. Their intention was to drive south along the A1 and to cross the border at approximately 1.30, allowing for the Permanent Vehicle Checkpoint on the approach to the border. Five members of the band travelled in the van, one man went home separately.

Just before 1 a.m. they approached the fake checkpoint on the outskirts of Banbridge and were flagged down by Harris Boyle. Boyle told them to get out of the van. He told them to line up on the side of the road facing away from the van. Wesley Somerville and Robert McConnell stepped up behind them, both carrying an SLR.

Jackson came back down the hill. Hoppy and Specs came along the ditch. They were carrying a Bose speaker cabinet between them. They put it down on the grass. Jackson opened the ammunition box and took out the device. It consisted of six sticks of explosive held together with masking tape, with a power timer unit attached to the side. The PTU was cased in black plastic. Agnew thought it looked like an industrial switch, an ugly functionality that indicated serious purpose. He could hear McConnell talking to the band members at the other side of the ditch. The motor of the van was still running. They had a Storno tuned to the police band, radio chatter hanging on the night air, the crackle, the short-wave lyric. It was warm and you could smell new grass, the elder trees in the ditch, the wry stink of them. The uniformed men moved easily around the van. Predation hung in the air. Jackson lifted off the cover of the speaker and placed the device inside, then began to screw the cover back on. Agnew still didn't understand what he was doing. He looked up and saw Robert. It was not long after the equinox and there was a little light in the night sky, which made Robert stand out in silhouette. Because of the angle Agnew looked from, Robert's body was slightly elongated, bent forward at the waist with malign regard, so that you thought of the hunt, of lone predators on night-time skylines, and as Agnew watched the man stirred and moved and descended and was enveloped into the shadow at his feet. Agnew did not want to meet Robert. He had the feeling of a thing hunted. He could feel the impulses, the neural triggers, the taste of metal in the mouth, that sense of light-footed and inexorable approach in the dark, the knowledge of being prey, that you might be stalked and caught. He felt haunted by primal awareness of creatures that make repast amid scenes of slobbering butchery. He looked down. Specs was trying to put the last screws on to the speaker cabinet.

'What are you at?' Jackson said. 'Hurry up, to fuck.'

Agnew turned and pushed through the ditch and out on to the roadway. He felt that he needed a sense of order. He was looking for guiding principles and in their absence the checkpoint's atmosphere of stern military resolve in the face of a ruthless enemy would do. Wesley Somerville was talking quietly to one of the band members. He heard them laughing, Somerville putting them at their ease. As Agnew watched, Specs came through the gateway into the field carrying the speaker unit. He put it down on the ground. Behind the hedge he heard Jackson's voice and then Robert's. He could not hear what they were saying because their voices were lowered but he thought that the tone was one of satisfaction, of furtive and long-planned-for events unfolding. Agnew saw one of the band members step out of line. Harris Boyle had taken a guitar case from the van and thrown it on the ground. Somerville punched the band member hard on the side of the head and pushed him back into line. McConnell lowered his SLR and told the band members to face the ditch, that he would shoot the next man to move. Agnew could see the five men tense. It was the first time he had looked at them. They had long hair and were wearing flares and platform boots. They appeared to him to be in the tradition of troubadours, gauds of ragged itinerancy, entrapped in conflict not of their making. McConnell was shouting at the band members now, his face in rictus, as the full delinquency of the uniformed entourage began to take shape.

Boyle stood at the back of the van. Somerville put his SLR on the ground and lifted the speaker cabinet. He carried it over to the van, where Boyle held the doors open. Agnew could see that Boyle had cleared space so that the speaker containing the device could be put in among the other equipment and thus disguised. Boyle was watching as Somerville tipped the speaker on its edge to put it in. Agnew wondered that none of the others seemed to be watching them, as the planting of the device seemed to be central to their mission. He could not see Jackson or Robert and the other men in uniform had started to clear the signage and the traffic cones, cursing each other as they did so, sweating, nervous, overcome by the depravity of their mission, the drab and nameless perversions of their night's work. Boyle heaved the speaker into the van and grasped hold of the bumper in order to follow, the back of the van gaping, a maw whereby oblivion awaited him, for the device ignited as he did so and the van was rendered invisible in a dense burst of flame which threw Agnew backwards on to the road, its lethal heat sweeping over him, the processes of its ignition, the vacuum at its centre, as all matter was propelled outwards, the absolute lack at the core of it that none could survive. Agnew got up off the ground and walked towards the seat of the blast. It seemed that there was to be a lull in proceedings of indeterminate duration which allowed Agnew to witness and give full testament to what had happened. The back of the van was ablaze with flame and oily vapours, metal compressed into shapes that seemed like the lewd figurings of an arcane and deadly vernacular. Several yards away he saw the limbless carcass of Boyle, blackened and smoking. He turned back upon encountering this and walked towards the margin of the road where the bandsmen had been standing, his feet dragging in the flesh slurry which coated the tarmac. Men in uniform stood around but a kind of inertia seemed to have overtaken them, an encompassing hopelessness. He saw that one of the band members was missing. Two of them still lay on the ground and one of them had stirred and risen to his feet. Agnew turned to see that Jackson was standing beside him. Jackson raised his rifle and shot the standing band member in the chest whereby it seemed that he was jerked from behind like some species of puppetry and propelled backwards among the elder trees that lined the road behind him.

'No witnesses,' Jackson said.

McConnell pointed his rifle at the face of one of the remaining band members and started to fire single aimed shots. Others stepped forward for this duty but Agnew saw Jackson raise his SLR in his direction and he turned and ran back towards the van. The vehicle was fully ablaze now and there were explosions from inside and out to accompany the sound of gunfire. Agnew looked back once and saw a figure with a pistol firing shots into one of the bodies. He could not be sure that it was Robert but neither could he recollect that any of the others had carried a pistol, and if so, why would they use it in preference to their rifle? He wandered through the smoke, which had now obscured the whole scene, his ears ringing from the sound of their butchery, and then he emerged on to the carriageway to find Specs standing in the middle of the road without his glasses, his uniform torn and smoke-blackened. The youth had his hands in the air and his fervent sightless eyes raised and he intoned in the manner of a preacher.

'I understand how I have fallen short of the glory of God,' he said. 'My righteousness is like filthy rags to God and my only hope is in accepting Jesus Christ as my lord and saviour.'

26

Lorna found the place in the sand dunes where the boys sniffed solvents, the sand covered in plastic bags, the insides covered in Evostik, in Ronsons. She thought once she might try it but she didn't like the smell it was too modern she liked musty old smells the insides of handbags old wardrobes etc. She wondered that she hadn't seen it in their eyes that look what was the name for it the pupils dilated little tiny slits. Agnew told her once that if you had concussion your eyes went slitty he was always telling her things like that he thought that you needed facts against the world maybe he was right. Now that she thought about it that was the right word for the boys who hung around the caravan park they looked like sad boys concussed with the things they did not know. They never tried to meet her eye or call dirt after her when she walked past perhaps they didn't like girls perhaps they were homo or perhaps it was just the solvent that kept their heads busy their thoughts going round and round. She kept on looking in Agnew's things she did not want to think about what she found the charge sheet from the case that put him in prison why did he keep it? That he did knowingly and feloniously. She thought that he was too small and lost to do fearful murder or foul conspiring. Though from what she could see he never did point a gun and pull the trigger on some poor man or woman he was just standing there watching. Maybe he told them a lie that he was just standing there when in actual fact he was doing the killing so that he wouldn't get life or whatever it was they gave to people who did murder. It would be like him to stand and watch that was what he did but it would also be like him to tell lies.

She wondered why it seemed that Robert never had a girlfriend or a lover. She thought that if she could have met him she would have been his lover and then when he died she would have worn black and gone to tend his grave which would have been sad but also soothing because he would be hers for all time that's right she realized there couldn't be a grave because they never found him that was a lonely thought. She wondered if maybe he was a homo as well there was only one mention of a girl Mary Parker and she said that she didn't really know him which meant that there was never any. She kept looking at his photograph to see what they said about him that he was handsome but she did not think that he was handsome that broken nose but also something about his eyes like he was standing a long way back in his head watching you. If he was homo it would have been against the law in those days. That he did wilfully. That he did feloniously. It had to be a secret in those days in public toilets in dirty hotel rooms all those handsome boys with secrets behind their eyes. It's no wonder Robert turned out the way he did if that was what happened. She never thought about boys that way much any more the doctor said it was because her body was undernourished no period no moonlight romance no lying awake at night wondering if any girl ever took him in her arms and said come to me now my secret love.

Mallon said there was no proof that Nairac was there at the Miami massacre.

'He was there,' Agnew said. 'I seen him with my own two eyes, standing on the hill, and then I hears him talking to Jackson.'

'But you can't be sure it was him firing the shots into the band member on the ground.'

'It looked like him. There was bullets from the Star pistol dug out of one of the bodies.'

'But you can't be sure. He might have just slipped off into the night before anything happened. There's no proof. The lead singer was shot twenty-two times in the face.'

'The good-looking one, that's what they said about him, wasn't it? The guitarist, Travers, he was hit in the shoulder by a dum-dum bullet and blew through the hedge. The bass player, he gets threw into the ditch by the force of the blast.'

'They find Somerville's body ninety fucking yards away.'

'The operation was a disaster. You'd of thought they would have run away instead of opening up on the band.'

'Jackson wouldn't have run away.'

'Neither would Nairac.'

'How did you get away?'

'I walked up the road and sat and waited for the police to arrive.'

Agnew remembered that he had allowed himself to become a bystander, held back behind barricades, behind incident tapes strung between poles. He fell into recognized patterns of behaviour, exhibiting along with others a repellent degree of voyeurism. He found solace in it. Other bystanders asked questions of him and he was able to reply with a degree of authority. He saw people gathering in knots. He saw people milling uncertainly. Stocky self-possessed women came out of houses in their nightclothes to stand at their garden gates. He saw a Wessex coming in to land on the hard shoulder of the road, a thunderous event, the majesty of a helicopter landing on a closed roadway, the epic discharge of soldiers into a zone of awful carnage. A fleet of ambulances carried the victims away into the tumultuous night.

'One conviction.'

'One conviction. The glasses was blew clean off Specs's nose. Somebody picked them up in the field. The poor bastard's eye condition was unique. In court he says he knew they were coming for him.'

'He refused to name accomplices.'

'If he named Jackson he was a dead man.'

'There's another theory about the device.'

'What's that?'

'That Robert had provided it. That he put an anti-handling mechanism on it. That the whole point was to take out Jackson.'

Agnew feeling the idea of conspiracy getting out of control now, spiralling deathwards. A sense of Robert picking up people and discarding them. Pseudo-gangs. He didn't believe that Robert wanted the Miami Showband to carry a device across the border. He thought that he had other motives, the things he had going on in his head, the shadowy ulteriors. Robert wanted the conspiracy itself in all its covert multiples, and he found himself in the company of men like himself, heretic plotters, the outcasts coming in from the shadowlands. Jackson, Boyle, Knox. The forsworn brethren, the Ultras. Ultra meaning beyond. Ultra meaning extreme. The word itself had a rustling cabbalistic tone to it. He wondered again who Mallon was working for, knowing as he did so that he would never find out. He knew also that Robert had been involved in other, even more terrible happenings, no-warning events of terrible intent and consequence, and that was the price that Robert had paid to connect to the currents of history, the secret fluxes. That was what Robert and the others did. They created secrets and forced everyone else to live in them.

That was what scared him. The knowledge of clandestine governance, the dark polity.

Knox had been withdrawn in 1978. His previous postings had included Iraq, Egypt, Sudan, Syria and Nigeria. Agnew received a letter from the Foreign Office confirming that Knox's final official posting had been to Greece following the overthrow of the government by the generals. Junta, the jackboot word. Junta meaning joining. Meaning a body of men joined or united for some secret intrigue. The hard, consonantal word, the overtones of repression. Agnew could see Knox standing on a dusty street in Athens, wearing a Panama hat, a solitary man looking vague and nonplussed, military vehicles streaming past on the main boulevards, political opponents sprawled in courtyards. Knox had stopped all contact with Agnew shortly before they had come for him. Mallon wouldn't say where the order for his arrest had come from, or who had provided the information, but Agnew suspected that Knox had something to do with it.

'Do you not think that he just lifted his protection,' Mallon said, 'that he stopped telling people that you were an asset?'

'How come they never lifted Jackson or any of them others?'

Robin Jackson had gone on killing until 1997, when he died at home from cancer, the rogue cells in the bloodstream. The body conspires against itself.

'Are you fucking joking me? Jackson was far too handy. They fucking passed him around among themselves.'

'What about me?'

'That's what I said. You were done. You were no use to man nor beast. The only thing they cared about was you keeping your mouth shut. Even at that they knew there wasn't nobody listening.'

'You're listening to me.'

'Do you think I'm listening to you? Am I listening to you or watching you?'

'I don't know. I don't even know where you work.'

'Don't pay no mind to where I work. Knowing that won't do nothing for nobody. It'd only be giving you a wrong view of things. You'd be inclined to make assumptions about things. Keep your mind on what happened. Do you think someone was running Nairac?'

'Hard to tell. MI6 were well in place. Special Branch had their own men. So had Army Int. The only outfit that weren't well dug in were MI5. They were desperate to turn their own assets.'

'So he could have been working for 14th Int in name but in fact have been an MI5 operative.'

'It's possible. Could he have made it through Ampleforth and Oxford without at least being contacted by the security services?'

'Not the type, though, was he? Keen on sports, that sort of thing.'

He was the type, Agnew thought. You just had to be able to spot it. The way he watched you. The way he constructed personas. The bluff, genial Guardsman with a feel for the common soldier. The PsyOps man. The falcon master. The legendary border operator. The boxer. In 1988 his college contemporary Julian Malins said that never was a man born who was less capable of dissimulation.

'Nairac would have enjoyed it,' Mallon said.

David flew from Aldegrove to Brize Norton in an RAF Viscount. He was escorted by the Special Branch men, Cooper and Mahood. In the plane he wanted to know what they were doing there.

'Man wants to know what we're doing here.'

'You're civilian police,' David said.

They had been giving him diazepam. He was finding it difficult to think clearly. He felt dim, low-browed and oafish, a struggler with basic concepts.

'There's crime involved here,' Cooper said, 'very serious crime.'

'You're a dangerous fugitive, David,' Mahood said.

'I can't be a fugitive. I haven't done anything and I'm not running away.'

'Nevertheless, you represent a flight risk. Will we put the cuffs on?'

'Maybe. Tell us this, David. Are you likely to try anything? Are you likely to resort to physical violence?'

'Don't put handcuffs on me.'

'Tell you what. Take one of these boys. It'll keep the head right.'

Mahood took a vial out of his pocket and shook a capsule into his hand. David swallowed it dry.

The interior of the aircraft had been cleared for cargo and was empty except for a row of metal seats facing the back. The interior fuselage was chipped and scarred and webbing hung from metal struts. When the plane banked left over the airport he could see the landing lights, blue and red, advancing on pylons. By looking over his shoulder he could see into the cockpit, the dials, the green light of the radar screen, the basic tones of tech euphoria. The world hummed with marvels. He wondered what was in the capsule given to him by Mahood. He was aware of the interior of the aircraft, the actual structure of it, ducts streaming with high-pressure lubricants, hydraulic fluids, the dense circuitry hanging in loops from the cabin infrastructure, the aeronautic hum. He felt happy with the way it felt with the seating and interior stripped out. He liked the workaday feel to it, solid, work-scarred. He felt that he understood things better now, the connections between them.

'Look at your man,' Cooper said.

'He's away with it all right,' Mahood said.

On 20 July David was incarcerated in Manderly Mental Faculty, a military hospital on the edge of the moors. It seemed a prerequisite of such institutions that they should be sited next to barren uplands. That there should be geographical scope for vision-haunted wanderings, that patients should be permitted to stand at barred windows staring across bleak and waterlogged hillsides, that they should be lost in morbid imaginings, flat-roofed concrete structures. There were intimations of silo in its construction, nondescript science buildings clustered around a test site. The interior corridors were floored with rubberized matting. There were bars on the windows. David was placed on ward seven. He was medicated each morning and each evening. His clothes were removed and he was given a hospital robe and slippers which were too large. He understood the signals. The slippers were intended to promote a shuffling walk. There was only one mirror in the ward. It had a scratched metal surface, so he was unable to shave properly and he understood by this that he was to let go of the self. He learned that there was a doctor in charge of his case but he was unable to see him. There was one other patient on the ward, a pilot who had been incarcerated for exposing himself in a series of public open spaces in the vicinity of Greenham Common airbase. He explained that he was reacting to the concentration of radio-wave activity in the vast windswept acreage of the airbase, the techno-clutter caused by the continuous take-off and landing of B-52s and AWACS. He explained that the signals were picked up by the fillings in his teeth. There was a suggestion of sinister implants. He stole tinfoil from the kitchen and used it to line his pillow.

After two weeks at Manderly David was brought to an office in a prefabricated building near the perimeter fence. An official from the Home Office called Watson was waiting for him. David sat down on a metal-framed chair at the other side of the desk from the man. He was aware how he looked. He hadn't washed for days. He waited for Watson to speak to him. He fixed his features in a lowly and unassuming expression. He had been subjected to demeaning procedures for some weeks now, invasive medical procedures, and he was inclined to the onset of blank-faced humility.

'Have you been charged yet?' Watson said.

'Charged with what?' David said.

Watson read from a sheet of paper in front of him. 'The Director of Public Prosecutions recommends that a prosecution be instituted against David Anthony Erskine in the matter of the murder of Joyce Anne McKinney.'

'I don't know what you are talking about,' David said.

Watson recounted the finding of Joyce's body close to her car at a beauty spot adjacent to Theipval. He said that she had been strangled with her own stocking. Police reports stated that her clothing had been interfered with but that an assault of an intimate nature was not thought to have taken place. He detailed the injuries that had been found on her body. He said that the police were concentrating in particular upon the use of the stocking as the murder weapon, the psycho-sexual overtones, the gross simulacrum of sexual activity that was implied. His voice was measured, with intimations of society's justified contempt for the perverse nature of the crime and its determination to apprehend the culprit.

'I didn't do anything to Joyce,' David said.

He knew that he did not sound convincing. His speech was dull and uninflected.

'She was a degenerate,' Watson said, 'and she died the death of a degenerate. The court will decide the matter of your guilt.'

'I want to go back to work,' David said.

'Your job doesn't exist any more,' Watson said. 'In fact the corridor doesn't exist any more. Information is being processed with greater speed and efficiency elsewhere.'

'I was just a bit tired,' David said. 'The stress was getting to me. I could go back to work now.'

Watson told him that there was no place for him now. That he would not be able to understand what was happening. New acronyms had been devised. Shadowy government departments were being set up at a bewildering rate. New technologies were being employed on the streets.

'This kind of war has never been seen before,' Watson said.

As if war did not establish its own fell dictate.

'Is Joyce really dead?' David said.

He realized that he was speaking in a whisper. It seemed the only way that he could muster what was necessary, the piteous imperative.

'She is dead. You are the main suspect. The police are, as they say, not looking for anyone else in connection with her death.'

David felt tears begin to roll down his face. He felt himself sobbing. Great shuddering gasps, his shoulders moving, harsh and wrenching. A man weeping. He knew he was the thing that people turned away from, gulping, anguished. People looking uncomfortable. There were harsh and terrible intimacies contained in the sound, the man noise. They knew how to deal with a woman crying. There was a different quality to the desolation. You weren't forced into proximity with it. There was a softness at the edges. You were not forced to deal with the fierce perplexities, the gruelling spectacle, the masculine soul attrition. It didn't last long. He found himself moving into a new range of vocal effects, snuffles, throat clearings. Sounds that lacked the authority of the previous utterings. When he looked up he saw that Watson had not in fact been embarrassed and was now studying him. His face wore a gentle, understanding look. Watson looked like a third-rate eugenicist with strong opinions on race theory and the supremacy of the Nordic peoples.

'Wipe your nose,' Watson said. 'The reason I'm here is to tell you that a plea of manslaughter due to diminished responsibility will be accepted. You can reduce your sentence considerably.'

'I didn't do it.'

'That's neither here nor there, David. If you don't take the plea and you are found guilty, then it is of course a mandatory life sentence.'

'I'll tell everything in court,' David said. 'I'll spill the beans on the whole thing. PsyOps, the whole lot.'

He felt his eyes narrow. He felt a cunning expression creep over his face. The kind of expression you expect from the criminally insane. Crafty, deranged.

'It won't do you any good, David. You are now discredited. You are incarcerated in a hospital for criminal lunatics. Who would believe you?'

David thought about it. The blood of cockerels. Occult scrawls in graveyards.

'What about Nairac? He's still out there, isn't he? I know the sort of thing he's up to. I'll go to the newspapers. I'll go to television.'

He saw himself being interviewed by a softly spoken man in his mid-forties with a sympathetic manner and impeccable credentials in the field of investigative journalism. He saw himself sitting in a comfortable chair and talking to camera, photographs of smiling grandchildren in the background, the whole set-up intended to convey distance from shocking revelations of deceit and murder. There would be night-time reconstructions on lonely rain-soaked border locations, theme music with an ominous string section.

'Will Nairac still be out there when you come to trial? That's the question.'

'What do you mean?'

'Captain Nairac has been in the field for almost seven years. It may be that his luck will run out. It may be that his style will conflict with operational policy now. There are other conflicts in the world where someone like Nairac would be useful.'

'You don't know who he's working for, do you?' David said slowly. 'He's out there and nobody knows what he's doing or who he's working for.'

'It could be Five,' Watson said. 'I always thought it was Five. There was a man at Ampleforth with the right credentials. He shared Nairac's interest in birds of prey. My information is that he used to visit Nairac in Oxford.'

'Maybe it isn't anybody,' David said.

'That is astute, David. Part of me feels that he has been oper-ating between agencies, everyone thinking he was working for someone else. Operating in the spaces between organiza-tions. If that is true, then he is a lot cleverer than we think.'

'If he's not working for anyone, then what is he doing?'

David's head was sore. He felt tired. He felt a yearning for the iron-framed bed in the ward, the deep textureless drug-slumber, the medicated void.

'I don't know,' Watson said. 'He is a hunting man, perhaps that's it. A predator. Hunting for the sake of the hunt. It happens, you know.'

Despite the drug regime David woke that night. He did not know what time it was. They were not permitted clocks in the ward but he felt that it must be close to 3 a.m. He could hear the other man make small noises in his sleep. This was the place for men to toss in their sleep, to cry out, to wake and run barefoot along empty corridors. This building had the echoes, sound reverberated in its lonesome galleried spaces.

David had woken thinking about Robert. He felt prescient and brilliant, as though some accident of medication had opened him to prophecy. He thought that he could actually feel Robert becoming a legend, moving at that very moment in a border location, map-referenced, alone, with a sense of deadly mission. Knowing that his time was limited. Knowing that matters were coming to a head. Knowing the responsibility that had been placed upon him in this matter. David knew that Robert would gather mystery to himself. The links to deadly killers. The men who were apparently seen by eye-witnesses removing a wounded man on the night of his death. The figure standing slightly apart at events of military and historic import. The fomenter of havoc. The plotter. The hatcher of villainy, of murderous schemes, alone in the prowled-through locale of his own mythology.

27

That night Agnew went over the evidence presented at the trial of Liam Townson for the murder of Robert. In the immediate aftermath of Robert's disappearance five statements had been made by men who were alleged to have been part of the group who had abducted him. These statements were made in Castlereagh Interrogation Centre. None of them mentioned Townson. Three statements were allegedly made by Townson. In the single unsigned statement that was ruled admissible, Townson was alleged to have said, 'I shot the British captain. He never told us anything. He was a great soldier.'

Agnew read the statements of the policemen who found the location where Robert was supposed to have been shot, the Flurry Bridge. They said that they were approached by two fishermen who produced several bullet casings. They claimed to have found them at the bridge. When this was investigated, the police found blood and teeth fragments. Neither of the two fishermen has ever been identified.

During the trial of Townson it emerged that the military authorities did not have any record of Robert's blood group. They could not therefore establish whether the blood at the bridge belonged to Robert. Mallon had brought Agnew a photocopy of the Joint Services Movement Card of Paul Harman, a covert military operative shot dead by PIRA in December 1977. This was the same card that was carried by Robert. Among the details on the card was Harman's blood group.

Townson and five others were convicted on charges arising from the murder of Robert Nairac. The convictions rested heavily upon the disputed statements.

Agnew walked to the window of the caravan. He could see the phosphorescence of the waves on the shore. High winds the previous night had covered the beach in jellyfish. He had walked the beach that morning, stepping carefully between their venomous tendrils in case they clung to his shoes, going down on one knee to look through the jelly to the cortex of them, violet and lobed. You had the impression of higher intelligence, sophisticated brain-stem activity, advanced toxins. It was the thing he had always liked about the caravan, its proximity to forms of mystery. Looking across the lough in daylight, he could just see the edge of the forest, the dark tree mass before it descended into the border region, the fissure in the mountains where Robert was said to have disappeared.

He was interested in a statement claiming that shortly before his death Robert had attended an intelligence briefing in Theipval in the company of 'an old man from London'. The man was said to have borne a resemblance to Sir Maurice Oldfield, the then Director of MI5. But Agnew wondered about Walmsley. He described Walmsley to himself as the falcon master. He wondered if the man would have referred to himself this way. He thought that he might. What little he knew about Walmsley suggested that he would have a weakness for the kind of self-regarding melodrama inherent in the title.

He realized that all the statements concerning the way that Robert met his death were compromised. The five obtained at Castlereagh Interrogation Centre were suspect because of the reputation for brutality that was associated with Castlereagh. Townson claimed that he had not made the statements ascribed to him, none of which he had signed. These were the sole accounts of Robert's death. These typed statements were the only access to the detail of that last hour, the actions he had gone over repeatedly in order to extract meaning from them but which had proved mutable, open to interpretation, the pistol-whipping, the attempted escape, the gun being put to his head then misfiring four times, the reputed bravery, along with the fact that Robert was said to have known that he was going to die, that he had cried.

The assertion that Robert had cried troubled Agnew. There was a ring of authenticity about it. It didn't seem to be the kind of detail that would have been added by a hard-nosed detective concocting a confession late at night in a dimly lit squad room. The other alleged incidents seemed to have a function: they brought an atmosphere of gratuitous cruelty, moved the action along, created shorter sequences of action within the main storyline. There was anticipation and irony. Robert lying on the ground, bloodstained, heroic. He imagined the detective working in his shirtsleeves, stolid, balding, adhering to narrative conventions. Agnew was familiar with fabricated statements. He knew that there were themes involved, recurring motifs. But nothing in all that he had learned about Robert had prepared him for the weeping. If it was true, he did not think that it was because Robert was in pain, or frightened, or remorseful. Robert had been on the border for twenty-seven months at that stage. He was drinking. Agnew was sure that he was drinking heavily. He had conspired and killed and felt his life folding back in on itself in layers of falsehood, dark canards, and now a border emptiness had enwrapped him, the deep soul vexation, the tugging void.

When he went to pick up Lorna that Friday Angela told him that she seemed better.

'We went shopping yesterday. Just the two of us. We had some good talks,' she said.

'What about?' he said.

'Don't worry, it wasn't about you. Just mother–daughter stuff.'

He thought there was a smugness about her as she said this. A sign that she had reached a meridian of female knowingness with her daughter. Talking together in the car.

Taking note together of the bounty that pertains to one-stop finance, to exclusive retail outlets.

'I don't actually give a fuck whether you talked about me or not,' he said.

He was trying to change the mood. He felt that she should be wary of abandoning the rancour that had sustained them this far. He felt that she was entering unknown territory. She shook her head sadly. She had a repertoire of head shakes. Despairing, faintly amused, indulgent. It was something he had liked about her when he first met her. He thought she had devised the gesture as a way of dealing with marriage to a rogue policeman, a man with a prison record. It suggested a woman who was prone to a mild form of world-weariness, easily got over. She had an affinity for tentative ironies. She turned and went back into the house, calling Lorna's name as she did so. Agnew found himself reaching out and touching her on the shoulder, the warmth of her skin through the light wool jumper, the bra strap underneath, the taut intimate thing. She stopped momentarily, bowing her head slightly so that she was looking down but not turning back towards him. Then she walked forward again so that his hand fell off her shoulder. As Lorna came down the corridor towards him he saw her look at her mother's face, as though she saw an expression that she didn't recognize. Agnew hoped that he deserved something in a range between stoic regret and out-right forgiveness.

Lorna talked all the way back to the caravan. She told him about the times she had seen her parents fighting. She sat at the top of the stairs and said prayers, incantations against dis-putatious adulthood, against divorce and other words she did not understand but nevertheless loomed in a conceptual manner. She seemed intent on full disclosure.

'I'm not saying it's your fault I'm not saying that I'm not so shallow that I blame what's going on now on past trauma the counsellor said that I know it's time for me to look forward and be resolute.'

Agnew noticed the way the words were coming out without punctuation. There was a headlong aspect to her disclosure that he did not understand. Those nights coming back to him. His daughter reeling off incidents. The night the police had to be called. The night he broke the window. The night he got into the bed beside her and cried while she held him. Testaments of dark parenthood, a rank-natured and unseemly office. Her eyes were bright. Normally her speech was slow, full of pauses to enable the full import of adolescent wryness to be appreciated by the listener. The crucial watershed events in a young life that were missed.

'It's quite good in a way you were a kind of anti-father,' she said. 'All the things that a father shouldn't be.'

'I'm not proud of it.'

'I was, because none of the other girls knew anyone like you. I think they thought you were glamorous, turning up drunk to pick me up at school and carrying a gun and things.'

'There was nothing glamorous about it.'

But he knew that he had believed it himself at the time. That he was glamorous, ruined in a complex way. He thought that people would detect an edge in him. That he had stepped outside their moral universe and therefore possessed a depraved magnetism, an unspeakable cachet.

That night she slept the night through without waking. He expected her to have the diary in the bed with her but he could not see it. He thought that there was more colour in her cheeks, that her breathing was more even. When the phone rang he moved quickly to answer it so it would not wake her. He wondered if the sound of the old-fashioned phone made her heartbeat quicken the way it did his. The sonorous and pressing notes, a sternness that betokened twentieth-century imperatives. When he lifted the phone no one spoke for a minute and he found himself lost in the line noise, the hums and static. When Mallon spoke he did not identify himself.

'I got a hold of somebody you might want to talk to,' Mallon said.

'Who is it?'

'A witness, you could say. The man doesn't have the full wits about him. The head is not what it might be. But he does have something to say.'

'Where is he?'

'He works in that meat factory, the one that Nairac was supposed to have ended up in. It's shut down now. Your man is the caretaker.'

'How do I get to talk to him?'

'We go up there tomorrow night. Are you on?'

The prospect worried Agnew. He realized that he had been working exclusively off the written record, the statements, the court records. He had spoken to few primary sources. He envisaged the man, contemptuous of the tentative truths he had arrived at through research. He would set up his account alongside the one that Agnew had worked at, the nuanced, flimsy thing.

'I'm your man.'

'Are you sure you're fit for this?'

'I'm telling you.'

'I'll pick you up at nine or so.'

Agnew sat down at the banquette and poured a Gordon's. He used to think gin was a drink for women. He pictured a divorcee with high cheekbones and a thin dissatisfied laugh. But it was the only thing he could drink now and that he was drinking only from habit. He could no longer find even the range of shallow emotions that drinking had once provoked in him and he missed them, the wheedling voices. He observed that his hand was shaking and that his fingers were yellowed from smoking. The doctor had given him tablets to take, things to place under his tongue, gels, capsules, sprays. Like drinking, none of them seemed to have any effect. The tongue was still coated, the blood pressure was still high, the nightmares still came.

He remembered being in court. The judge asked why, in relation to the conspiracy-to-murder charges, no one else had been charged. He took this to refer to Jackson. He realized that he was the only one still alive with any real knowledge of that period. He wondered if the trip to the factory was a trap. If Mallon was working on a scheme involving elaborate irony, having him killed in the same place where Nairac's body was supposed to have been disposed of. As he imagined the meat factory, it seemed an appropriate place to die, one of those settings of harsh, quasi-urban romance, a place of yards and sheds, with motifs of desolation and ruin. He saw himself sprawled on concrete, Mallon pocketing a gun with an air of grim satisfaction.

Lorna woke him. He had fallen asleep across the table.

'Old habits,' she said. 'I didn't want to wake you.'

He had the sensation that she had been watching him as he slept. Her speech had returned to its normal pattern. She handed him a cup of coffee. He saw that there were deep marks on the inside of her wrists.

'She didn't tell you?' she said. 'That happened a long time ago. A cry for help apparently. I won't be going there again.'

He realized that she always wore sleeves so long that they almost covered her hands. He wondered what other marks were concealed on her body, what torments she had inflicted on herself. She sat down opposite him, pushing aside a file.

'What about the boy soldier?' she said.

'Who?'

'Nairac. Like I always thought he was a boy soldier.'

'He was a bit more than that.'

'I don't mean it in the way that he was young and didn't know what he was doing. I mean it that he sort of didn't care what he did.'

'A deadly boy, then.'

'Something like that.'

'I don't know. The closer you get to the last days, the harder it is to find material. Apparently he told people that he was close to an intelligence breakthrough. That's about the only thing we know about that period. We have other details. The car he was driving. Nothing more.'

'Like he was getting ready to disappear?'

'A part of me likes to think that he did that. That he just slipped away.'

'Just slipped away,' she said. 'That's good.'

'There is a church window dedicated to him. In a church called St Mary de Lode.'

'Really?'

'And a bravery award named in his honour.'

'That's pushing it a bit.'

'He got a George Cross as well.'

'What's that?'

'A medal. Strange enough, it's one that you give to civilians. Am I supposed to be talking to you about all of this?'

'Why are you asking that question? Is it my youth? Is it my well-known and documented vulnerability?'

'Don't be at that stuff now.'

'All right. Sorry.'

'He had this kestrel in a film. A film called Kes about a lonely boy. One of the birds they used belonged to Nairac.'

Robert would leave Bessbrook Mill and drive to the lough, going down the road that ran along the bank of the ship canal until he reached the lock gates. The lock was heavily over-grown and the gates were welded shut, having been damaged in a collision. Robert would fish for small perch. When he caught one he would rig it with a metal trace and treble hook, then cast it into the deep lock basin and allow the dead fish to sink to the bottom. When a pike took the perch Robert waited for a long time before striking. He would wait for the perch to pass into the pike's gullet and then strike to lodge the hook there. Then he would feel the pike on the end of the line, mov-ing slowly at first, almost a deadweight. This was the part that Robert liked. The connection you felt to the predator.

Even though you knew that it could not harm you, there was a primal dimension that meant you felt drawn into its cold regard, the mask-like head turning in your direction. On the surface of the water it would thrash, but in the deep water you could only sense malice unconfined.

That July Robert had caught a thirty-pound female pike. It took an hour to get it on the bank. He was in the undergrowth below the lock gate. The surface of the water was covered with rank weed. Dragonflies hovered over the water like something of vivid import from the beginnings of the world. Robert remembered that Knox had raised several in a tank in his office on the corridor. He had explained the principles of metamorphosis to Robert, the shedding of the pupa stage, the emergence into the light. The oil spill blues and greens. Lustres from a time of genesis.

Robert heard voices on the roadway above his head. A man's voice and then a woman's. Lovers, he thought. The way they dropped their voices slightly when they spoke to each other. As if there was a covert element to their relationship. As if there was something about them that the world must not know. Robert knew that they could not see him through the alder trees above his head. The female pike, which he had gaffed and dragged on to the grass, moved its tail and lay still. The lovers stopped above his head, less than six feet away. Robert thought that they must be kissing. There was something in the silence. It was almost historic, the calm you get around old buildings, at heritage sites, panelled rooms with dust motes floating. The fish moved again. Robert went down on one knee to remove the hook, careful to avoid the jaw, the backward-angled teeth for gripping, for tearing. The mouth of the fish was wide and flat, with lines that suggested cruelty, implacability, and the fish appeared to be watching him with the eye of a barbarous misanthrope. Robert took his pistol from the holster under his arm and reversed it and used the butt to strike the fish between the eyes. He watched it die. He could hear the couple above him, the rustles, the adjustments, the breathing quickening, working their way towards the corporeal priorities, the girl sounding as if she was in pain, as if a voluptuary tariff was being exacted from her.

Robert sat by the side of the water until they had finished. The pike no longer moved and its colour was fading. He pushed it off the bank with his foot and watched it sink away from the light. He sat alone in the smells of the river, the alder, the dried vegetative matter, the hogweed and various other stinging and burning river plants. Their smells and ammoniac stinks.

In his room at Bessbrook Mill Robert had put more OS maps on the wall. This time there were no markings on them. He had decided that he was approaching the terrain in the wrong way. He had added nothing to these maps. He was looking for mysteries in them, ancient pathways, mystic linkages. He had started to read literature that was themed around ancient civilizations and their art. He studied aerial photographs of mystery lines on desert floors. He scanned cave art for images that suggested connections to advanced civilizations. He kept paperbacks by his bed, books written by bearded men with authoritative Middle European-sounding names. Erich von Daniken.

In the early days he had found that army surgeons would give him post-mortem images if asked. He had used his own Polaroid at scenes of lonely assassination. At night-time he pinned these photographs to the wall beside the maps. Close-ups of wounds, the matter of the body exposed, and he sought correspondence between the exposed veins and nerve fibres of the body and the map, energy flows. He read a magazine article on Asian belief. He tried to look beyond the carnage. He thought he might be able to detect the Vedic channels.

He did not seem to be able to keep his room tidy. He took trays of food from the mess and slid the remains under the bed. There were piles of damp clothes. There were scale-encrusted items of fishing tackle. There was literature relating to falconry. There were P-cards, SigInt documents, photo-fit sheets from local Special Branch. There were loose shotgun cartridges, personal effects removed from houses during night-time cross-border searches. There were empty bottles of Gordon's. When he looked at himself in the mirror he thought he was starting to resemble one of the photo-fit pictures. The hair was long and matted. The eyes were staring, haunted with delinquent knowledge. He looked like a drifter, a man sought after by police forces. There was something about his face that seemed badly put together, that seemed to show the joins the way the photo-fit did. He felt an affinity with these men, with their composite selves. He told people he was Danny McErlean from Ardoyne. He told them he was a PIRA operative with street knowledge of small towns. He thought perhaps he knew too much.

The day Robert died he said that he was meeting a man in Cross. In fact he was seen at lunchtime that day in conversation with a man outside the courthouse in Newry. That night at the Mountain Inn the owner of the premises stated that he saw Robert in the company of two men in the car park. None of these men have been identified.

The Dolomite was not used exclusively by Robert. The Q-cars were rotated between brigade areas so they would not become too familiar. Food wrappers spilled out of the door pockets. There was caked mud in the foot wells. There was excess play in the steering.

He had forgotten the Browning and had to return to his room for it. There were foot patrols going out of the gates at a run. There were helicopters abroad in the night sky. He signalled to the Greenjacket in the Sangar and the man swung the steel doors open. Sappers were erecting anti-mortar netting on the outside of the Sangar, a new Com mast was going up with cameras on the top. The phrase wars of attrition came into Robert's mind. Attrition meaning wearing down. He drove through the gateway and turned southwards. He remembered that it was important to vary your route but he could not remember which route he had taken the last time. He drove through the tunnel under the railway embankment. Further down the line he saw a Wessex hovering where a device had been placed on the track, its Nitesun fixed on the scene below, the white glare, the eerie corpse light. As he exited the tunnel he saw a shape slip from the whins by the side of the road, a fox with its brush held low and its ears flat against its skull, a sense of delinquent purpose about it. It turned its head towards him and bared its teeth in a look of obscene ingratiation, slobber dripping from its opened jaws. Robert found himself looking into the fox's yellow eyes, at the taint that lingered there, and then the fox crossed the road and went under a barred gate and was gone.

Robert parked at the top of the car park at the Mountain Inn, from where he could scan the building. He used the Storno under the dash to call Bessbrook. It was 9.58 p.m. He told Captain David Collet that he was about to enter the Mountain Inn. Collet logged the call. He said afterwards that he particularly remembered the call and acted quickly later that night when Nairac did not return. He did not know why the call had stood out but he thought that it might have possessed the melancholy allure of last transmissions.

Robert entered the Mountain Inn and sat at the bar. He realized that he had left the Browning in the glove compartment of the Dolomite. He thought that it would look suspicious if he went back to the car to get it. He drank White Horse. He drank Double Diamond. The bar was quiet, filling slowly. The band was setting up on the corner stage. He told the barman that he was Danny McErlean from Belfast. He found that the accent came easier after he had taken a drink. The punched-out consonants. He knew that he had arranged to meet someone in the bar but he could not recall the man's name. He had written it on the back of a cigarette packet. He went into the toilet, where he searched his pockets, but he could not find the packet. He knew that he was to meet

236

someone but he did not know to what end. That was when the sadness began. He went back out to the bar and sat down. He could feel the sadness growing in him now, the desolation. He knew that the band would start soon and they would play country songs, anthems of loss, and he would understand why they did it. He knew that he had been working towards this sadness. That this was what filled the empty places in the maps. He greeted people as they came up to the bar. He thought that they might be able to see his sadness, the enveloping woe. He kept ordering drinks. He bought rounds for them. He told jokes. He knew that he was going to get up on the stage and sing for these people. He knew that his sadness was big enough to encompass all of these elements and all of the positions that a man might take in his own heart. Several times he felt tears in his eyes and he had to go into the toilet to wipe them. He thought, if only he could remember the name of the man he was supposed to meet. He remembered how his father had shown him the structures of the eye. Lacrimae meaning tears. He knew that they would be waiting for him outside. He knew that he would meet his sorrow with their own. He saw himself standing over a man on the ground, pumping bullets into him. At the end of the night the bandleader came up to him and asked him if he was all right, if he wanted to go home. He shook his head. There were narrative conventions to be observed. Closure of a kind was to be effected by means of the obscured episodes, the dream sequences. The struggle in the car park. The abduction. The report of a wounded man being removed from outside a nearby hotel by men with English accents. The attempted escape. The man kneeling and weeping. The body, if there was a body, being removed, being conveyed through the darkness in delinquent cortege. Cortege meaning procession. Nocturnal meaning night.

That morning Agnew received a classified document in the post. It was an inventory of material recovered from Robert's room. Agnew had asked Mallon to get it for him several months earlier. When he opened it he found that whole paragraphs had been blacked out. Agnew was glad to see this. It opened up new fields of speculative discourse. He thought that the person who had released the document knew that this was the responsibility that he bore to the material. That it should reek of concealment. The references to the pathology photographs remained. There was a detailed list of the fishing tackle, swivels, hooks inventoried by size. There was a box of falconry hoods and jesses. There were shooting magazines and gun cleaning materials. There were gun parts and empty ammunition boxes. Agnew wondered what had been left out. He did not sense the reported chaos in Robert's room. There was a sense of bare inventory about this list. Of meaning carefully revealed. Agnew felt that the unknown censor knew what he was doing. There was a powerful sense of subtext to the way the document had been handled. Agnew thought that he was being directed towards some subordinate but nonetheless compelling truth about the whole affair. He imagined an unassuming man with glasses, a classicist with a high forehead who had difficulty communicating with co-workers, a struggler with shyness. He felt that he was being directed by a man who understood the power of the hidden.

Standing at the doorway of the caravan, he saw Lorna. She was walking through the dunes, a small hurrying figure sometimes obscured by the marram grass. The hunched figure, busy, furtive. He thought she was going in the direction of the pilot jetty. He walked across the beach towards it. He found her sitting in the old wheelhouse. The wheelhouse felt different from the times he had sat in it with Mallon. Then the cracked dials and brass fittings encouraged a salty camaraderie. Lorna brought her own quality to each place she went. The feeling that she was sequestered in that location. You felt she was in a place where rigid pieties adhered to her. Agnew thought that she was like someone who had bound herself to an obscure and canonical dogma.

She was standing with her hand on the brass wheel, looking out to sea. Agnew stood beside her without speaking. Out on the lough the wind carried spume off the crests of the waves so that it struck the glass in front of them.

'What's that?' she said, pointing out towards the channel.

'A naval patrol boat,' he said.

It was a small steel-hulled vessel with a single gun turret on its forward deck.

'It's a Second World War minesweeper,' he said.

'What's it doing out there?'

'I don't know,' he said. 'It just patrols.'

The lines of the vessel were stubby and archaic. It looked like something from a lost era of naval architecture. As it came closer they could see rust patches on its hull. The wheelhouse roof was covered in antennae. There were two small radar domes to the front. As it passed, Agnew noted the contrast between the exterior of the vessel and the interior. The way the hull was salt-streaked and paint-layered and crested the waves as though it took part in an uplifting wartime drama with mildly dated themes of sacrifice and courage under fire. He imagined the interior of the wheelhouse with its navigational aids, the GPS, the radar, the wheelhouse interior fizzing with static, otherworldly noise. He put his hands on his daughter's shoulders and they stood watching the ship go by. An ensign fluttered at the stern. It gave the ship a self-important look. Concerned with the ruins of empire, gathering information as it went, creating new secrets, searching them out. The ship carried on up the channel until it was twenty feet away. A window of the wheelhouse was open and a man turned his head in the direction of Agnew and Lorna and they saw that he was wearing opaque goggles and headphones. They could not see his eyes through the matt glass of the goggles. He bent his head again to an unknown task beneath the level of the window. The man reached up and adjusted the goggles as the ship started to move away from them. Agnew imagined that he functioned as custodian of eerie noises, the sonar blip, the electron hum, the hubbub of data flux. The ship kept travelling up the channel until it rounded the point and was gone. Agnew was glad to see it go. It was freighted with dangerous knowledge, new systems, cutting-edge surveillance modes. It made the work of men like him seem a shambling and uncouth thing.

28

David spent another two months at Manderly. Out of boredom he found himself attending group therapy sessions with the other patients. He invented a childhood of casual neglect in an imaginary inner-city area. He explored the possibility that he may have suppressed traumatic sexual experiences with a close family member. He hinted at exposure to satanic practices. In late September the two Special Branch men came to see him again.

'How's David?' Mahood said.

'Looking fit, son, looking fit,' Cooper said.

'They say that the mind needs a rest as well as the body. I'd say that David's mind was tired out when he killed that girl.'

'I'd say the bap was near away with the fatigue all right.'

'I didn't kill anyone.'

'He says he never done it.'

'You never can tell. Maybe the man can't recall as such the foul events of that night.'

'Can you say for sure you never killed no one, David? In your line of work.'

'Maybe somebody got rid to death in that whorehouse of yours.'

'What do you two want, anyway?'

'Do you mind Captain Nairac?'

'I remember him.'

'Well, the bold captain goes and gets himself done in.'

'Nairac dead?'

'Well, that's the funny thing. There's them that say he's dead and there's them that say he isn't. You see, the body was never found. We have a rake of statements, but we don't have the actual body of the deceased.'

'Makes it a bit tricky in court. Habeas corpus and all that.'

'Why are you asking me?'

'Well, we know you were seen meeting with him at Theipval, in the car park, and there was talk that you might have had some notion of who his contacts were or what he was up too, because, by fuck, nobody else seems to have a baldy.'

'It wasn't a meeting. I was going out to my car. I stopped at the Four Square Laundry van. It was in the car park. Nairac came over to me.'

'What did you talk about?'

'This and that. I can't remember. We talked about using proxies, about taking the gloves off.'

'That's Ultra talk, so it is. You reckon Nairac was recruited?'

'Please, gentlemen. You're not still on about the Ultras.'

'Don't mind us talking,' Mahood said. 'We're just provincial cops. Bit of brutality in the interrogation room, fair and good, but don't be asking us any politics.'

'I'm not saying that.'

'There was talk about MI5,' Cooper said.

'Gentlemen, I don't know anything about MI5 and I'm very wary about all these conspiracy theories.'

'Do you mind what you said yourself, David?' Mahood said. 'Them boys decide they want shut of you, what happens? You find yourself falsely arrested, you find yourself in the mental.'

'Do I have to make a fucking elaborate show of looking at my surroundings to make the point?' Cooper said.

'Hold on here. You're saying you know that I shouldn't be here?'

'We know nothing, David. We are mere servants enforcing the power of the civil authority in order to keep murder and mayhem off the street.'

'At which job our success can only be described as modest in the past few months,' Cooper said.

'If the evidence says you done it, David, then you done it,' Mahood said.

'I want to talk to Knox.'

'Knox's gone as well.'

'I hear tell he got sent to Greece. Or Italy. One of them places out abroad.'

Italy or Greece. David was thinking juntas, Red Brigades. David was thinking trans-European webs of intrigue.

'Who is in the corridor now?'

'That's not for you to know. All you need to know is that there's nobody there gives a flying fuck about you. It's like, do you mind David Erskine, the mad bastard that killed the girlfriend?'

'There's nobody going to help you forby us, David.'

'I don't know anything.'

'Then there's nobody can help you at all.'

David lay awake that night. It was quiet in the hospital at night, less a silence than a medicated void. He thought of Robert the last time he had seen him. He didn't want to start seeing him as a legend now that he was gone. David knew how that worked, the processes of it. The charisma of premature death. He had run a poster campaign involving photographs of bomb victims, children and young women. You had to project a sense of young lives brutally cut short. He thought that if they let him out he could manage the news of Robert's disappearance. The fearless young captain. He imagined a memorial service on a windswept base, regimental flags cracking in the wind. It had to be somewhere in the field, VIPs sharing the hardship of the ordinary soldier. He thought of creating something lasting, a project that would reflect aspects of Robert's personality. It would have to be a project with an outdoors feel to it. An athletics scholarship. He thought he would mention it to the doctors the following day. He thought it might provide evidence of his mental alertness. It would be a way of demonstrating positive thoughts. As well as good ideas like this one, there were other methods, such as a jaunty walk and cheery hellos to patients and staff.

The following day David was told that he had another visitor. When he was led to the visiting room he saw Knox sitting behind mesh. He was told that an orderly would be present throughout the visit. He sat down. Knox was wearing a Barbour jacket and a check shirt and looked as if he had just come from a day's stalking on the moors. Stalk meaning approach under cover. Stalk meaning to steal.

'Good afternoon, David,' Knox said. 'Sad business, this.'

'I didn't do anything.'

'I'm sure that it will all be sorted out in due course. A series of regrettable misunderstandings. You have my full support. You have heard, of course, that I have been transferred. To Greece. Damned hot over there.'

'What are you doing here?'

'Simply to show my support. Strange how much the politics of one troubled country resemble those of another.'

'I suppose they have Ultras there as well.'

David letting his mouth hang open, staring at Knox, a look that he knew Knox would associate with the hospital, sullen, vacant.

'Ultras? No such thing. A product of the fevered left-wing imagination. A nonsense of post-colonial theorists.'

'Why did you leave Theipval? Were you fired?'

'Look here, David. There is no such thing as fired in this business. One simply attends to the currents within one's sphere and permits oneself to be carried along. I saw the way things were going and reactivated a dormant reposting.'

'They pulled you out.'

'They wanted to diversify operations. They wanted an aggressive integrated approach. The gloves are coming off. They see it as a matter of internal security. My brief is international conflict.'

David thought about the meaning of the words, internal security. They had an undertone of bloody suppression.

'There is no conflict between my aims and theirs, David. It is a matter of different emphasis.'

'You are one of them,' David said. 'You are an Ultra.'

'And what were you, David, what were you?' Knox said. He got up. 'Goodbye, David.'

'What about Nairac?' David shouted after him. 'What about Nairac?'

That night David envisaged Knox discussing his case, the sad but resigned tones. He regretted talking about the Ultras. The idea had a feverish aspect to it. You thought of whole societies in the grip of paranoia. You thought of one man in a secure hospital ward, his schizoid babble.

That night David realized that he was going to be convicted. He saw himself in prison, falsely convicted, a man at peace with himself through his innocence, earning the respect of inmates and staff alike with his dignified refusal to accept his fate. He saw growing public disquiet, a groundswell. Prisoners would come to him for legal advice. He would give freely of his time. He saw himself standing in the middle of the road outside the Court of Appeal, pale, stooped, determined. Outside he thought he could hear cries, birds wheeling over the moor, night falcons, he thought, hawks, wheeling on the nocturnal updraughts.

In March 1978 David Erskine was found guilty but insane on a charge of murder and was sentenced to be held at Her Majesty's Pleasure at Manderly. Following two suicide attempts and an assault on a member of staff, he was transferred to Broadmoor.

29

Mallon picked Agnew up at nine o'clock. He hadn't been able to find Lorna to tell her where he was going and he scanned the dunes looking for her, but he knew she would be impossible to see in the growing dusk, lost in the textures of the grasses and the sand.

'How come we're going out here at night?'

Agnew feeling that Mallon was creating a sense of theatric peril, storm clouds coming over the mountain, dusk shadows.

'Take her easy,' Mallon said. 'The man's a night watchman. He doesn't start until the evening.'

They left the shore area and drove up the dual carriageway that followed the edge of the lough, past the docks and then the marshes, the drained land at the head of the lough, the flat salt marsh. They drove up the hill towards the border and past the car dealers, the sellers of marked diesel, the currency dealers, the reprobate frontier commerce, until they reached the border itself, the road crossing a stretch of bog, built up on a raft of stones and rubble, the shapes of old customs posts clearly visible in the tarmac, exacting who knew what phantom excise, until they reached the entrance to Ravensdale, the road itself going in a long curve under mature pine trees that enclosed the road, dense and encroaching. Mallon pointed to his right.

'They would have took him down that road on to the main road,' he said.

'Were there ever any forensics on the car?'

'I don't recall. They probably took her over the border and burned her.'

They drove past the left-hand turn-off which led to Flurry Bridge and the reputed seat of the killing without comment and took the next left, which led towards the meat factory. The black metal gates were closed and appeared fused with rust, but they opened when Agnew got out and pushed against them. A long, straight concrete road led from the gates down to the factory, which was at the bottom of a small valley. The road was pitted in places and weeds grew on it. They drove slowly down and Agnew saw that the factory was spread over a large acreage adjacent to a small river, with concrete blood channels that ran to the banks of the stream. There were miles of metal fencing. Agnew thought that the plant resembled some abandoned Soviet-era industrial site, run down in an awesome way, rotten with pollutants. He saw five or six titanic sheds and subordinate shedding. The asbestos sheeting on the roofs was broken and missing. The sheds were constructed around a central area of cattle pens. There were sodium lights on over the pens and in the sheds, although many of them were broken. They got out of the car and walked through the nearest shed. Agnew thought that it had a border crossing's harsh aesthetic. Mallon told him how its closure had been gradual. Lights going out in the truck block, the freezer block. It had been used for rendering carcasses for a few months. Then it had been used for tanning hides. There was an air of environmental catastrophe, industrial seepage. A conveyor for carcasses with meat hooks hanging every few feet ran the entire length of the shed. Several chain-mail filleting vests had been left on the hooks. Spaced out along the conveyor were huge steel baths, stained with nameless ordure. A chain swung in the draught that came through the open doors and struck the side of the shed and Agnew jumped as though someone had started the conveyor, sent it clanking into hideous life.

'This is the place,' he said.

'This is the fucking place all right,' Mallon said.

They passed through the shed and emerged into the central holding area. They made their way through the pens, stepping over channels full of ancient filth.

'That's your man over there,' Mallon said.

He pointed to a glass kiosk which stood between the cattle pens and the killing shed, where a man would make tally of the cattle led to slaughter. The glass kiosk was lit by a flickering fluorescent tube and the outline of a man appeared intermittently with the flickering, so that it seemed as if there was some doubt as to the substance of him. As they approached the kiosk the man stepped out from it. He was wearing a black beret and thick glasses that reminded Agnew of the glasses Specs had worn at the Miami ambush. Specs's glasses had given him an air of mystery, but the impression Agnew had of this man was of a sinister vacancy that was enhanced by the jerky way he moved and the way he shrank back when Mallon stepped forward.

'This is Wingnut,' Mallon said. He pointed to Agnew. 'And this is ex-Sergeant Blair Agnew.'

Wingnut stared at Agnew from the shadows at the side of the kiosk, where he had retreated. The fluorescent tube stopped flickering for a moment and Agnew saw the man's head for the first time, the jutting forehead and the deformed skull partly concealed by the beret, a hydrocephalic look to it, babyish, something monstrous in a jar on the back shelves of a provincial museum.

'Tell Agnew what you seen,' Mallon said.

'I did see the captain and they brung him here,' Wingnut said.

His voice was wettish, muffled.

'Where did you see him first?'

'I did see him in the Mountain Inn and then I come here to work.'

'What was he doing in the Mountain Inn?'

'Sung a song. Sung Danny Boy, so he did. Took a lock of drink, so he did.'

'Was he drunk?'

'He did take a lock of drink.'

Agnew felt rain starting to fall. Mallon motioned them into the kiosk and they stepped in. They sat down. The rain drummed on the Perspex roof sheeting. The sound of the rain and the flickering light brought an element of dementia to the proceedings.

'Did you see what happened outside the Mountain Inn?'

'I never seen nothing, for I was gone to work here.'

The rain grew louder. The idiot seemed to roll his eyes and look at the ceiling in fear. Agnew turned to Mallon, as if to ask what they were doing here in this glassed-in antechamber to a noisome killing line. Mallon did not look back at Agnew. His eyes were fixed on Wingnut and as he watched the man seemed to take command of himself and started to speak unprompted.

'You do take the road past the Flurry Bridge for to reach this place and I goes down the road that night and I sees a car stop a way down the road and they get out with the captain and him fighting and all but they never stopped, they did toss him into the field and follow him in after. I hears some man and a gun fires off the one time and then I do be afeard. I goes up to the bridge and I hides there, for I do be good at the hiding. I hears the captain. He did cry and cry and they asked to him did he want a priest, but they were doing nothing but sporting him, for they never brung no priest.'

'Did you hear what happened then?'

'I was afeard and I run down the road and come to the factory to work. I done cleaning machines at night when the machines did be switched off at the switchover in the plant room.'

There was a long silence. Somewhere a piece of metal moved with a creaking sound in the wind. Agnew saw a movement in the pens, a rat that ran alongside a low wall and then disappeared.

'They do live in the blood tanks,' Wingnut said. 'The captain was took here. Somebody was took here. The car come down the hill and I was cleaning in the offal pit and they took a man from the back of the car and they carried him into the machine room, where they do put the carcasses into the mincer for the dog food and the like.'

'Could you see who it was?' Agnew said.

'It was dark and I could see nothing, not the face of the one carried in nor the faces of the men that done the carrying. All I seen was this man carried in.'

'How do you know it was Nairac?'

'Who else was it?'

'How did you know they put him in the machine?'

'I did hear it start up. I did see the meter turn in the electric room. They did run the machine. I never seen them come out, for I runs and I hides in the trees. That is my speak and I go now, for I do have work to do. I do watch for them. I watch at night for them.'

A gust of wind swept through the stockyard and a gate swung and clanked against a pillar and then the wind died down again. Wingnut turned and walked away from them, leaving them standing in the deserted charnel house until they turned away also and walked back to the car in silence. They got into the car but Mallon did not turn on the engine.

'We know they brought him here,' Agnew said.

'We think we know. We got something that might or might not have been seen by a fucking retard.'

'Still, he seen something.'

'My investigation is over anyhow,' Mallon said. 'I done as much as I can.'

'I didn't know there was an investigation.'

'Doesn't matter now.'

'Who was running it?'

'To tell you the truth, I don't know. I'm a civil servant. I do what I'm told.'

'What did they want?'

'The body,' Mallon said. 'They wanted the body.'

But Agnew thought it was more complicated than that. They wanted to put an end to the Nairac story. They wanted to stop it intruding into their sphere. They were the keepers of mystery. They were the holders of secrets. They could have controlled Nairac if he was alive. They could have practised

250

policies of containment. Agnew imagined him as an embittered and disillusioned Special Forces operative. A subject of gagging orders, D-notices, draconian press restraints. But the lost Nairac was encroaching on them. Agnew thought of him as existing in maverick dreamtime. They wanted rid of him. He was a source of persistent rumour. That he led death squads. That his body had been spirited away. That he was still alive somewhere, in deep cover, awaiting an unknowable outcome. That he knew who they were and what they dreamed of.

Mallon started the car. If this was the place where Nairac's body was disposed of, Agnew thought, then this was where the dreaming still lingered, in the tainted place, the boneyard, the drab ossuary, and as they drove off the sense lingered that there was someone there, watching, alone in the necrotic dark.

They found Lorna late the next morning when the tide had receded. She was wedged between rocks close to the pilot jetty. They brought Agnew to her but they would not let him touch. Her eyes were closed. He thought her skin was the whitest thing he had ever seen, like an unknown coral, a deep-sea calcified structure. Her brown duffel coat was gathered round her like a habit, so that she resembled a member of a mendicant order, a pale anchorite honed by years of fasting and prayer, and her thinness seemed metaphysical, a gateway to higher understanding.

There had been hailstorms all morning, the blue-black clouds interspersed with dense, silvery light. Hailstones fused with cold blocked small gulleys and inlets on the beach. The light glistened off the roofs of the caravans as if they were constructed from a new substance, a phenomenal alloy. The air seemed infused with icy vapours, freon, neon, gaseous compounds. Thunder rolled beyond the mountains. There were intimations of unseen lightning. The wet rock of the mountains in the distance suggested deep-sunk metallurgical deposits, massed elementals, the deep ore veins.

Agnew looked up from his daughter's body to see ambu-lancemen, policemen and then, formed in an outer circle, the boys who had always hung about the beach and now stood there, as though to bear witness at this place and time had been their purpose all along.

Hailstones swept across the lough again. The water seethed. Backlit, the hailstones seemed to evoke complex neural happenings, nano-events, the logic threads, the pulses, the data stream, something that had been dreamed of in quiet rooms with polyester carpets, the hum of open terminals. Agnew got to his feet. He was told that she had been seen that morning lowering herself carefully into the sea from the pilot jetty. A look of ritual to the way she did it, a sadhu's immer-sion in the sanctified waters for purposes of cleansing, for purposes of purification.

When he got back to the caravan Angela was already there. She was looking at the photograph of the Miami Showband. She held it up for him. Her eyes were bright. He could see the pleading in them.

'We saw them play,' she said.

'Did we?'

'In the Roxboro.'

'The hotel?'

'Yes, the hotel. The ballroom. It was a dinner dance. Some-body's dinner dance. The Lions. The Round Table. One of those charity business things.'

She had liked to see herself as well meaning, he remem-bered. A fellowship of convivial philanthropy with a sense of an inner circle about it, men and women in evening dress, sweet-natured and provident.

'I can't remember.'

'I was wearing a dress I copied from a Vogue magazine. Something of Grace Kelly's. Covered in sequins, hand-sewn sequins. You wore a dinner jacket.'

Urging him towards the memory of it. The hand-sewn

sequins. Grace Kelly. The exhortation to remember. Women in long dresses, gloved to the elbow. All working towards the Grace Kelly look, the Lana Turner look, for one night to be small-town regal and exalted. He could tell that she needed him to remember. That there were imperatives of remembering and that this was the way she would get through this, to recite what there had been of her daughter's life and to mark each point of it with grave observances. Agnew did not know how to help her. She turned away from him and left the caravan and he heard the noise that burst from her, less a cry than a whole body tumult. A sound to encompass all the things that could not be borne. He turned away. He looked at the bed and saw the shape of Lorna's diary under the bedclothes. He took it out. The binding had come loose and the cover was foxed and stained. It had the feel of a document that had lain unopened in an archive for decades. He opened it at the last entry.

30

My last will and testament I Lorna Agnew being of unsound mind that's not even funny. I wonder if they see me my mother or my father they are always looking away they can't see what is in front of their own noses sometimes. In science they made us cut up frogs the sinew the membrane the eyes the vitreous humour. I thought I would be sick still it is good to see the way the eyes work. My eyes aren't good to read that much any more or to write she is going to take me to get glasses I could be the speccy girl at school unloved but brainy or just unloved. I think Robert Nairac was a bit unloved I wonder was he speccy I wish I had somebody like him we could do things together we could fish we could hunt with eagles we could live in the mountains like brother and sister I don't think he was that interested in girls at least not that way. I wonder will Agnew be all right if I leave him alone I know that she will be she has her new husband.

Agnew looks so old so sad now I think he is lonely for that graveyard he talked about the nice grave that no one visits except I can say I beat you there at least you have company now. She used to talk about him that he was mixed up with the wrong people all his life they were a kind of mafia all I can say is that Lorna Agnew she sleeps with the fishes ha ha.

They think the problem is weight food not eating but I know that is not true I know where the pain is they gave me a new young body but they put old bones in it said there you go girl try to creak around in those bones see how it feels. The day I heard Mallon talking with him in the wheelhouse I was hid under the side of it. They were talking about the days when Agnew was a policeman gone bad and

Mallon was his grim captor I don't blame them for talking about it I would want to understand it as well. They talked about Ultras I don't know what they meant by that. You get stockings tights etc that say ultra sheer there is a colour ultraviolet but I don't know how men can be ultra. It is a good word though I hope they understand that I am ultra tired and ultra sick of creaky bones. My tongue is yellow my eyes are dark my prognosis is grave the doctor says if only she knew I'll show her grave. I will miss Agnew the only one I think even though he is a rogue. All girls love a rogue. I wish he would go to the hospital take his pills not drink so much this could be my last will and testament for him or a request from beyond the grave a watery grave that is. I suppose not though that would be blackmail really he wouldn't look after himself then he would feel terrible I think he's got enough things to fell terrible about without that. The previous sentence will be struck from the record the jury will disregard isn't that what they say. A list of things I regret. I regret my mother I let her down I'm sorry I'm sorry. I regret not ever having a husband I would say to him come to me you handsome pouting brute God the lips the eyes the hands. Note. That is not a real regret. I regret my immortal soul I saw a man preaching in the square he stood on a box and had a microphone he said the wages of sin is death he told about Mrs Peggy Hodgeson and her four children living in Enfield England who were afflicted by demons he said depart from me ye cursed into everlasting fire. I will depart.

I can't help thinking about Robert I look at his photograph I look into his eyes. I can't see anything there. Maybe that is the meaning of the word ultra. That you are ultra secret and do not give anything away no matter what. That they look and look and look and cannot find you. When I was small I hid in the dark and they called but I did not come out. Each to his own Robert had to learn his own secrets I had to learn mine but I think his secrets were about killing people lots of people and mine are just sad secrets a bit pathetic really that you learn to stop them getting near to you to stop them feeding you when you don't want. That to wear big clothes to hide you. That to drink water then more water to fill you and clean you clean as a whistle on the inside. To hang your hair over your face to hide you. That to hide you that to hide you.